Ybor City Blues

Gwen Mayo
Sarah Glenn

Mystery and Horror, LLC
Clearwater, FL

Ybor City Blues

Sarah E. Glenn, Editor
Cover by Patty G. Henderson
at Boulevard Photographia
Copyright © 2024 by Gwen Mayo and Sarah E. Glenn
Published by Mystery and Horror, LLC

ISBN: 978-1-949281-33-0

Table of Contents

Dedication

To my sister, Deanna Familton. Your presence in our lives means the world to us. Your kindness is a light in the darkness.

A Command Performance

"Time flies when you're having fun. Much more so when you've been arrested," Teddy said. She smiled, but the kohl lining her eyes was damp.

Cornelia Pettijohn scowled. "I was there, and no it didn't." Her gruff voice made the words sound harsher than she had intended. Her month-long vacation in Florida had been anything but restful. The thought of returning to Fort Fitzsimons filled her with blessed relief. Managing three dozen nurses was many times easier than taking care of the two dear souls she had spent the past month herding.

Steam hissed from the locomotive behind them, adding to the morning humidity. The metallic-tasting vapor rolled over the platform, engulfing everyone in a thick cloud of fog-tinged pink with the light of dawn.

She struggled to think of something to say that didn't sound cross. The past few weeks had been trying, but Teddy and Uncle Percival both loved her. They had come to the station at what Teddy considered a revolting hour just to say goodbye to her. The least she could do was put on a brave face. She would miss them once she was far away from their chaos.

Cornelia's leave was exhausted, and the Army required her to return to Colorado by the first of March. Her uncle had decided to see more of Florida before choosing a place for his winter home, and Teddy was staying with him. They claimed they would look out for one another, but Cornelia was skeptical. Both her perpetually seventy-five-year-old uncle and her impetuous companion had a penchant for getting into mischief. The thought of how much trouble the two of them could create together was cringeworthy, not that worrying would do any good at all.

She smiled at the pair of them and shook her head. "I'm not going to bother telling either of you to behave. But please try to stay out of danger for a few weeks. I'm not going to be able to help you much from Fort Fitzsimons."

Cornelia wiped moisture from her temple. Her traveling suit was too sticky for the humid conditions, but she'd be needing long sleeves once she got north of Jacksonville.

She handed Uncle Percival her bag and folded the silver-haired Teddy in her arms. "I'm going to miss you so much."

Teddy clasped her close. "We had hardly any time to relax together. I'll be happy when you muster out for good."

That wouldn't be until summer. By the time she caught up at the base, it would be time for her to leave. "I won't know what to do with myself then."

"I'll come up with something," Teddy said. "I'm sure Percival will help."

Cornelia turned to her uncle. He looked so much better than he had at Christmas. The warm climate had helped him get over the pneumonia and put roses in his cheeks—although some of that was due to sunburn. "I'm sure he will. Set that bag down, Uncle Percival, so I can give you a proper hug good-bye."

Her uncle complied, and they embraced. Even at his advanced age she still felt safe in his arms. She closed her eyes and breathed in the spicy scent of his hair tonic and the warmth of his skin.

"You take care. Don't swim if it's too cold," she cautioned, and stepped back to look at him. The twinkle in his dark blue eyes and the snowy beard made him look even more like the jolly old elf in the *Night before Christmas* poem. It was pure deception; her uncle held an enduring slot on Santa's naughty list.

2

"I'll be fine, Corny. We'll both stay in the sunshine until we meet again."

Cornelia's eyes blurred, but she nodded. Hoisting her bag, she tried to ignore the painful burns on her legs as she climbed into the Pullman. Her time in Florida had hardly been fun-filled.

There were advantages to traveling with one bag; she secured a window seat while the clutch of other passengers dickered with the baggage handlers outside. Leaning back, she closed her eyes and let out a long breath. This would be her last return to Fort Fitzsimons General Hospital. The next time she saw her family, she would be retired. Her entire adult life had been encompassed by Army postings around the globe. In her twenties, she'd answered her country's call for trained nurses immune to yellow fever and became a volunteer in Cuba, tending to Roosevelt's Rough Riders. That was where she'd met Teddy. They had faced every dark moment of their lives together since. Now, she was a captain in the Army Nurse Corps, helping soldiers who were still struggling with war injuries.

Teddy was invalided out of the Army due to injuries in the Great War before the country had seen fit to grant relative rank. She had already made the move from Colorado to Cornelia's farm in Kentucky. Before Florida, and all the nonsense about marrying her uncle had begun, their plan was for Cornelia to join her after mustering out. Beyond that, she had planned nothing. The path ahead would begin in the middle of nowhere on a farm that she was ill-trained to manage. Teddy'd had eight years to adjust to civilian life. Cornelia didn't have a clue of what she would do with herself as a civilian.

Cornelia's legs prickled under her stockings. They'd gotten burned in a St. Petersburg beauty shop, and had healed enough to itch. She leaned back in the seat and closed her eyes. Her mind drifted between thoughts of her family and those of the nurses she supervised. She'd spent the last year grooming Lieutenant Ruth Gardner to take on her role as Fitzsimons' chief of nursing services, and was confident her protégée would do an excellent job. At least she would if the Army kept the facility open; the hospital was suffering from budget cuts and neglect. As usual, Congress didn't care much about war casualties once peace was restored.

The noise outside increased. Cornelia tried to ignore the shouting. Someone was clearly taking liberties; the railroad police were commanding the miscreant to stop. The biggest thing she would not miss about Florida was dealing with the police. She hoped the train would get underway soon, so she could catch up on her sleep.

Heavy footsteps rushed into the carriage, and abruptly stopped beside her.

She opened her eyes. A heavyset man with dark hair, slicked back and short on the sides, leaned over her. It was Sal Borrero, one of Charlie Wall's men. He held his gun low, so it was unnoticed by the other passengers.

"Get up, quietly," he said. "Behave, and nobody has to get hurt. You understand?"

Cornelia started to comply but froze when she spotted his companions approaching the Pullman. The two thugs that arrived behind Sal were young and lacked his discretion.

She clutched her purse and tried to remain calm.

Around her, passengers shouted and screamed as armed men pushed through the crowd, brandishing their guns.

Sal and his goons emerged shortly thereafter, dragging her with them.

Cornelia was putting up a fight. She clouted one of the men with her purse, making him howl.

His grip stayed firm, though, and she was borne away.

"Corny!" Uncle Percival was aghast. He and Teddy rushed after the kidnappers, making haste with their canes. More than one gaping witness was brusquely shoved aside by the old man, who had worked with heavy farm equipment

4

since before their birth. Teddy, smaller and more mobile, simply squirmed between people.

Railroad security men were also in pursuit but stopped when the leader of the trio slowed long enough to put his gun to the woman's temple.

"Back off!" he commanded.

Teddy's shriek echoed above all other cries of dismay.

The three men, unhampered, departed with their prize. The travelers clustered around the ticket office also parted for the gunmen, and the thugs bundled Cornelia into an Oldsmobile parked at the curb.

While railroad police hurriedly contacted local authorities, Teddy and the professor ran—well, hastened their walk—to Cornelia's Dodge Brothers Touring Sedan, which she had left behind for their use. Teddy, gasping for air but still in the lead, flung the door open and tumbled into the driver's seat. She yanked the choke and pushed the starter button. The Dodge rumbled awake.

Cornelia's uncle arrived. "Move over!"

"I was here first!" she heaved, and gestured him around.

The old man began to argue; Teddy reached for the gear shift.

He wisely decided that speed was of the essence and climbed into the back. The car lurched forward, and he grabbed for handholds.

Teddy wrenched the wheel hard, and they turned north onto Fourth Street, tires screeching.

The slender woman was still gasping for air; the professor feared she would pass out from her scarred lungs. Teddy had no business running after anyone, armed or not, but sense wasn't one of Teddy's strengths. Neither was driving. Cornelia claimed that she drove better drunk than sober, but he doubted the validity of that claim. Drunk or sober, the woman was a moving highway hazard.

The car careened through a busy intersection, narrowly missing a truck carrying laborers to one of Saint Petersburg's many construction sites. Horns blared, men clutched the wooden railings of the truck bed, and one narrowly escaped falling into traffic. Teddy continued to stand on the accelerator.

"Theodora, you must calm down." He reached over the seat back for her arm, but she swatted his hand away, causing the car to veer uncomfortably close to the green benches near Williams Park.

"Do you see them yet?" she barked.

The professor glanced at the street signs ahead. "Where are we going?"

"Tampa!"

"They're headed to Tampa?"

She took in a long, ragged breath. "Have to be. That's Chago's car."

Cornelia glared at the young red-haired man who shared the back seat of the Oldsmobile with her.

He glared back, rubbing at the bruise already forming on his sunburned face. Her purse was tucked under his arm. No surprise there; she'd hit him hard with it.

She turned her gaze to Borrero, who was driving.

"Where's Chago?" The young gangster was more Teddy's friend than hers, but she'd seen his car enough to know it on sight.

"He's in the can."

Sounded reasonable. "Mr. Borrero, kidnapping a military officer is a federal crime, and in this case a useless one. Why did you grab me? I don't have any money. The Army isn't going to pay to get me back, and I doubt my uncle will, either. He views himself as thrifty."

"The boss wants to talk to you," Sal said.

Charlie Wall? Mitch Grant, a reporter they'd met during their time here, had told her that Wall was the biggest crime boss in Florida. What business did he have with her?

"Why would your boss want to talk to me? He doesn't even know me."

Sal leaned forward, pressing harder on the accelerator. "He'll tell you when we get there."

"Isn't he in Tampa?"

"Ybor City," Sal said.

6

That explained why they were turning onto the Gandy Bridge. A great span built of concrete and steel jutted ahead of them, stretching over the clear blue waters of the bay. Before the bridge was a toll booth, though, and Cornelia saw her chance to escape.

Unfortunately, so did her captors.

"Hold her, Lobster," Sal ordered, and the young man next to her seized her arms.

"Help me!" she screamed at the sleepy attendant, causing him to straighten and peer into the car. Sal shoved a fiver at the hapless man.

"Ignore my wife, buddy; she doesn't want to see her in-laws."

His companion in the front seat snickered.

"No!" She struggled with the Lobster fellow, but they were already hurtling away from the shore and any hope of rescue.

The car bounced beneath them; fighting wasn't safe.

Cornelia stopped moving and sighed. "I see I have no choice in this."

Borrero replied, "You've got it, sister."

"Then let's get this over with."

Lobster let her go.

Cornelia glanced out at the waters, dark and sparkling in the morning sunlight. She straightened her clothes and ran her hands over her hair, shoving a loose lock back into its bun. After a moment, she eyed her bag, located near the young man's feet. "I'm certain I look a fright. Could I have my purse, so I can use my comb before meeting your boss?"

Lobster shrugged and handed the bag to her. He didn't think the condition of her bun was going to make any difference to Mr. Wall. The stout, gray-haired woman was no looker. He couldn't imagine what the boss would want from her, but orders were orders.

"Thank you." She reached inside, and pulled out her 1911 Colt .45, pointing it at the young man, who yelped.

"Now, Mr. Borrero, I need you to stop this car."

The passenger in the front seat turned, aiming his own gun. "Put it down, lady."

"No! I presume your boss wants me alive."

Sal kept driving. "There's nowhere to go but Tampa. It's not like I can turn around in the middle of the bridge."

Cornelia knew he was right, but was determined to escape. "Stop the car anyway. I'll walk back."

"No."

"I'll shoot."

"Then shoot," Sal snapped. "I'm more scared of the boss than I am of you. Besides, you're smart enough to know better than to shoot the driver in the middle of a bridge. We'd all wind up in the bay."

Cornelia growled and put the gun away.

The toll booth collector leaned out to address the flushed silver-haired woman in the Touring Sedan. "Ma'am, could you please call the police? I believe that a woman in the last car was abducted."

"She was," the woman said. "We're in pursuit. Could you tell me how to get to the El Dorado Lounge?"

He and the old gent in the back gave the woman startled looks. "Begging your pardon, ma'am, that's no place for a lady like yourself to go."

"But that's where they're taking her!"

The man gave her directions.

"Thank you." She handed him a fiver to match the one he'd just received.

As the sedan lurched away and gained speed, he wondered what the unofficial mayor of Tampa would want with the abducted woman. She didn't look the sort to have truck with trouble boys. Then again, her two would-be rescuers didn't look like the sort to take on Florida's criminal underworld.

The El Dorado was a three-story red brick building with an ornate wrought-iron balcony on the second floor. The business name was painted on the south side in five-foot-tall script. Inside the café, a few late-morning patrons

8

lingered over coffee. It was obvious that Cornelia could expect no help from that quarter. None of them had the guts to make eye contact with her or her companions as they ushered her through the dining room.

The young man they called 'Lobster' held open the door in the back of the café for Cornelia. She stepped through and paused to let her eyes adjust to the dim light. Instinct kicked in as she mentally noted the exit behind the bar and the door to the stairs. Cornelia had never been inside this kind of casino before; her curiosity threatened to be her undoing as she watched a nearby roulette wheel spin instead of paying attention to her captors. Illegal gambling tables filled a room nearly as large as the ballroom of the Vinoy Park Hotel. Heavy cigar smoke hung in the air above the players, most of whom looked like they had been here all night.

Sal's gun poked her in the small of her back. "Don't keep the boss waiting."

Cornelia hadn't realized what a disagreeable man Borrero could be when she'd met him. "Either shoot me or put that thing away. I'm not taking another step."

He must have given a signal to his companions. The two hoodlums lifted her off the floor and carried her into the office in the back corner of the gambling den.

The painful burns on her legs made her wince, but Cornelia wasn't about to give them the satisfaction of knowing she was injured. These brutes would probably hurt her worse.

A short but burly young man with wavy hair stood watch outside Wall's office. He stepped aside as they approached.

Charles Wall was unperturbed by the methods his men used to bring her to his office. He stood and bowed when Sal's boys strong-armed Cornelia into the room. "Miss Pettijohn. Thank you for coming."

"It wasn't my idea," she snapped. "This is kidnapping."

"I apologize for my tactics," he said, "but the constraints of time made extreme measures necessary. By the time my men located you, you were leaving town."

"Of course I was! The Army expects me to be back in Colorado by March first. If I were you, I'd have someone drive me to Jacksonville where I can rejoin my luggage."

"I apologize about the luggage. We will provide a new wardrobe and take care of anything else you need while you are my guest." He gestured to an overstuffed chair. "Please, have a seat."

She straightened her jacket before sitting. "I wouldn't need anything if you hadn't kidnapped me."

"True enough, but you will have to make do with what we have."

Cornelia eyed him haughtily. "Your men also took my purse. That adds theft to the kidnapping charges."

He glanced at Sal.

"She had a gun in it," Sal told Wall as he set the bag on his boss' desk. "She also bounced it off Lobster's face. He'll have a doozy of a shiner."

This produced a smile. "I expected her to be full of surprises."

"So are her friends, and they aren't far behind me," Sal said. "A car followed us from the station. I thought we had lost them, but Eddie saw it again on the Gandy."

"Show them in when they get here, but frisk them for weapons first. Miss Pettijohn might not be the only member of the family who carries a gun."

"Yes sir."

"Thank you, Sal. Please leave us and close the door behind you."

Sal gave Cornelia a sidelong glance but left the room.

Wall sat behind his desk and opened one of the top drawers. "Chago told me about you three. You seem to get into a lot of trouble for people old enough to know better."

"You can hardly blame that on us," Cornelia said, although she did think there was a grain of truth in the statement when it came to her uncle.

"The point is, your companions were each arrested for separate murders in separate cities in the same month." Wall tapped his pen on the desk. "Charges were dropped in both cases, based on evidence you turned up, Miss Pettijohn. I find that impressive."

"They were both innocent. To be fair, though, you're not giving my uncle credit for his filmmaking."

"I still remember the footage he got of Tiny Belluchi dumping Benny's body. In my business, that's the sort of thing that gets you dead. You did a respectable job of looking out for him."

Cornelia shifted in the chair, uncomfortable with this topic of discussion. Earning the attention of a crime boss would not look good to her superiors. "What does this have to do with my being here, instead of on a train back to Fort Fitzsimons?"

Wall spread his hands. "I need your help."

Her heavy brows drew together, and she studied the tall, well-dressed man across the desk from her. He looked the part of a distinguished businessman, except for the utter lack of concern in his features. This man had had her abducted from a train at gunpoint in front of dozens of witnesses. He clearly had no fear of repercussions from the authorities. She couldn't help wondering why he would want her assistance.

"My help? You had me kidnapped so I would help you? I'm sure you could afford any medical attention you needed without abducting a nurse."

"That's true, but it is your detective skills I need—or, rather, our mutual friend Chago needs."

Chago Aldama was more of an acquaintance than a friend, although Teddy had an exceedingly high opinion of the young gangster. He had been quite accommodating about supplying her with booze when they were in Homosassa. Still, Wall had her attention. Cornelia remained silent and waited for him to continue.

Teddy pulled to the curb behind the Oldsmobile. There was a slight scrape of metal when the bumpers met, but not enough to do severe damage. She was surprised by the screech from the back seat. She had never thought of the professor as the nervous type. He was out of the car before she turned the engine off.

The El Dorado didn't look disreputable from the street. A small café in the corner of the building smelled pleasantly of coffee and fresh-baked bread. There was no question they had found the right place, though. Mr. Borrero was standing in the doorway, arms crossed, glaring at her. "The boss said to show you in when you got here. He's not going to be happy when he hears that you banged his Olds."

Professor Pettijohn clutched the shaft of his cane in one hand and stepped in front of Teddy. "You're nothing more than barbarians," he shouted, waving the silver wildcat knob inches from Sal's face.

Sal Borrero took a step back to avoid being struck by the old gent's stick. "Do you have any idea who you're talking to, *anciano*?"

"Yes, I am speaking to a pack of jackals who kidnapped a defenseless woman from the train this morning. I'm addressing the loathsome creatures who have the audacity to snivel over a lump of steel when a lady is being held against her will. If you have harmed a single hair on—"

"Simmer down, Gramps, I'll take you to her. Jeez."

"Well? What are you waiting for?" Teddy asked.

Sal glanced from the professor to the slender silver-haired woman behind him. Small beads of sweat trickled down the back of his neck. Memories of how much trouble they had been during their last encounter reminded him not to underestimate either of them. He would rather trade places with Chago than tangle with these old people. The big house had to be better than dealing with this trio.

"I've got to search you first. Boss' orders."

The old man's face turned so red that it gave his beard a pink glow. "You'll do no such thing. Search me if you must, but lay one hand on this dear lady, and I shall beat you within an inch of your life."

12

Sal could feel Lobster and Eddie the Hat staring at the back of his head, waiting to see how he handled the situation. He didn't want to hurt the old man, but orders were orders.

Cornelia could hear her uncle's voice through the closed door. She was on her feet in an instant and headed to his rescue.

Wall rushed to get ahead of her. He opened the door. "What's going on here?"

"Just following orders, Mr. Wall." Sal pointed to the professor. "This one objects to his lady friend being searched."

Charlie Wall stopped in his tracks. He blinked as if that would change the scene unfolding in his casino. He recognized the professor and Miss Lawless from the stolen film footage, but the movie didn't do justice to the real articles. Despite the snow-white hair peeking out of his expensive fedora, Professor Pettijohn was a dangerous man, entirely focused on protecting his companion. Given his advanced age, Sal could take him, but not before the old man landed a couple of blows from the head of that cane. Judging from the way his suit fit, there would still be power behind those blows.

The short man, still standing near the door, turned to Wall. He bore a V-shaped scar on his cheek; clearly no stranger to violence.

"Are you sure you want these two in your office, Boss? Sal and I can find them seats in the lounge if you like. Or maybe the curb."

"No, things will go faster if they're present. If you give me your word of honor that the lady is unarmed, Professor Pettijohn, we can forgo the search." Wall didn't wait for an answer. "Sal, you and the boys can let them through."

"What about your car, Boss?"

The professor lowered his cane. "Miss Lawless pulled to the curb a little too fast. I'll cover any damages, of course, provided my niece is returned immediately."

"Your niece is my guest, sir."

13

"Are all your guests invited at gunpoint?"

Wall opened his arms wide. "Not all, sir. In this case, necessity required me to improvise. I was about to explain the situation when you arrived. Please, join us in my office. Johnny, bring some extra chairs."

Once they were situated, Wall started over. "I summoned Miss Pettijohn to request her assistance on behalf of our mutual friend, Chago Aldama. He's been arrested for murder."

Teddy raised one hand to her throat. "Oh no!"

"Pardon me for making assumptions," Cornelia said, "but isn't that an occupational hazard in his line of work?"

Wall almost smiled. "Set your assumptions aside for a moment. For the last few months, Chago has been courting a young woman, Jaquinda Duarte. You may have heard of her under her stage name, Jackie Dart. She was a singer in my clubs."

"I see you are using the past tense," the professor said.

"Someone found Jackie's body two days ago in an alley near The Cuban Club. Last night, they arrested Chago for her murder."

"On what grounds?" Cornelia asked.

Their host reached into the drawer of his desk and pulled out a large brown envelope. "Everything's in here, including the police photographs. I must warn you though. It isn't pretty."

Cornelia hesitated. She didn't want to get involved in another murder. Curiosity overrode common sense, though, and she reached for the envelope. "Nothing in a photograph could be worse than what we saw on the battlefields of France. But if you have access to the police investigation, what do you need me for?"

The look on Wall's face was somewhere between a smile and a grimace. "Chago is Cuban, as was Jackie. Neither was white enough to warrant a thorough investigation by local authorities."

"I see," Cornelia said dryly.

14

"The police investigation comes down to the following: they had a lovers' spat, she was killed with blows to the head, and Chago owns a Louisville Slugger. I need someone who will look beyond the obvious and find the truth."

The report itself was sparse in detail. Jaquinda Duarte, twenty-two years old. Occupation: cigar factory, singer. Race: Cuban. Body found yesterday morning in alley; victim bludgeoned to death. Fractured skull and ribs, injuries on face, arms, and torso. Family: mother and younger brother living, father and older brother dead. Residence: Tampa, with "the scrub" handwritten beside the street address.

Cornelia braced herself before looking at the photographs. The young woman was lying on her back, hips twisted to one side. Her gown, elegant but blood-spattered, looked to be either white or silver. Rings adorned her hands: one cluster ring, one filigree, and one heavy ring with a stone. A broken strand of pearls still clung to her neck. Beside the body rested a broken bat, very likely a Louisville Slugger.

Teddy peeked over her shoulder. "It looks like she was dressed for a performance. That's an expensive gown, and the pearls look real. Those shoes are dark, too dark to be gray or silver. Perhaps they were dyed?"

What Teddy didn't mention was Jaquinda's face. Cornelia had seen uglier injuries in the field, but the brutality of the murder was unmistakable. A fashionable bob framed a face that had been battered beyond easy recognition. The left side was mostly pulp. She pitied whoever had been called to identify the woman. Oddly enough, though, there was less bleeding from the mouth and nose than such heavy injuries should have produced. Cornelia wondered if Jaquinda had already been dead when her face was disfigured. The cruelty of the act had to be personal.

Her thoughts were interrupted by her uncle. "Are there no private investigators in Tampa that can be trusted?" the professor asked.

15

Mr. Wall studied him for a long moment. When he spoke, his tone was soft and measured. "As you surmise, sir, there are a number of private investigators for hire. What I need is someone unknown to my enemies and not likely to arouse their suspicions."

Cornelia hesitated before speaking. Whoever had killed this woman, though, had been someone close enough to have strong feelings. "What if the truth leads to Chago?"

"No!" Teddy cried.

Wall simply shrugged. "Then he is in no worse trouble than he is now. What do you say, Miss Pettijohn? Will you take the case?"

Cornelia stood up. "Mr. Wall, I am sorry, but the army is unforgiving of oath breakers. Leavenworth is not where I envisioned my retirement. Now, please get me back to my train."

There was a trace of a smile on his lips as he reached into the drawer of his desk again and took out a telegram. "There's nothing to worry about on that account. Your leave is extended."

Her eyes widened as she read the telegram:

Mr. Charles Wall,

As requested, Brigadier General John S. Parker has granted Captain Cornelia Pettijohn additional leave up to 22 days to assist in this life-threatening emergency.

Sincerely
Governor John W. Martin

"Would you at least give him twenty-four hours of your time? That much delay won't make you late returning."

"Even if I knew how to conduct an investigation—which I don't—that amount of time wouldn't be enough to solve a murder."

"Perhaps not, Miss Pettijohn. But it is time enough to hear Chago's story and discuss it with your companions."

A Gilded Cage

Sal escorted the trio from the office and back to the street, where Chago's Oldsmobile awaited them. "Get in. The boss has arranged accommodations for you during your visit to this side of the Bay."

"Our car is right behind yours," Teddy protested. "We can't just leave it there; it could be hit. I parked it ... badly."

"Not gonna argue about that," the heavyset man said. "I'll have Eddie move it."

Cornelia raised her chin. "That's *my* car you're talking about. My property. I don't want strangers driving it." She was surprised her uncle had let Teddy drive it at all. She loved Teddy, but, sober, the woman was a disaster behind the wheel.

"So you can take off in it? Mr. Wall would have my hide for sure." Sal waved to the man at the door. "Get Eddie to grab that Dodge and follow me."

He turned back to his captives. "Now, get in the car. Miss Pettijohn in front, since she's full of surprises."

The professor glanced at Cornelia. After receiving a curt nod, he assisted Teddy into the back seat. Sal opened the front passenger door for Cornelia and remained close until she sat. He quickly circled the vehicle and got into the driver's seat. They pulled away from the curb.

Cornelia scanned their environment. She'd been too distracted by her abduction before to notice things; it was time to orient herself. The streets around them were lined with carts selling sandwiches and crab cakes. The scent of coffee and scalded milk wafted from the open doors of cafés. She glanced at Sal and decided not to mention that she hadn't eaten since before dawn. He might see hunger as a way to control her.

She leaned back in the seat and focused on the neighborhood. The signs above shop doors were written in Spanish rather than English, although a few had smaller script with German, Italian, or English. Once or twice, she spotted Chinese under the Spanish shop name. The plethora of languages surprised her.

"This must be Tampa's Cuban district," Cornelia said. "We were stationed in Havana during our first tour of duty. This place reminds me of it in some ways, although the buildings are much newer."

"This is Ybor City," Sal said. "A town in itself. You'll get slapped if you call it Tampa."

"I will keep that in mind." She and Teddy had been young nurses when they arrived in Cuba, new to the language and each other. Under other circumstances, it might have been pleasant to visit this side of the bay. Instead, she was here by force, clutching an envelope with repulsive contents.

"Where are we going first?" Teddy chirped from the back. "The scene of the crime?"

"Not yet," Sal said. "The boss has arranged lodging for you in Tampa. No sense in going back to Saint Petersburg."

"Our clothing and luggage are both in Saint Petersburg," the professor objected. "Except for my niece's luggage. Hers was on the train where you accosted her."

Sal raised his hand. "Calm down, Professor. We'll get your clothing for you. As for Miss Pettijohn, I was told to provide for all her needs."

Teddy squealed. "Wonderful! I haven't shopped in Tampa yet."

Cornelia cringed.

When Sal told them that Mr. Wall had arranged lodging for them, Cornelia had pictured one of the boarding

18

houses near his establishment. Instead, they left the Cuban quarter and were now traveling through an area closer to Saint Petersburg in appearance. This had to be Tampa.

The professor leaned forward from the back seat. "Mr. Wall may be our host, but what about our possessions?"

"We'll send someone to the Vinoy to collect 'em," Sal said.

"Send a car with a big trunk on the back," Cornelia said. "Those two do not travel light."

Sal grunted.

Foot traffic moved faster than the Oldsmobile as they neared the river. They crept in silence until they reached the Lafayette Street Bridge.

Teddy gasped. "Cornelia, look! That's where we nurses from New York stayed while waiting for orders to invade Cuba. Colonel Roosevelt's Rough Riders had tents along the waterfront. Doesn't it look like a castle?"

The professor craned his neck to get a better look at the crescent finials rising from the long red-brick building. "It is certainly big enough to be a castle. I would say it is at least a quarter mile long."

Sal grunted again. "A big red elephant, if you ask me. I doubt it's been full since the Army checked out."

"No one asked," Teddy snipped. "Our stay was a historic time. The New York nurses were traveling with Clara Barton. In the evening, the officers would sit on the porch and plan the invasion. The newspapers took to calling it the Rocking-Chair War."

Sal's dark eyes flashed sparks of anger. "If the United States had done what the Cuban people asked, the Cubans could have won the revolution by themselves."

Teddy glared at him. "How can you say that? A lot of American boys died for Cuba's freedom."

"My grandfather died fighting for independence ten years before your navy came to Cuba. My father, my uncles, and many of my cousins fought in the rebellion. We buried an uncle and two cousins because they believed that Cuba should be free. We held the Spaniards at a standstill for

19

years, sometimes fighting with nothing but farm tools. We asked the United States for guns and bullets, not the lives of her soldiers."

"Sinking the *Maine* was an act of war."

Sal shook his head. "Spain could not have sunk your ship if the ship had stayed home."

Cornelia interrupted. "Traffic is moving again."

Sal shifted gears and stepped on the gas. The Oldsmobile lurched forward. Soon, they were turning into the drive of the Tampa Bay Hotel.

No wonder Teddy thought of the Tampa Bay Hotel as a castle. Cornelia could easily picture Theodora as a young woman traveling with people of her own social class. This was a far cry from her own journey from Jacksonville to the Port of Miami and on to Cuba. There were no grand hotels for the nurses in her company. Tents and army cots were her introduction to Florida. If she hadn't been brought here by brute force and held against her will, she would have admired Mr. Wall's taste in hotels. It must have been quite grand with the Army in residence.

Up close, the facade was even more impressive. It was a massive structure set between the Hillsborough River and the bay, on a property that was almost as large as the farm Cornelia had inherited from her mother. She had never seen a building quite like it: classic Victorian details mixed with a Moorish design. There were three sets of double doors leading to the lobby; tall keyhole windows flanked them. The roof was adorned with steel minarets which were each topped with a crescent moon. It was a pity that she would not be staying long enough to explore the grounds.

Sal opened her car door. "The boss had me arrange a suite for you here. He thought you would be safer on this side of the river. We hadn't expected your whole family to show up, but that shouldn't be a problem."

He glanced at Teddy. "They have plenty of rooms."

Cornelia's sedan pulled in behind them with a sullen-faced Eddie behind the wheel. The young man was taller than Sal and wore a broad-brimmed white fedora that hid his eyes. Lobster pouted next to him.

"Wait here," Sal ordered. "I'll square things with the desk, then you two can drive the lady's car to St. Petersburg and retrieve their luggage."

Cornelia's eyes narrowed as she scowled at Sal. "So, you've stolen my automobile as well as my purse. Is there no end to your crimes, Mr. Borrero?"

"I wish you no harm, Miss Pettijohn." He handed Cornelia her purse. "I need to hang on to your gun for now. Maybe after you talk to Chago, you will understand why he needs your help."

It was clear Teddy was happy with the present situation. The moment they entered the hotel, her face took on the dreamy look of someone lost in memories of happier times. Cornelia could picture her walking into this enormous two-story lobby with its polished marble pillars and life-sized sculptures for the first time. Before the war became bloodshed and mangled bodies, before the plague of flies, mosquitos, and yellow fever, there were dashing officers making bold plans and young men practicing drills on the lawn.

She left Teddy to her dreams and found a seat to wait for Sal to return with their room keys. Cornelia looked through the evidence again, trying to figure out why she'd been dragged into this situation. She was no detective. She didn't know her way around the city or understand enough about the crime to know what pieces of the puzzle might be missing.

There was plenty of reason for Chago to be a suspect. It was his girl, and maybe his bat, but the case against him was thin. One lover's quarrel was not a strong motive. She didn't see anything in the file that indicated there was a history of fights between them. In fact, there was no history that Chago had ever lifted his hand to a woman. It was true that he had a record of breaking arms and legs. She'd expected that. After all, he was a career criminal.

What bothered her was that the file held no indication the police had looked at anyone else. They hadn't really looked for other motives or interviewed anyone but Chago.

Maybe Mr. Wall thought there should be other suspects, or that she would be able to find another. But that didn't explain why she had been kidnapped. She was unlikely to find anything that an actual detective couldn't discover. Why detain her?

Nothing about this situation made sense to her. Charlie Wall had the power to get the governor to arrange additional leave for her; surely he had the power to get Chago released without her help. She stuffed the evidence back into the envelope and tucked it into her purse. The only thing she wanted to investigate was how to get back to Colorado.

What she needed was an escape plan. There had to be a way to get past Sal.

Professor Percival Pettijohn had a chat with the concierge while he waited. The young man was an accommodating fellow who provided him with a list of the hotel amenities, local attractions, a map of the grounds, and both the train and streetcar schedules. Pettijohn scanned the schedules, committing them to memory, and quickly put them away. It wouldn't do for Sal to catch him looking for transportation. This wasn't the city he had in mind when he decided to explore more of Florida, but the professor had long ago decided to make the most of whatever life handed him.

Of course, the information had would also be useful to Cornelia. He could tell from the way she'd ignored Teddy's disagreement with Sal that her mind was elsewhere. Besides, his niece had spent most of her leave getting him out of trouble. Now that *she* was in trouble, he was duty-bound to rescue her from the clutches of these hoodlums.

He closed his eyes and reviewed their surroundings. Mr. Wall had chosen a strategically excellent location. The Tampa Bay Hotel was isolated from the surrounding metropolis: located in the heart of a large park on the edge of Hillsborough Bay, and cut off from Ybor City by the

Hillsborough River. Their chances of reaching Ybor City without capture were slim. The bridge was a perpetual traffic disaster. It had taken precisely fifty-two minutes to cross by automobile. That left them only two options: boarding a train at the platform behind the hotel or cutting cross-country to reach the downtown area. Considering the limited number of passenger trains operating in Florida, there was not much chance of getting anything but a local.

He ruled out an escape by streetcar. Frequent stops would make it too easy for Mr. Wall's men to apprehend them. Their hotel had a stable, but he did not relish the idea of trying to escape on horseback or on foot. He and Teddy both had health issues and he, at least, hadn't been on a horse in years. Cornelia was an excellent horsewoman, but she was recovering from painful burns caused by an incident with an electric hair-styling device. She'd tried to explain the mechanics of the permanent wave machine that caused her injuries, but despite having patented hundreds of inventions, he couldn't quite fathom why anyone would build the monstrosity she described. In any case, the train was their best chance of escape. What he needed was a way to incapacitate their captors until the train departed.

They had taken Cornelia's gun; a pity, but not unexpected. They were hoodlums.

"Gramps," indeed; Mr. Borrero had dismissed him as a doddering old fool. He and his companions didn't realize that the greatest weapon any man possessed was an inventive mind. Man's ability to examine his environment and use what was at hand to improve, refine, and repurpose the materials available was what allowed them to build all the marvels of the modern world.

Professor Pettijohn closed his eyes for a moment and focused his mind on what materials he had that could assist them in disabling their captors. A devious smile appeared on his face. When he opened his eyes, there was a new spark. He reached into his pocket and took out his ever-present notebook and pencil and began to sketch potential weapons he could improvise from their possessions. He was so intent upon his drawings, that he didn't notice Sal's return until he heard him asking Cornelia if she was ready to see Chago.

Cornelia insisted that they speak to the Tampa police first.

"Okay," Sal said, "but you're not gonna get much from them."

When they entered the offices on Florida Avenue, Sal asked to speak to Sergeant Nelson. They were directed to a row of chairs.

She sighed. More sitting.

"Is the sergeant friendly to Mr. Wall?" Teddy asked Sal.

"He's friendlier than some."

While they waited, Cornelia studied the offices. In a city of Tampa's size, she'd expected the office to be bustling with activity. The staff there were very busy, but there weren't many of them.

"Is there a special event going on today?"

"No."

"Not many employees for a city of this size."

"The city wasn't jumping like this a few years ago. They can't even keep up with the car thieves. Someone stole a car from the police, and the insurance goons found it last year."

"That took nerve."

Sergeant Nelson arrived at the station and met with the trio. He wasn't much help. In fact, rather the reverse.

"It's clear what happened," he said. "She was a canary with a lot of cats chasing her. Aldama had a public argument with her at the Cuban Club. Wasn't the only argument that happened that night, but it was the loudest." He glanced at Sal. "Takes a lot of passion to kill a woman that way."

"Won't argue with that part," Sal said.

"Aldama had a baseball bat in his car with blood on it. If you saw the photos, you know where it came from. Of course he got his elbows checked."

Cornelia fumed as they headed for the jail. Teddy and Sal were wise enough to let her be.

Teddy took a seat in the small interview room of the Tampa jail and folded her hands in her lap. While she waited, she thought about awful it was for a young man to be locked in jail for a crime he didn't commit. He was innocent. Well, innocent of this. She had no illusions about her friend's involvement in other crimes. He was a gangster, but not the sort of man who beat an unarmed woman to death. She knew what kind of man it took to do that.

She kept her thoughts to herself. Cornelia was in one of her moods and had barely spoken to her or Sal since the meeting with the sergeant. She glanced over her shoulder to the firm set of Cornelia's square jaw and the barely controlled rage in her eyes. The stubborn old dear had her back up about being abducted. She was practically standing at attention in the interview room. It was a shame, too. It was going to be hard to get her to put her ill temper aside and help Chago.

The sound of chains rattling caught her attention a few seconds before the door opened. That was long enough for her to compose herself and put on a brave smile for her friend. Poor Chago; his white suit was rumpled, and his jet-black hair needed a comb. He always took such pride in his appearance. Even in shackles, he had straightened his tie and finger combed his hair.

Teddy stood up and reached out to embrace him. "We've got to stop meeting like this, Chago. People will talk."

His smile warmed his brown eyes, but did nothing to erase the dark circles under them. "Miss Teddy, I wasn't expecting to see you at all. Why are you here?"

"Mr. Wall asked Cornelia to investigate."

Teddy ignored Cornelia's grim expression and continued smiling at the young man as if there were nothing wrong.

"By asking, she means that your boss had three of his men kidnap me from the morning train and bring me here at gunpoint," Cornelia replied. "He even went behind my back and had the governor convince my superiors that I was needed here for a medical emergency."

"He didn't say medical, he said it was 'life-threatening,'" Teddy corrected. "I think that's a fair assessment of Chago's situation. Don't you?"

Cornelia's only response was a look that would have made a lesser woman flee.

Teddy was undaunted.

"I am very sorry, Miss Pettijohn. I didn't know what he was planning." Chago reined in his emotions with difficulty and lifted his chin so he could look her in the eyes. "I don't wish to keep you from your duty."

"Well, I'm here. You might as well tell me what happened."

He lowered his head. "I don't know what happened. We had an argument after her first set. She left, then I left. I found out she was dead when the police showed up at my door."

"Where was this?"

"The Cuban Club, *Senora* Pettijohn."

Teddy took a tiny notebook from her purse and began writing. "What did you argue about?" she asked.

"I can't tell you that."

Cornelia moved a few steps closer. "If I am going to help you, Chago, you must be completely honest with me. There can't be any secrets."

He stiffened, then relented. "I was angry that the woman Jaquinda used to work for had recorded her music. She is not the sort of woman a man wants his girl to associate with. I called that woman a name that I will not repeat in front of you ladies. Jaquinda threw a vase of flowers at me and told me to get out. Between the shattered vase and me slamming the door, the fight sounded worse than it was."

"Where did you go when you left the club?" Teddy asked.

"I was mad. So, I took a walk. I needed to clear my head before I went to work."

Cornelia raised an eyebrow. "Did you see anyone you knew or talk to someone while you were out walking?"

26

His chains rattled as he shifted from one foot to the other. Then he shook his head. "I wasn't paying attention. I don't even remember what streets I took."

Teddy slipped a small silver flask into the pocket of his suit as she hugged him. "Keep your chin up. We'll figure this out."

Sal was waiting when the ladies stepped out of the jail. The morning was slipping away. He wasn't sure why the boss wanted Miss Pettijohn here, but orders were orders. Not that she seemed all that keen on playing detective for him. In fact, the storm clouds behind her sharp blue eyes made him glad he had taken her gun away. He opened the door to the big Oldsmobile and waited for Cornelia to settle in before speaking.

"Where to next?"

Her spine was rigid, and the hand that clutched that big purse she carried was white-knuckled from the tightness of her grip. Cornelia gave him a look that made him think of a few places she would probably like to tell him to go to, but the lady had enough self-discipline to keep her mouth closed.

He let her be and helped her friend into the back seat. Tomorrow, he was going to make Eddie the Hat play chauffeur to the two of them. No, they were going to the Scrub. It would have to be Clevon.

As usual, the friend was talking. She rarely shut up. "What do you think, dear, should we go to the scene of the crime next, or see if we can locate that club Chago told us about?"

"Why did you promise Chago we would figure out what happened?" the Pettijohn woman said. "We don't even know if he's telling us the truth. Besides, we are nurses, not detectives."

"People in Ybor City and the Scrub won't talk to detectives, police or otherwise," Sal said. "They will let Chago fry before they'll squeal, even if he makes it to trial."

Teddy gasped. "You think someone will bump him off?"

27

There was a trace of a smile on Sal's face when he started the engine. No matter what her friend thought, Miss Lawless was not going to let her back out of helping.

"It would be easier to show you what Chago is in for once he is arraigned." Sal pulled away from the jail and headed north. They had driven about half an hour when he spotted what he was looking for.

"This is what they do with prisoners," he said, pointing to a large work crew building an intersecting highway. He slowed a little as they neared the intersection.

Cornelia could see the work crews in prison stripes. It was a common practice in many states to have prisoners work for their keep. She didn't like the practice, but ...

On the grass some distance from the other workers, she spotted what Sal wanted her to see. Four prisoners, face down in the grass, their bare backs cut to shreds by the man flogging them. Guards with shotguns stood by, watching, doing nothing, while the torture continued. Despite a lifetime of seeing the horrors of war, she felt tears burn in the corners of her eyes.

Behind her, Teddy muffled a cry.

Sal drove on in silence until they were out of sight of the work camp. He pulled to the side of the road and handed Cornelia his handkerchief. "I am sorry if I shocked you. Chago is my friend. It was important that you understand what he is facing."

"Chago is a smart man. He wouldn't do anything that would get him in trouble with the guards."

"You're right, Miss Pettijohn, but he doesn't have to do anything wrong. In this county, we have professional floggers. You can hire one to flog anyone: men, women, even children. The county jail pays them to flog four men in the work camp every day. If no one has committed an offense, they pick four at random."

Cornelia's mouth gaped. "That's insane."

"Perhaps, but the sanity of the floggings doesn't change how the system works. Once he is arraigned, Chago will be transferred to the Hillsborough County Jail. He will be there weeks, perhaps months, before standing trial. Bond is not granted to men charged with murder. They will send him to one of the work camps. Those men on the ground were just picked out of the line for flogging because the county wants prisoners to be punished."

"Mr. Wall had the power to get the Army to allow me to stay in Florida. Surely, he can get Chago out of jail."

Sal's voice was soft as he explained. "There are favors Mr. Wall can request, and ones he cannot. It is easier for the governor to request additional leave for a nurse than to help a known criminal escape justice. Of course, an escape could be arranged, but that would make Chago a fugitive. He couldn't go back to work or even stay in Tampa. He would be hunted the rest of his life. It would also leave the murder unsolved, and let Jackie's killer go free."

It was lunchtime when Cornelia and Teddy reached Ybor City. Teddy suggested they get Cuban sandwiches from one of the street vendors, but Sal pulled to the curb near the Kress' Five and Dime. "Woolworth's is next door if you prefer, but Mr. Wall would have my hide if I let his guests eat from a street vendor's cart. I'm told that the soda fountains are a suitable place for ladies to have lunch."

Cornelia arched an eyebrow as she watched him grow increasingly more uncomfortable. "I take it you've never eaten at either store?"

Although his voice remained steady, she could see his earlobes turn red. He didn't look at her. "I won't as long as the Cuban Club stands. I should take you there for dinner, but not lunch. The roof might fall on me if I walked into the club with a woman during the workday."

"Perhaps they need stronger beams."

"Cornelia, be nice," Teddy said. "Mr. Borrero is just being a gentleman. Have some respect for his culture."

Sal kept his distance as the ladies sat at the counter of the soda fountain, nibbling on sandwiches much less tempting than the fragrant offerings of the vendors outside. Teddy had cream of tomato soup instead of potato chips.

Teddy glanced at their guard before leaning closer. "Do you think he's right?"

"About what?"

"That we shouldn't have gone to Cuba."

Cornelia thought for a moment, sipped the milkshake she had decided to treat herself to. "The American people wanted us to go. The press wouldn't stop screaming about Spanish atrocities, even before the *Maine* incident."

"Grandmother was against it. She said going to war would profit very few people."

"Acquiring a number of new territories was probably very profitable for the country," Cornelia said.

"Yes, but what if all those young men died when they didn't have to? That would be awful."

"It *was* awful," Cornelia replied. "It would be better if no one ever had to die at all. But we were not part of that decision."

Teddy put her spoon down next to her bowl. "But we *were*. We each signed up to nurse the troops. We wouldn't have even met if the war hadn't happened."

"Then we must view it as one good thing that came from the war," Cornelia said, patting Teddy's hand. "Maybe the best."

After lunch, Sal took the ladies to the place where Jaquinda's body had been found. Maybe they should have gone before their meal, but Cornelia didn't expect to find much gore remaining at the scene. She was surprised to find almost none.

"There's very little blood," she said, taking the police photo out to make a comparison. "Rather tidy, considering what was done to the poor woman. Nelson didn't notice *that*."

"Tidy isn't the word I would use," Teddy replied, frowning down at the detritus near the wall of the brick building that flanked the alley. "There's trash, and cigarettes, and a cigar, and—oh, look." She bent and pointed. "Here's a couple of pearls. Not real ones, beads."

"They could be from the lady's necklace. It was broken."

"Indeed." Teddy took her handkerchief from her purse and picked the beads up. "Mr. Borrero?"

Sal, stationed close to the street, came closer. "Yes, *senora*?"

"Does Chago smoke cigars?"

"Sometimes."

"There's a cigar band here that looks new. I mean, discarded recently." She lifted it with the kerchief. "Does he smoke Infantas?"

"He'll take what he's offered, but he's partial to Rigoletto."

Cornelia checked the brick wall of the building more closely. "I don't think she was murdered here. There should be blood all over the place. I believe she was dumped."

"If Chago had done it, he would have moved her in his car," Teddy said, pointing at the Oldsmobile. "Did the police search it?"

"That's not his car. It's Mr. Wall's," Sal informed them. "They found traces of blood, but ... not fresh. Accidents occasionally happen."

"Of course," Teddy said. "Did they find any beads?"

A scowl added more creases to Sal's already-creased face. "I don't think so."

"Let me go through the report again," Cornelia said. After a moment, she slid it back into its envelope. "No beads listed, but that's hardly exculpatory. The prosecutor will say that he cleaned his car."

"But carelessly left a cigar band near the body?" Teddy threw open the door of the car and burrowed into the back. Cornelia shrugged after a moment and joined her.

"If you do find a bead, it won't help Chago's case."

"No," Teddy said, her voice muffled, "but the real killer had to break in to get his bat. We might find something else."

Several minutes of searching yielded nothing useful. Teddy swiped the sweat from her forehead before climbing out of the car.

"There are bloodstains back there," she told Sal. "They've been cleaned, but on close inspection I could still tell what they were."

Teddy watched the muscles tighten in Sal's face.

"That don't prove nothing," he said. Besides, this is Mr. Wall's car, otherwise the police would have kept it."

Cornelia joined them. "The police have taken samples."

"Are you sure?" Teddy said.

She frowned at her companion. "There was a note in the file. If the blood type matches Jackie's, it will look bad for Chago."

"So where do we go next?" Sal asked.

Teddy grinned. "Shopping."

Both Sal and Cornelia scowled.

"Don't look at me that way." Teddy said, examining Cornelia's sweat-soaked traveling suit. "We need to visit both Club Tropical and the one where Jackie worked before. You can't go dressed like that. You need an outfit suitable for the evening, and one that is appropriate for the climate for daytime. You'll roast alive if you keep wearing those long sleeves in Florida."

The line of cars crossing the Lafayette Street Bridge seemed interminable. The chugging of motors idling was a steady rumble, punctuated now and then with the hiss of steam. Cornelia had her own internal buildup of steam going, despite the cooler dress she wore. While they were in the store, Teddy had insisted that she also purchase a night dress, new underwear, and foundation undergarments. Sal had been nearby, standing guard, the entire time. There was no point in contesting her need for underwear, but she had felt embarrassed and humiliated. Even now she could see the remnants of the deep blush on Sal's neck.

Teddy, who had sat in silence for longer than normal, spoke up. "Mr. Borrero, thank you for taking us everywhere today."

"It's my job."

32

"Well, yes, but I'm sure your normal day is quite different."

"I would agree."

"Since we're stuck here, perhaps you could help provide Cornelia with more information for her investigation."

'Her investigation' sounded so silly. Cornelia wasn't in charge of anything, even if Teddy was determined to make her try to help Chago. It was Mr. Wall calling the shots.

Teddy continued. "Do you normally work with Chago on a daily basis?"

"Usually."

"Who would want to send him to the pen?"

Sal shrugged. "I couldn't name everyone. It's one of the occupational hazards Miss Pettijohn referred to."

"Mmm, yes. Who would be the most recent person or persons to hold a grudge?"

"I wouldn't know."

He was dissembling. Cornelia said, "I think you do know, Mr. Borrero. We have imposed on you in more ways today than I would have ever wanted to, but clearly you want us to help. I don't think you would have detoured to show us Chago's future otherwise."

Sal was quiet. Teddy started to speak again, but Cornelia gestured for her to stop.

"The last guy Chago might have offended was Gabriel Vacco," Sal allowed. "We were asking him about someone, and he was not forthcoming."

"Who was the someone you were asking about?"

"He might have been offended, too, but won't be a problem. They fished him out of the Hillsborough River on Wednesday."

"Before Miss Duarte was killed, then."

"Yes. Although—" Sal turned, foot on the brake "—we were talking to Vacco about Renzo, Jaquinda's brother. Renzo was selling *bolita* tickets in the Deuces and got knocked off."

"Where are the Deuces?" Cornelia asked.

"Saint Petersburg. It's where the colored folk live. A little nicer than The Scrub." Sal looked uncomfortable suddenly. "Renzo was darker than his sister. Her mother had him with her first husband, who died. He never got to see her on stage. He was only permitted to enter the *Sociedad La Unión Martí-Maceo*—the segregation laws divided the original Cuban National Club into two groups."

The car behind theirs honked and Sal lifted his foot, letting the Olds close the three-foot gap that had opened.

"When was Renzo killed?"

"Last Friday night, maybe early Saturday morning."

"Could his death and Jaquinda's be connected?"

The car behind them honked again. Sal muttered an uncomplimentary remark about the other driver's ancestry in Spanish. "Maybe. Vacco wasn't too happy about how Chago persuaded him to talk. And he wasn't a friend of the Duarte family."

Cornelia rubbed her chin. "Where would we find Mr. Vacco?"

"He's an employee of the Gangplank, plus some other folks out of state."

"The Gangplank!" Teddy broke in. "We've been to the Gangplank. Visiting again would be lovely."

"I don't think me or any of the boys would be welcome," Sal said. "Vacco's boss and mine don't exactly see eye to eye. The chump will also remember who was with Chago last Saturday."

"We'll have to work something out," Cornelia said. "This Gabriel Vacco sounds like a prime suspect for the frame."

"Could be," he said. "But I want to speak to the boss about it first."

By the time they pulled up to the entrance of the grand hotel, Cornelia was stiff-legged and longing for a hot bath. *The train would have been just as cramped*, she told herself. And their suite did have a nice large tub. If only she could relax in the tub and then crawl into bed for a week. The burns on her legs prevented her from anything more

34

than a sponge bath. She suppressed a sigh. Returning to her post at Fort Fitzsimons would be more of a vacation than her so-called 'vacation' had been.

As they went up the lift, Teddy and Sal talked about the Gangplank. Teddy was keen to go there tonight, but Sal argued that it was too late to make such a long trip. The club was on the Gulf side of Saint Petersburg, a lengthy drive. Cornelia silently rooted for the Cuban.

Putting their room on an upper floor was a good bit of strategy. It would be more difficult for them to escape without a direct route to the outside grounds. She hoped Uncle Percival hadn't been too bored in their absence. He'd probably already eaten dinner; perhaps she and Teddy could order from Room Service.

Sal unlocked the suite and held the door open for the ladies, and they entered. Cornelia had expected to find her uncle reading in one of the comfy chairs or tinkering with something at the table, but the room appeared empty. Had he gone to bed so early?

"Aha!" The professor stepped from behind the open door and pointed a pipe at Sal. A three-foot piece of plumbing pipe, as far as she could tell. He'd had time to find materials. Who knew what he'd built in their absence?

"Stop right there, you scoundrel," he ordered. "Quick, Cornelia, tie him up. The ropes from the curtains are on the couch."

"Oh, how clever!" Teddy cried, and ran to fetch them.

Cornelia interposed herself between her uncle and Sal. "Please, stop! It's all right. I've decided to stay and help Chago. Put that down before you hurt someone. Like me."

The professor lowered his makeshift weapon. "So, we're working with them now?"

"Yes. I am not completely convinced of his innocence, but the police are no longer investigating. If he is innocent, he needs help."

Teddy, holding the tiebacks, looked disappointed. "We're not taking Sal prisoner?"

Cornelia glanced back at their guardian-*cum*-captor, who was madder than a wet hen. "No."

35

"I suppose we should all sit and work together, then." Her companion began clearing the table, which held miscellaneous items that didn't belong in a hotel room. Tools, for one. Several round stones next to a handmade slingshot. Pieces of pipe and gravel. *Loose bullets?*

"How sweet, Percival," Teddy said. "Is this slingshot for me?"

The professor smiled. "Of course. I've heard of your skill."

"You two are crazy!" Sal sputtered. He snatched the pipe away from the old man. "Give me that. Who the hell threatens an armed man with toys?" He slammed the end of the pipe on the ground, and it exploded upwards. Pieces of the ceiling sprayed everywhere.

Percival Pettijohn laughed as Sal dropped the pipe gun and jumped back. "Never underestimate an engineer, young man. A gun is nothing more than a hollow tube and a firing mechanism."

Teddy stared upwards. "Good construction. It didn't go all the way through. We won't get a leak in the roof."

"It is fortunate for him I only found one length of pipe. A double barrel might have brought the roof down."

"Where did you get the bullets from?" Cornelia asked her uncle.

Percival grinned. "I filched the cartridges from your purse earlier. He took your gun, but not the ammo."

"Very clever."

"I was wrong," Sal said. "All three of you are crazy."

"Mr. Borrero, I don't think you would consider attempting to escape crazy if you were the one taken hostage. I suspect you are embarrassed that my uncle was able to turn the tables on you."

After a brief discussion, they decided to go to the Cuban Club. It was the last place Chago had seen Jaquinda alive, and close to where her body had been found.

Teddy headed off to change, but paused at the door to the bedroom she was sharing with Cornelia. "Are you going along with us, Percival?"

36

"Oh, he's going," Sal said. "I don't like what he gets up to when he's left alone."

The professor's smile returned. "Why, thank you, Mr. Borrero. I don't normally stay up late, but I could use a break from being cooped up in the suite. And, as you noted, I find ways of alleviating boredom."

Even Cornelia chuckled as she and Teddy dressed for dinner. "The look on his face when that pipe went off was priceless."

"It will teach him not to underestimate his elders," her companion replied. "Here, Corny, let me put some powder on your face. It's too shiny."

"A stressful day brings the oil out. And don't call me Corny. You've picked up that bad habit from Uncle Percival."

The Cuban Club was an imposing four stories of yellow brick and white stone. A double stairway lined with slender balustrades and coral risers led upwards to a pillared grand entrance. Couples and small groups of people stood on the steps, chattering in Spanish. Underneath the chatter, they could hear music.

"Look at the embroidery on that gown," Teddy said, studying the crowd. "Gorgeous. And the woman with the broad-brimmed hat. She has a bare shoulder—so striking."

"We saw lots of that in the Philippines."

"But this was for effect, dear." The woman wasn't the only one dressed for effect. Teddy was dressed to the nines, with a glittering blue gown and shoes made of silk and leather. Her uncle wore a well-tailored suit and carried his favorite cane, the one with the head shaped like a wildcat's.

Cornelia would never wear a gown with a naked shoulder, but she did admire the woman's hat. With its black and broad-brimmed shape, it wasn't that different from the one she wore with her uniform in the field. It was more festive, though, with a sparkling buckle.

Their escort, Sal, had also changed into a suit. He'd had one in the trunk of the car. Cornelia wondered if he kept a suit there just in case, or if he had brought one just for them. Who knew? He guided them up the stairs, nudging people to make way.

The music grew louder as they entered the club. People turned to glance at them, then quickly turned away. Since they'd never been to Ybor City before, Cornelia assumed that they recognized Sal. That could be good or bad.

Once they were clear of the entrance, the heavyset man faced Cornelia directly. "Where shall we begin, *senora* Cornelia?"

"I think we should find out where the argument took place. Some of those people may be here tonight, especially the staff. May I rely on you to make the introductions, Mr. Borrero?"

"Of course. We'll need to go upstairs to the ballroom. That's where she was performing."

They began their trek upwards. Sal and Cornelia went up the stairs rapidly while Teddy and the professor lagged behind, hampered by their respective handicaps. Overall, Cornelia thought the climate was beneficial to Teddy—perhaps because they were closer to sea level than Colorado had been—but her uncle's knees were another matter. The old dear must be nearly ninety by now, despite celebrating his seventy-fifth birthday multiple times.

When they reached the next flight, she noted the stained-glass window facing the street, the one with the flag of Cuba. She'd also spotted a sign in Spanish indicating where the pharmacy was. This was a true community center, not just a glorified dance hall.

The ballroom was on the fourth floor—of course it had to be the top floor—and a party was in full swing. Some people were dancing on the center floor while others were gathered at tables surrounding it. A live band played on an elevated stage. A sign with "Alligator Mojo" sat to the side; she presumed this was the band's name. They had a drummer, a piano, at least one guitarist, and a fellow on banjo. Two women, clad in matching black gowns, also played instruments: one, an alto sax, the other, a clarinet.

38

She noted that the piano player wore dark glasses. Did stage lights bother him, or was he blind? Cornelia knew that some soldiers, blinded in combat, relearned instruments they had been able to play before their handicap.

Sal nudged her. "That's Jaquinda's band, the one she performs with at Club Tropical. He indicated the man on trumpet. "Fernando Garcia. He's the band leader."

Nearby, Teddy was tapping her shoe, entranced by the music. She edged closer to the dance floor, and a young man at one of the tables stood. He spoke to her, she nodded, and he led her to the floor.

"We've lost her," Cornelia said. "With luck, she'll stay out of trouble. Uncle Percival, would you like to sit?"

"That might be best," he replied. "You proceed with the questioning; I'll see if I can make friends." He ambled away to the tables.

They needed to speak to the band, but that would have to be later. Cornelia scanned the room, looking for serving staff. She caught the eye of a waiter and gestured for him to come.

The young man approached, noticed Sal, and hesitated. Sal repeated her gesture and the waiter continued.

"Are you looking for an open table, *senor, senora*?"

Despite the heat of the room, Cornelia felt the cold prickle of awkwardness. It didn't help that Sal was watching her. "Soon," she blurted. "What I really need is a moment of your time."

"Come this way." They moved to a spot further from the stage, where it was easier to hear."

"What is your name, young man?"

The waiter eyed Sal. "Ricardo. How may I assist you, *senora*?"

"The musicians on stage. Are you familiar with the young woman who usually sings with them?"

"I'm afraid that she is—no longer with the band." He shuffled his foot.

Poor lad, he was trying to be polite. "I have heard that she had a misfortune. Were you here when she gave her last performance?"

"Yes. Her singing was *glorioso*."

"But there was an argument?"

He shifted his dark eyes to Sal, then back to her. "After the performance. She announced that she had made *un disco—*"

"A record," Sal translated for Cornelia, which was unnecessary since she was fluent in Spanish. If he didn't know she understood, though, keeping that knowledge to herself might come in handy later.

"A record with Opal and the Gemstones."

"They're the house band for The Black Opal. They don't perform here," her escort/translator added. "They are not suitable."

He seemed to share Chago's opinion; very interesting. "What happened then?"

"The people clapped. They loved her."

"But not everyone was happy."

"No. The Mojos were surprised, and *Senor* Garcia was *enfurecido*. He followed her offstage and they had an argument in the dressing room."

"Did you hear what was said?"

"Only a little. I was serving drinks to a table near the stage and heard him say that she had betrayed him and would never perform with the Mojos again."

"And what did Miss Duarte say?"

"She said that other musicians would be glad to replace them."

"What else?"

"He called her rude names I will not repeat to a *senora*. I had to serve other tables after that."

Cornelia glanced up at the band. "*Senor* Garcia is the trumpet player, correct?" It never hurt to double-check.

"*Si*. He's the leader."

"Thank you, Ricardo. What about *Senorita* Duarte's young man? The one she has been seeing, Santiago Aldama. I can describe him if you like."

40

Ricardo fidgeted. "I know who you mean. He was sitting up front in his usual spot when she made the announcement."

"You must have been nearby, then. What did he do?"

"He was as surprised as the band, and unhappy. He stayed in place and said nothing, though, until she joined him after the performance."

"Was this after the argument she had with Mr. Garcia?"

"Yes. She was defiant; her face was set. He spoke to her quietly at first, but she didn't reply. He grew louder."

"Did he threaten her?"

"No. He entreated her to set the recording aside and no longer associate with the women."

Cornelia doubted that 'entreat' was the correct term, especially if it were done loudly. "Which women?"

"The Gemstones are an all-female band. Opal, their leader, co-owns the Black Opal club."

Interesting. They would definitely need to visit the place. "What happened next?"

"She said it was not his business, but hers. He then offered to buy the recording, pay a fair price for its not being heard. The *senorita* stood, grabbed the vase on the table, and threw it at him."

This tallied with what Chago had said. "What did he do?"

"He picked up a napkin and wiped his face and jacket."

"What happened next?"

"The *senorita* said that they were finished, and she never wanted to see him again. She left then, angry."

Cornelia nodded. "Did Mr. Aldama follow her?"

"No, but—"

Shrieks from the dance floor interrupted. They turned and saw a crowd gathered near the stage. Uncle Percival was heading towards it at full gallop, his cane punctuated every step on the marble floor.

Teddy!

Cornelia charged into the cluster of well-dressed young people, Sal at her heels. "Move aside, I'm a nurse. *Por favor, soy enferma*." She knew exactly what had happened. Why, oh why, did Teddy always have to dance? Hadn't she rushed around enough today?

Sal moved ahead of her and parted the crowd, revealing the collapsed figure on the floor. It was Teddy, just as Cornelia feared. Her dance partner, who looked younger than the doughboys she'd treated in the trenches, was fanning her with his hand.

"*Soy enferma*. Lift her up—this way—so she can breathe easier." She checked for a pulse and found it, quick and hard. Teddy's makeup concealed her true coloring, but her mouth was open and Cornelia saw the pale gums. Her companion had fainted from overexertion ... again.

The old nurse reached into the purse she always carried, the practical one issued to her by the Army, and drew out a small bottle.

Teddy came back to life when the smelling salts were waved under her nose. "Ugh!" She twisted away.

"If you don't like the scent of ammonia, you need to learn your limits," Cornelia told her. "You know you shouldn't dance for more than a song or two."

"I am so sorry," the young man said. "She will be okay?"

"Probably, despite her best efforts. Can you sit up on your own, dearie?"

Sal brought a chair, and the two men boosted Teddy up into it. A waiter offered her a glass, and she downed the contents. This was followed by a spate of coughing, and Teddy waved the glass for a refill.

"Let me guess. Brandy?"

"Rum," Teddy managed, and held the glass higher. "May I have a little more, *por favor*? It seems to be helping."

"Doesn't it always?" Cornelia looked around, but Ricardo was no longer in sight.

Uncle Percival appeared at her side. "Shall we get a table where we can sit together until she recovers?"

They ordered *tostones* and tea. Cornelia declined the coffee; she remembered how strong the coffee in Havana had been. She needed to sleep tonight.

"Did you learn anything?" the professor asked.

"A little," Cornelia said. "Jaquinda argued with Chago, but she also had a set-to with Mr. Garcia, who is the band leader, about a record she'd just made with a different group. He's playing trumpet."

They all glanced at the stage.

"I presume the next step is to interview him and the other band members. Mr. Borrero, we may need your help in translation." Teddy looked at her curiously, and Cornelia shook her head slightly. She'd used a few phrases, but wanted to keep Sal in the dark about how much Spanish she understood. He was working for Charlie Wall, not them.

"Of course."

The plantains arrived and they dug in. Sal did most of the eating. Cornelia felt guilty; she hadn't thought to order a sandwich for Sal when they had their late lunch. Her uncle had spent most of the afternoon scheming, but might have ordered room service. She would have to consider Sal's needs in the future.

After eating a few of the fried slices, the professor excused himself. "There's card playing downstairs and other games. Some gentlemen here were very helpful when I asked for assistance in translating the menu, so I queried them about activities other than dancing. Perhaps I can learn more."

Sal scowled but let him leave.

Teddy, no longer pale, turned in her seat to watch the band. "They're excellent. I enjoy the liveliness of the music— perhaps I enjoyed it a little too much. I'm sorry, Corny; I didn't mean to scare everyone."

"Don't call me Corny."

The Mojos finished their set and disappeared behind the curtains flanking the stage. Two of the men emerged and headed for a balcony. Sal rose and waved to the women; they went to the same balcony, which overlooked one of the streets. When she looked down, Cornelia's neck prickled; below was the same alley where Jaquinda had been found.

The men were smoking, not unusual behavior for musicians on break. The air was also cooler than the ballroom, which was likely welcome after their time under the lights.

Sal approached the pair and spoke to them in Spanish. He told them that he was an employee of Mr. Wall, and the *senoras* wanted to ask them some questions about Jaquinda Duarte. Mr. Wall would be obliged if they were cooperative. The men nodded.

Introductions were made; the men were Roberto Garcia and Louis Fernandez. Cornelia learned that Alligator Mojo was a family band. Fernando Garcia, the one with the temper, was the leader. Roberto, his brother, played guitar; the other, Jose, played fiddle. The female clarinet player was their sister, Isabela.

Louis, the drummer, had been in the same year in school as Fernando when they were growing up. Cornelia noted that he had a line above his lip, a scar. Perhaps he'd had a cleft lip repaired, although she'd seen better work.

Teddy, their ambassador, laid on the enthusiasm. "It must be wonderful to make music with your family," she said. "My brothers both played piano, but I'm the only one who kept up with it."

Louis grinned, revealing a gold tooth. "What did you think of Blind Billy?"

"He plays divinely." She clasped her hands. "I'm so glad it's in his nickname; I didn't know how to ask without being rude."

"Theodora." Cornelia nudged her. "Let's not take too much of their break. We want to ask you a few questions about your former singer, Jaquinda."

"A true tragedy," Fernando said. "How may we assist you, *senora*?"

"On the last night she performed with you, she announced that she had recorded a disc with another band. The Gemstones, I've been told."

Fernando didn't quite frown, but the muscles in his face still showed distaste. "You are correct."

"You were angry."

"It was a surprise, and not a pleasant one. She flattered us, saying that she wanted to perform with such a fine band, and I thought she would be a great asset to the Mojos. Then she turned on us. I was ... disappointed."

"It was loud disappointment," Cornelia said. "And Miss Duarte had unkind things to say."

"She didn't mean them," Louis said. His lisp was faint, but present. "Jackie was angry. You should've given her time to think things over, Nando."

"The deed was already done." Fernando turned away to flick the ash off his cigar. "You're just softhearted because you liked her. That *senorita* turned your head."

"Jackie liked me better than she liked you. I know how to treat a doll."

Fernando raised an eyebrow. "So you say, Lefty, but I've yet to see you with a sheba."

"They look at his face and run," Roberto said.

There was no need for insults. "What did you and the other members of the band do after the argument?" Cornelia prodded.

"The show was over. Roberto took Jose and Isabela home; they're still in school. Bobby and Sadie gave Billy a ride home."

"And you?"

I went to the El Dorado to cool off. And think. We need a new singer."

"Where did Jaquinda go?"

"She left the stage to join her man. He wasn't looking too happy with her plans."

"I've been told they argued. Did you see it?"

Roberto put his cigar out on the concrete barrier of the balcony. "She wasn't my problem any more. I put my instruments away and left."

Cornelia nodded, then glanced at Louis. "Where did you go?"

"Off to The Yellow House, ma'am. I had a *bolita* ticket, and they were drawing."

They made their goodbyes and went to find Uncle Percival. Once they were on the stairs, the temperature of the air dropped. Conversations in Spanish echoed up the ornately decorated walls as they descended.

"She must have been striking on that stage, with her elegant gown and those rings," Teddy said.

"She was," Sal said. "She was a beautiful woman."

"And those shoes," Teddy said. "Tell me, what ..." She stopped walking and stared at the stairwell across from them.

Cornelia stopped as well. "Tell you what?"

"Red. Her shoes were red." Teddy scanned the stairs below them.

"Yes, *senora*. She had red shoes," Sal said.

Cornelia scanned the stairs and the walls. "Is there a poster of her I've missed?"

"No, I saw her just now. Rose-colored pearls, white gown, and red shoes."

Just now? This was concerning. She thought Teddy had fully recovered from her faint. "What do you mean, you saw her?"

Her companion pointed. "I saw her, running down those stairs. An arm reached out and seized her, and she vanished."

"Are you sure that was just rum they gave you?"

Teddy ignored the question. "It was a well-dressed arm with a gold ring on the left hand. A man's arm."

Cornelia was still concerned when they entered the casino room. Sal had said nothing, but he'd seemed startled as well. From what Teddy had told her about the Lawless family, her mother had been a practitioner of Spiritualism for several years, having visions and the like, but the only spirits Teddy was usually interested in were the liquid kind.

Uncle Percival was all smiles when they reached his table. "Good evening, ladies. I hope you were able to learn more about Miss Duarte." His hands were folded across his belly, arms covering bulges in both pockets.

"We did. How were the card games? You look pleased with yourself."

"The folk here are so friendly and helpful when you don't know the language," the professor said. "I'm afraid the closest language to Spanish I learned in school was Latin, a bit behind the times. Perhaps if we were in a monastery ..."

"You memorized the cards, didn't you?"

"Cornelia, dear, I have no choice in the matter. I remember everything at some level and my attention was on the game. Besides, that wasn't the game I did best in tonight. They introduced me to *bolita*."

Cornelia remembered the game from their time in Cuba. "You bet on which ball they would draw out of a bag? I didn't think you would gamble on something so dependent on luck."

He winked. "Sometimes men make their own luck, Corny," he replied, and stood, turning to face Sal. "Mr. Borrero, I have enjoyed the pleasures of your city, but have given nothing back. Would you be able to arrange for my winnings tonight to be given to Miss Duarte's family? Even death is expensive these days."

Surprise crossed Sal's face, but he nodded in agreement. As they left the club, Cornelia was certain the Cuban muttered something about her uncle needing to be watched at all times. It was a lesson *she'd* learned years ago.

Who's Calling Now?

The next morning, they breakfasted in the room. Despite the late hour of their return to the hotel, Cornelia felt rested. The mattresses of the hotel were markedly softer than the ones at Fort Fitzsimons. Between the Vinoy and the Tampa Bay Hotel, her back was becoming spoiled. Her return to duty would be a rude awakening in more ways than one.

Teddy was talking to Uncle Percival about their plans for the day. She was wearing a cotton frock; next to her, folded neatly on the sofa, was her newest jacket, a pale pink. The jacaranda hat she'd purchased from Berber's rested atop it. Cornelia knew she was dressing for the Gangplank, but they'd be visiting the jail first. She finished the fish patty—an unexpected item on the breakfast menu—and spread jam on her toast.

When the knock came at the door, Cornelia opened it, expecting to see Sal. Instead, it was one of the bellhops.

"I have a telephone message for a Miss Theodora Lawless."

Hearing her name, Teddy set aside her needlepoint and stood. "Did you say a telephone message? For me?"

"Yes, miss." He indicated the folded paper in his hand.

"I can't imagine who would be calling," she said, crossing the room. "If it's our host, I imagine he'd direct it to you, Cornelia."

"When did this call arrive?" Cornelia asked the young man.

"I'm not certain, ma'am. It was forwarded from the Vinoy."

"Perhaps it's from Shirley, then. We talked about visiting some of the other beaches." Teddy took the note and opened it.

Shirley was a young beautician Teddy had befriended during their time in Saint Petersburg. As Cornelia watched Teddy's face, though, her companion looked puzzled, then surprised.

"You say this was forwarded from the Vinoy?"

The lad nodded. "Yes, miss."

"I don't believe this," Teddy said, looking at the note again.

"What is it?"

"It's from my mother. She wants me to call her."

Telephones were provided in the rooms; Teddy pulled a chair closer to it and spoke into the mouthpiece. "Long distance, please. Erie County, Pennsylvania." She checked the note and gave the exchange to the operator. "Yes, I'll wait." She played with the lavender strands of Bakelite beads she'd chosen for her outfit.

The wait was not a short one. Teddy gave her mother's name and number to multiple operators. Meanwhile, Cornelia feared that she would pull the necklace apart. It had been years since the women had spoken. The last contact from Mrs. Lawless had been a curt letter delivered by Army mail when they were stationed in Panama, informing her that her grandmother had passed away. Later, when the second letter arrived from the dowager's banker, they knew why the letter had been so terse.

Then she sat up straight. "Hello. Is this Mother?"

Cornelia waited.

"No, we're in Tampa now. It's just across the bay. How ... how may I help you?" Her brow puckered as she listened. "No, I didn't know my arrest had made the paper

50

there. I don't know why they would even bother." Listening more, then: "Well, it was a given that I would be a suspect. He was murdered, and I was the ex-fiancée. No! How could I have avoided him if I didn't know he was in Florida?" Pause. "I didn't choose the hotel; the professor did. It was for his birthday."

Cornelia looked at Uncle Percival. He sat nearby with his hearing device plugged into his ear and undoubtedly turned to full volume. One white eyebrow lifted at being mentioned.

Teddy crossed her ankles. "Yes, the professor is my fiancé. We haven't been engaged long; it was sudden." She uncrossed her ankles. "I was surprised, too."

"As was I," Cornelia muttered. Her uncle's swift fabrication to explain Teddy's presence in the Vinoy might have worked with the police, but they weren't in Saint Petersburg anymore. Why did the two insist on continuing the pretense?

Teddy was tugging on the beads again. "I've always liked smart men; you remember how much I liked listening to Judge Thomas as a child. Father had to chase me from the room. Percival is a professor of engineering. With the University of Kentucky, although he retired a few years ago."

A few years ago? That was stretching the truth by at least a decade. The University of Kentucky was still the Agricultural and Mechanical College when Uncle Percival retired. They were building the first women's dormitory when he left.

"They put our pictures in the paper? We haven't had engagement photographs made yet, how could they—oh, really?" The necklace snapped, and she flung it aside, flushing to the collar of her frock. "Who gave them permission to do that? I see. I need to speak with dear Percival for a moment."

She covered the speaking portion of the candlestick phone with her hand. "The *Evening Independent's* society reporter shared photographs from the morning of my arraignment," she hissed. "I hate that Hornbuckle woman!"

51

Cornelia fought her own surge of anger. How humiliating for poor Teddy to be embarrassed in her hometown, which she had never visited in all the years they'd been together.

Teddy was listening to her mother again. "That's him. Yes, he does look a bit like Santa Claus."

The professor's mustache quirked in a smile. He edged closer.

"We just celebrated his seventy-fifth birthday."

"Again," Cornelia muttered, just loud enough for her uncle to hear.

Teddy swatted her armrest. "Applesauce! He's not *that* much older than I am. Newspaper photographs are notoriously unflattering." Pause. "No, not buildings; most of his designs are for farm equipment, although he did recently create a clockwork wildcat for sporting events. A wildcat, that's the mascot of the university. He's partnering with a Mr. James to produce smaller ones for purchase."

Teddy listened again. "No, he is not a farmer, although he does have a farm. Well, it might make him a farmer." She turned to Percival. "Dearest, are you a farmer?"

Cornelia winced at the word "dearest."

"I am a farm owner. I hire someone to manage the farm."

She repeated this to her mother. "He spends his time inventing things in his workshop. He's frightfully clever."

Uncle Percival beamed. Teddy, meanwhile, was silent. Silent, and growing pale.

"Lovely of you to call," she said, and made her goodbyes.

"What did she say?" Cornelia asked, concerned.

"She wants to attend the wedding. Said she wouldn't miss it for the world."

When their escort arrived, it was a young ebon-dark man rather than Sal.

"Hello," Cornelia said. "Who are you?"

The man doffed his gray fedora. "Greetings, ma'am. My name is Clevon Martin. Mr. Wall has assigned me to be your driver today." Clevon was clearly a snappy dresser; he wore a navy pinstripe suit that was broad at the shoulders and tapered to the waist.

"Is there a way you could prove that?"

His smile didn't fade. "If you come downstairs, ma'am, you'll recognize the car. I also have your uncle's winnings from last night." He opened his jacket and pointed to a packet lodged in the inside pocket.

What did she have to lose? She'd already been kidnapped once this weekend. "Come in, Mr. Martin. This is my uncle, Professor Pettijohn, and Teddy Lawless, my—"

"—My fiancée," Uncle Percival completed.

Not again.

"I'm pleased to meet you both; congratulations on your engagement."

Teddy gave her most charming smile. "Pleased to meet you as well. Are you from Tampa?"

"Yes, I am. Born and bred. That's why the boss sent me."

If he were a kidnapper, his manners were much better than Sal's. "So, he wants you to take us somewhere in Tampa today?"

Clevon turned. "Yes. Your uncle wanted to donate the proceeds from last night to Mrs. Duarte's family. They live in The Scrub, where I grew up. The boss wants you to visit them and make the donation personally. That way, you can ask them any questions you want, but you'll have a different reason for being there."

The professor frowned. "We are not going to *pay* that unfortunate family for information," he said. "They have suffered a great loss. We cannot restore their daughter and sister, so I am offering the only assistance I can."

Teddy placed her hand on his arm. "Mr. Wall thinks we *can* do more for them, dear; find justice for Jaquinda and save Chago. We will go bearing gifts, but I think they'll tell us what they know because it makes sense."

"Of course," the professor said, mollified. "Did Mr. Wall say anything else?"

"He suggested that you not partake of the games he runs. He approves of what you want done with the winnings, but he'd prefer that you game at his rivals' establishments. Are you a card sharp?"

Cornelia smiled. "He's sharp in a number of ways. Let's go. We have a long day ahead of us. Where's Teddy?"

"She went back to her room." Their visitor pointed at the couch. "She took off her jacket and left it there."

Of course she had; they were changing destinations, and Teddy always dressed for the occasion. She reappeared wearing her black cardigan jacket and cloche hat. She normally wore a sparkling brooch with the outfit, but had chosen a somber look.

She made a turn in front of Clevon. "Do you think this will be appropriate?"

"I think that is an excellent choice, ma'am."

Teddy smiled, then swept up the pink jacket, the flowered hat, and a large straw bag that sat beside the couch. Cornelia wondered why she was taking one of her big bags, then realized that the slingshot her uncle had made was no longer on the table. Clever girl.

Teddy adjusted her hat. "I'm ready to visit the family. How far is it?"

"We're not going there first," Cornelia said. "We're going to the jail. I want to speak to Chago again before I see the Duartes."

Clevon was correct about their recognizing the car; he was driving the same car that Chago and Sal both used. While he assisted Teddy and the professor into the back of the vehicle, Cornelia climbed into the front passenger seat. The valets attending the more moneyed clients of the hotel eyed them curiously. A private driver implied a level of income that the used Olds just didn't confirm.

They had missed the morning rush of traffic; it didn't take long to reach the jail. Nothing had changed for Chago since their visit the previous day, including his clothing. He looked exhausted, and a little more dust had gathered on his

54

pants and sleeves. He nodded to Clevon, who nodded back. Then his brown eyes shifted to the ladies.

"Ladies," he said. "I'm honored by your visit. How may I help you today?"

"We need more information for our investigation. We visited the Cuban Club last night, which seems to be the last place anyone saw Jaquinda alive."

"I wish I had followed her when she stomped out of the ballroom. Instead, I turned away and nursed my anger."

"We all have regrets; you didn't know what would happen." Teddy pulled a comb from her bag. "Here. I thought you might want to use this while we're here. I have a mirror if you need it."

Chago gave her his old grin. "Thank you, *Senora* Teddy. No need for the mirror; there's no one in here I want to impress."

Next time, I will remember to include a clothes brush."

He already looked better; Teddy had given him a bit of his pride back. Cornelia allowed Chago a few moments to make himself tidy before questioning him. "You look more like yourself now. Now, this first question is a difficult one: when we searched your car—or the one Mr. Wall lets you use—we found traces of blood in the back. I presume this is also where you kept your baseball bat. Whose blood is it?"

Chago looked down and shuffled his foot. "I visited a dance club with some of my friends. One tripped on the floor and got a nosebleed. He lay in the back seat while I drove him home."

Well, that was inventive. Unfortunately for him, Cornelia had heard scores of stories from young soldiers explaining why they had black eyes, how food could mysteriously disappear from a locked kitchen, and that they couldn't possibly have venereal disease.

She fixed him with a stern look. "I'm sure your adventures have extended beyond the dance hall from time to time. Is there a chance that you might have been carrying your bat to a game, when it slipped and accidentally hurt someone?"

Teddy, who was taking notes again, muffled a snort of laughter.

The young Cuban stared at the ceiling. "Accidents do happen."

"Who was the ballplayer the last time your bat slipped?"

He lowered his head and curled his lip. "A shortstop named Vacco."

That tallied with what Sal had told them.

"Is Mr. Vacco still in the game?"

"Yes, but he needs to stay in the infield."

Enough fencing. Cornelia decided to be more direct. "I've learned that Vacco had problems with Jaquinda's brother. Do you think he would take his anger out on her, too?"

"Not because of him, no. That was business. If he hurt her ... it would be because of me. And he would have taken a huge risk, coming so far into the boss' territory."

"So, not likely. But it might be worth finding out." She fixed her gaze right between his eyebrows, which she often used on reluctant informers. "Now, Santiago, I need your advice on another subject, one of more delicacy."

The young Cuban straightened at her use of his proper name. "How may I assist?"

"We're going to visit Jaquinda's family today to give them a gift. I've learned that this is one of a series of tragedies. What do I need to know before I start asking questions?"

"That you shouldn't ask them anything. They have suffered enough."

Cornelia nodded slowly. "I would agree with you under normal circumstances. But in this case, circumstances have dictated otherwise. Would you give me more information, so I can minimize the amount of pain I cause? Did the problem begin with Renzo?"

Chago sat down on the visitation room's bench. "No, with Renzo's father. He worked in the cigar factory with Jaquinda's mother, but made money on the side selling *bolita* tickets. Everything was fine until those *norteños* from

56

Chicago decided to expand their territory in Florida. One night, the father didn't come home. When he was found, he was dead. He'd been beaten for a long time; they probably wanted info on the boss that he didn't have. Renzo, who also worked at the factory, took on the *bolita* job. The boss sent him to the Deuces last week and he turned up dead, too. I apologize that my plain language may be too brutal."

"I have seen brutality in person; words can be harsh, but ones spoken honestly and without malice are not brutal," Cornelia said. "Just tell me the truth so I can sort this mess out."

"Yes. We sought justice for Renzo. The man behind that attack could not be responsible for Jaquinda, since he is already dead—although not by my hand. But Vacco worked for him, and he had reason to hate me."

"Her poor mother must be in great pain. Does she have any children left?"

"Only one. Her youngest, Bembe. He's too young to work in the factory because of the laws. He's been selling *bolita* tickets since his father died, but the boss is keeping him closer to home."

The Duarte home was located in a neighborhood adjacent to Ybor City. On the police form, it had been listed as "The Scrub." When Clevon turned down Central Avenue, Cornelia saw a street bustling with business—dressmakers, barbers, small groceries—all operated and visited by Negroes. Segregation had left its mark.

Two fashionably dressed young women waved from the sidewalk, and Clevon tipped his hat to them. "Good morning, ladies!"

"Neighbors?" Teddy craned her head to look.

"Everyone's my neighbor here. This is where I grew up."

Teddy studied the buildings. "This must be where the Buffalo Soldiers were welcomed when we were preparing to leave for Cuba. The white shopkeepers were very rude to them, turning them away. But the black population celebrated their arrival with music and entertainment."

57

Clevon's grin became more guarded. "Were you here then, ma'am?"

"Yes, I was here with the Red Cross nurses. They kept us at the hotel you just picked us up from. Just me, though. Cornelia was an Army contract nurse, and she came through Jacksonville with the Seventh Army."

"Women were serving that long ago. Imagine that."

"Women have always served in war, one way or another," Cornelia said. "Some even disguised themselves as men."

They turned off the brick street onto one where shotgun houses faced one another, porch to porch, tied together by clotheslines across the sand. No brick roads here. The businesses on the main street might be flourishing, but there were no playgrounds, no parks. Just identical houses with tin roofs, broken up by the occasional rain barrel or well.

Clevon pointed to one of the lookalike houses, distinguishable only by the dark wreath on its door. "There's where Jackie's family lives. I'll try to park close."

One of the Duartes' neighbors called Clevon's name from a nearby porch. He turned to wave. "Later, Matty. We have business."

They climbed the steps and stood to the side of the door while their guide knocked. The curtain of the front window moved aside, and a boy's face peeked through. As quickly as it appeared, though, it was gone. Cornelia heard whispers inside.

"Mrs. Duarte, it's me, Clevon. I'm here with some people you need to meet."

How intrusive Cornelia felt as a stranger standing on a porch, while the grieving woman inside decided whether to answer the door or not. She could feel the disapproval that peeked out from behind the curtains of neighboring houses.

Clevon removed his hat. "Mrs. Duarte, the boss sent me."

More whispering. Then they heard the bolt slide and the door cracked open.

A small, slender woman looked up at Clevon. She pulled dark netting across her lined face. *"Por qué estás aquí?"*

"I'm here with some people who want to help."

"There is nothing that can help us now."

"These people have a gift for you."

She studied the three Anglos: a somber, stout woman of middle age, another woman, expensively dressed, with silver hair and kohl-lined eyes, and an elderly gentleman with a cane.

"Who are they?"

"These are the Pettijohns," Clevon said. After her expression of puzzlement, he added, "Mr. Wall asked me to bring them here."

"Why?"

Clevon turned to Cornelia. "Perhaps you could better explain."

Cornelia disagreed; everything that came to mind sounded ludicrous. This was a ludicrous situation. How was she supposed to explain that Charlie Wall had decided that she was Sherlock Holmes?

Her Watson spoke up. "We're friends of Chago's. He loved your daughter so much."

The woman moved forward, filling the door. "Santiago is in jail for killing my daughter."

Teddy lowered her eyes. "I'm sure he's done some questionable things, but he did love Jaquinda. We think he's innocent. We want to help you and your son, especially since Chago's not in a position to do it himself."

"What can you do for us?"

Uncle Percival came to Teddy's side. "Help you with the funeral costs, if nothing else," he said. "I've outlived enough of my kin to know the responsibilities that follow death."

Jaquinda's mother turned toward him and lifted her veil, revealing an oval face and eyes very much like her late daughter's. "Please tell me your name again, *senor*?"

He bowed slightly. "I am Percival Pettijohn. This lovely lady, Theodora, is my fiancée, and this is Cornelia, my

59

niece. We met young Santiago when we were in Citrus County, looking at property for a winter home."

Cornelia gritted her teeth at the word *fiancée*. Her uncle had really seized onto the idea, and Teddy wasn't discouraging him at all. The old fool couldn't really be *in* love with Teddy, could he?

Everyone was looking at her for some reason. "My apologies," she said, squelching a stammer. "I think I missed that last part."

"I was telling Mrs. Duarte that Mr. Wall had engaged your services as an investigator," Teddy said. "You've saved at least two people from prison since we've been in Florida."

Cornelia suspected that her self-appointed Watson had not added that those two people had been Uncle Percival and Teddy herself.

"Thank you for the introduction. Mrs. Duarte, would you be more comfortable speaking to us inside the house, or would you prefer that we speak here? I don't want to intrude more than necessary."

"Come inside," Jaquinda's mother said, and they entered. The interior light was dim due to the dark draperies added to the usual curtains. The room was oppressively warm, probably for the same reason. It was only February, but February in Florida was like late May in Colorado.

The furniture was old but immaculate. Cornelia sat in the armchair their hostess indicated, while Teddy and the professor sat on a coral sofa inspired by a Chesterfield design.

"Young men are not always the best judge of what is in a woman's heart. Chago thinks they were in love. Did Jaquinda feel the same?"

Clevon's hands fumbled with the brim of his hat as he repeated her question in Spanish. He couldn't bring himself to look at either of them.

A trace of a smile flitted across Mrs. Duarte's face. "Jaquinda was young and beautiful, with the voice of an angel. Many young men loved her. But her music, her dream, that was what Jaquinda loved."

60

Teddy interrupted. "So, she wasn't serious about Chago?"

Mrs. Duarte looked at Clevon, who reluctantly translated.

"She liked him, maybe falling in love. But he would always be second in her heart. Chago does not seem the sort of man who could settle for that."

Cornelia frowned. This wasn't helping Chago's case. "You said there were other young men who loved Jaquinda. Did any of them frighten her?"

The question led to a long exchange in Spanish between Clevon and Jaquinda's mother.

Cornelia sat quietly and listened to the two of them discuss what she had meant by "frighten" and the possible beaus who gave her concern. The most interesting person mentioned was an unknown admirer who left presents and amorous notes in her dressing room. More worrying, was the fact that Clevon didn't tell her about the mystery man when he translated an abbreviated version of their conversation. He also neglected to mention the woman at the Black Opal who made advances. The latter, she suspected, was because he thought it unsuitable to share.

Clevon explained that the bandleader frightened Jaquinda. He repeated much of what they'd learned at the Cuban Club. He also mentioned that a member of Antinori's mob tried to entice her away from her current club. When that didn't work, he resorted to threats.

"Was that all?" Cornelia asked. He reluctantly added that someone had been leaving "gifts" for her in her dressing room.

"Which location?"

He turned to Mrs. Duarte and asked.

Club Tropical.

"Does the band have a shared dressing room there?"

Clevon nodded. "There's one for men and one for women. She shares the space with the dancers."

"How many people have keys to the ladies' dressing room?"

Clevon's brow wrinkled. "There's no locks on the dressing rooms. People come and go all the time."

"So, anyone in the club could have left these 'gifts' for her?"

His eyes widened. "Not just anyone. They would need a reason to be backstage."

Cornelia's dark blue eyes met his. "And Mr. Wall has someone there to ask about those reasons? Is it the same someone every night?"

Clevon grinned. "Exactly."

"I need to talk to Mr. Wall's man backstage. Can you arrange that?"

She didn't wait for him to answer before turning to Mrs. Duarte to say goodbye and thank her for seeing them.

The professor pressed a fat envelope into Bembe's hands. "Now that you are the man of the house, you need to take care of your mother."

Bembe's shoulders squared, and he straightened his jacket the way Cornelia had seen Chago do many times. The boy must have watched his sister's beau closely to mirror his mannerisms so perfectly.

Not the best role model, she thought as she turned to go.

They were barely out of the front door when Teddy stepped close to Cornelia and whispered, "So, when are we going to the Black Opal? Should we postpone going to the Jungle Prada and visit there tonight?"

"Teddy, you're incorrigible. You just want to find out which of the Gemstones tried to steal Chago's girlfriend."

Teddy giggled, which provoked a fit of coughing.

Professor Pettijohn removed a small silver flask from his vest pocket and held it out to her.

She took a much smaller sip than usual and passed the flask back to him.

The drink helped, but she was still wheezing as they walked.

Cornelia hovered beside her, worrying that she might swoon. Thankfully, she managed the short walk back to where Clevon had parked the Olds.

They were near their parking spot before Teddy recovered enough to speak. "Learning which Gemstone got the icy mitt isn't the *only* thing I want to find out, but it is pretty near the top of my list."

Teddy was not happy that they didn't return to the hotel after their visit with the Duartes. Instead, Clevon made a stop at the El Dorado. "Wait here," he ordered.

Cornelia's eyes widened. He had been such a polite young man all day. She hadn't expected churlishness.

"I didn't mean to frighten you. The boss doesn't want your uncle tempted to do any gambling," he added.

Cornelia glanced in the back seat where her uncle was giving her his most innocent look. She wasn't fooled. The old dear couldn't be trusted to behave. Among his many talents was his uncanny ability to find or make trouble wherever he went.

Instead of Clevon returning, the young red-head Sal referred to as 'Lobster' slid into the driver's seat. He didn't look happy to be their driver. Cornelia suspected that his ego had taken a beating over the black eye she gave him during the kidnapping.

"Where's Clevon?" Teddy asked.

He started the engine and pulled away from the curb. "The Boss doesn't think visiting the Gangplank is good for Clevon's health. I'm taking over for him." He glanced at Cornelia's stony face. "That's not a problem, is it?"

The ice in Cornelia's voice could have frozen boiling water. "Not if your manners have improved since we last met."

He swallowed hard. "I am sorry, ma'am."

There was a certain amount of satisfaction in watching the color creep up his neck and turn his ears a brighter shade of red than his hair.

"You should be. Manhandling a defenseless woman is barbaric."

"Defenseless! You nearly killed me."

"I was protecting my virtue."

His entire head, down to the roots of his hair glowed bright red. He opened his mouth, but no words came out. After several seconds, his mouth snapped closed and stayed that way until they reached the Gandy Bridge.

Now that Cornelia was a consenting passenger, she realized how beautiful the view was crossing the bridge. The bay spread out for miles on each side of her in sparkling waves, blue in the deeper areas and greenish-blue where the shallower waters were. Near the shore an osprey snatched his lunch from the sparkling waters. The fish glinted silver in the sunlight as it struggled to free itself from the bird's powerful claws.

It was a shame her field glasses were packed with the rest of her belongings and on their way to Colorado. She would love to have a closer look at the osprey and the flock of egrets gathered in the mangroves below him. There were so many beautiful birds in Florida, not that she had been able to enjoy watching them on this trip. Between her uncle and Teddy, the birds she saw most often were jailbirds. She had even joined the flock for a brief time. Cornelia retreated from that thought and went back to scanning the horizon for birds of the feathered variety. Her reward was a glorious view of pink feathers. "Teddy, look."

Teddy glanced where she was pointing. "Is that a real flamingo?"

"We're a bit too far north for those," Cornelia replied, "not that Florida has many. Hunters nearly wiped them out in the last century. That's a roseate spoonbill wading in the shallow waters along the shore. I can't believe our luck. This is my first sighting of one."

"You like birds?" Lobster asked.

"You sound surprised," Cornelia replied.

Lobster smiled. "Nah, my grandma likes birds, and loves hummingbirds. She planted a garden for them and the butterflies. You should see how many show up at her house on their way north."

Cornelia's whole demeanor changed, and the hostility disappeared from her voice. "My mother would never let my father cut down the milkweed that grew wild along the fence rows. She claimed the butterflies depended on it for food. I haven't thought about that in years."

By the time they reached the St. Petersburg side of the bridge, they were chatting like old friends. Their conversation came to an abrupt halt when the professor caught sight of the giant road sign proclaiming "No Jews Wanted Here."

"What kind of town puts up a sign like that?" he groused. "I cannot believe I was considering buying a home in St. Petersburg."

Cornelia glanced back at him. "I can't believe you considered buying a home anywhere in Florida, at the prices they are asking."

"Cornelia, aren't you shocked by that sign?"

"Appalled, but not shocked. We humans are guilty of far worse behavior."

"I don't know why you are so shocked, Percival," Teddy chimed in. "Surly you're aware that Mr. Brockman was living on his yacht because he wasn't welcome at any of the hotels."

"Wasn't he? I didn't notice."

Teddy patted his hand. "Really Percival, you have to be the most single-minded man I've ever met."

"That's because I must focus. If I let all the details of daily living into the forefront of my mind, I wouldn't get anything done." He paused. "I hope you don't find that too distressing."

She smiled. "Not distressing, but it is amusing to see how your mind works. Think about the land offices. At least half of the ones we visited had signs proclaiming restricted deeds, and that Cubans, Jews, and colored were barred from buying."

The professor leaned back in his seat and closed his eyes for a brief time. "Yes, I see now that all of them did. Some were less pointed in tone, but no less insulting."

Lobster parked the Oldsmobile under an ancient live oak across the gravel lot from the Gangplank. He turned to Cornelia. "Now that we are here, ma'am, what's the plan?"

"There is no plan. I am going to go in and ask to speak to Mr. Vacco."

Cornelia started to open the door, but Lobster caught her by the arm. "Say you ask for Vacco, and he doesn't want a sit-down? You put him on the spot like that, he might start throwing lead."

"Nonsense," Cornelia replied. "He might have his staff tell me he isn't there, or order us to leave, but he won't start a gunfight in his club in the middle of the day. That's bad for business. Now, let go of me."

Lobster sputtered. "The boss will kill me if I let anything happen to you."

Cornelia lifted his hand off her arm and dropped it. "Then come along. If trouble starts, I'll be more than happy to get out of Mr. Vacco's club."

He muttered something unintelligible as she got out of the Oldsmobile, then hurried after her.

The stained-glass windows of the bar probably helped the room stay cool but provided little light. After more than an hour of driving in the midday sun, the Tiffany lights did little to brighten the room. Cornelia stopped just inside the heavy mahogany door to allow her eyes to adjust before making her way to the bar.

"What'll it be, lady?" the bartender asked.

He was a small man, probably no more than five feet tall, with black hair and deep brown eyes. The lines of his face were hard enough to be chiseled from marble. His eyes were arresting in their intensity. Cornelia couldn't help thinking that this was a man who would do anything for the right price.

She swallowed hard. "I need to speak to Mr. Vacco."

He scowled at Cornelia.

Professor Pettijohn pulled a Jefferson from his pocket and held the bill directly in the bartender's line of sight.

The bartender's eyes flicked to the bill and back. "Have a seat, lady. I'll tell him you're here."

"Thank you," Cornelia said as she turned to find a table.

The professor laid the twenty on the counter. "You'll find me in the billiards room, dear. Call if you need me."

The room wasn't crowded like it had been the night she and Teddy had visited. There was no live music, either, but the strains of "Farewell Blues" floated from a Victrola behind the bar. A few patrons still lingered over late lunches. Cornelia chose a table as far from the other customers as possible. There was no point in sharing her business with anyone but Mr. Vacco.

The bartender pocketed the money, then disappeared into the back room.

A short time later, Gabriel Vacco limped into the room. The Italian wasn't a big man, about the same height as her uncle. His eyes were the color of ripe olives and accented with thick black lashes and heavy brows. Vacco might usually be handsome, but he was sporting a black eye, busted lip, and a swollen face.

Judging from the raw knuckles and multiple scrapes, he had put up a fight.

"Good afternoon, Mr. Vacco. My name is Cornelia Pettijohn. I've been engaged by Mr. Wall to investigate the death of a singer known as Jackie Dart."

His eyes narrowed as he looked at her, a middle-aged woman seated in the corner of his club. She also felt the incongruity of her request with the person she normally was.

"Lady, what kind of a chump do you think I am? I'm a busy man. I got no time for ..."

"Yes, you do," Cornelia replied in her most authoritative tone. "You do a brisk business in the evenings, but your customers haven't gotten off work yet."

Behind her, Lobster sucked in his breath.

67

He snorted. "You're over the moon. There's no way Charlie Wall would send someone like you to poke around in my business. Who are you, his grandma?"

"No, I doubt his grandmother would have to work. However, I do. Jackie Dart is also known as Jaquinda Duarte. She sings in nightclubs. She had a brother named Renzo, whom I know you had an acquaintance with."

"A very short one. We weren't close."

"How droll," Teddy said. She had taken a seat at the closest table.

Vacco pointed a thick finger at her. "What are you looking at, sister?"

"I love to watch Corny grill the suspects," she replied merrily.

"Don't call me Corny," Cornelia snarled, but she was overridden by Vacco's spluttering.

"I'm not a suspect! What information I had on Renzo, I already gave to Wall's men." He waved at the marks on his face. "As you can see, they weren't polite about asking me."

"I agree that they weren't subtle. Still, the deaths are suspicious. First Renzo's father died, then Renzo, and now Jaquinda. None were by natural causes."

"The sister's dead? I'm surprised that the mug with the baseball bat isn't here instead of you. I heard he was dizzy for her."

So, the blood in the car could be Vacco's. She hoped it was *only* his. "I'm surprised you haven't heard, being such a wise head. Mr. Aldama is being held as a suspect."

Vacco smirked. "What a shame."

"If he loved her, why would he kill her?"

"Everyone wanted that dame. The horn blower in her band, the drummer, the barkeep at Club Tropical were all sniffing at her heels. Then there were those women at the Black Opal. Maybe they were more to Jackie's taste."

Cornelia hadn't realized that Lobster could turn even redder than his sunburn. "You think she was giving someone else the tumble?"

"I wasn't familiar with her social calendar. I'm just the bearer of bad tidings here."

68

Her conversation with Vacco came to an abrupt halt as he bolted from his seat and limped off to see what had caused a disturbance in the billiard room.

Cornelia sighed. *What had her uncle gotten into this time?*

"What's going on here?" Vacco demanded.

"The old guy with the white beard is a menace, boss. He's either cheating or some kind of sharp. Either way, he's not walking out of here with our money."

Professor Pettijohn was standing quietly by the billiards table, examining his cue stick. The wires of his hearing device hung from the pocket of his suit with the earpiece dangling. When he saw Vacco, he returned the earpiece to his ear and watched him cross the room.

Vacco casually picked up the chalk cube and examined it, then looked at the professor. "My boys claim you're cheating. What do you have to say for yourself, Methuselah?"

The professor cleared his throat. "Your boys are a bit confused, Mr. Vacco. I have been playing billiards since I was a cadet at West Point. Until today, nobody has ever accused me of cheating. I find it an extraordinary claim, considering that the young man making the accusation presented me with a cue stick that has a slight bend."

He rolled the cue stick down the table, causing the warped wood to bounce.

Vacco held up the chalk cube. "What about this?"

The professor grinned as he pulled an identical cube from his pocket. "The wet chalk? I noticed it immediately. That's why I got a cube from the rack and kept it in my pocket while we played. My hands have never touched that cube."

The gangster turned and looked at the shorter of the two young men. "Rut, how exactly has he been cheating?"

"The geezer claimed he had never played Nine-ball. I racked the balls and gave him a rundown of the rules. From first break, he called every shot."

Vacco's face darkened with rage. "So, you told him the rules, gave him a bent stick, wet the chalk, and tried to shake him down. When your cheating didn't work, you accused him of being a cheat. Right?"

He didn't wait for a reply. "What were the stakes?"

"A hundred points, dollar a ball." The younger man replied.

He winced at the scowl on his boss' face.

"He passed the barkeep a twenty just to fetch you from the back. I figured he had money to throw away."

"You figured wrong. Pay the man, Rut."

"But boss ..."

"I said, pay the man."

Rut stared at his toes.

Vacco swore. He reached into his own pocket, peeled five twenties from his bankroll, and dropped them onto the billiards table. "Do us both a favor and stay out of my club, Methuselah. These boys are too wet behind the ears to know when they're outclassed, and I can't afford educating them at your prices."

Dinner and a Show

Cornelia had expected the Black Opal to be another speakeasy, but if it were, there was no sign of a bar. The place seemed to be more restaurant than night club. Tables crowded close to the small dance floor. Waiters in black trousers and white shirts hustled about with heavy trays. Their feet echoed the rhythm of the band as they made their way across the black and white tiles, spreading the tantalizing aroma of Southern comfort food through the room.

She could hear Teddy's toes tapping beside her and knew it was just a matter of time before her companion forgot all about their investigation and her lung problems. Nothing could keep Theodora Lawless from dancing. Cornelia wanted to be angry, but it was impossible to stay mad when music brought so much joy into their lives. She checked her bag for smelling salts while she waited for the hostess to seat them.

Mr. Wall had sent Clevon Martin with them this evening. The young man, who had been seated with them in the same booth matter-of-factly, was trying to appear nonchalant. He was failing miserably. His eyes nearly popped out of his head when a young woman kissed her girlfriend while they were dancing under the crystal chandelier in the center of the dance floor.

"Miss Cornelia," he whispered. "Are you sure you want to question the band here? Mr. Wall could provide you with their addresses."

"We'll be fine, Clevon," she whispered back, thankful that the hostess had arrived, ending the exchange.

While she handed them menus, the house lights dimmed. A large black woman dressed in white stepped into the spotlight in center of the stage. Cornelia looked up just as the chandelier over the stage was caught in the light. The sparkling crystal prisms cast rainbows of light on the woman's white tuxedo and top hat. The effect was beautiful. *She* was beautiful. When she sang, every other sound in the room melted into nothingness. There was only the deep soprano ache of her blues ...

> *The storm is risin', the rains begin to fall.*
> *I'm all alone by myself, no one to love me at all.*

Cornelia felt goosebumps prickle on her arms. The table conversations around them had stopped; all eyes were on the singer. Beside her, Teddy and Clevon sat rapt.

After the moment passed, she looked past the gleaming woman to the musicians behind her. The band was all female. A young woman in a long black gown and evening gloves played a careening accompaniment to the melody. The drummer wore a man's suit and had short-cropped hair. As her hands moved, sparks of light flashed from her heavy rings. The saxophone player sported an Eton curl above a black form-fitting tuxedo. Her vest was embroidered with pearls.

When the tall siren finished her sad tale, she moved to a livelier song. The doors to the kitchen opened and out came the wait staff, trays laden with food. The scent of fried chicken and fatback wafted behind them. Cornelia's mouth watered. She looked at the menu eagerly.

A voice got her attention. "Clevon! I don't believe I've ever seen you here before. Who are your friends?"

"Miss Lulu!" their guide stammered. "These ladies are guests of Mr. Wall. This is Miss Teddy and Miss Cornelia."

"Pleased to meet you both," Lulu said, extending a hand.

Cornelia shook it firmly. "We're here to—"

Lulu cut her off. "Food before business. What will you ladies have?"

"I'd like the fried chicken," Cornelia said, "and the cornbread and collards. I haven't had good greens since we were stationed in Alabama."

"Honey, you are in for a treat. You won't find a better mess of greens this side of the Mason Dixon. Lord knows, those folks up north don't know how to cook greens."

They all had a good laugh.

Teddy was looking over the menu. "How's the lemonade?"

"Swell," Lulu said with a wink. "I'll send your waiter over."

The Gemstones finished their set, and another group of local musicians stepped onto the small stage, opening with a lively ragtime featuring guitar and banjo.

Their waiter cleared away Clevon and Cornelia's empty plates, then looked at Teddy's practically untouched meal. "Should I bring you something else?" he asked.

"Another of these."

She held up her empty glass.

Lulu wasn't wrong about the food. Not that Teddy seemed to notice. She was much more interested in her gin-spiked lemonade than the thick ham steak on her plate. *So much for her promise to stick to the medicinal dose of alcohol*, Cornelia thought.

She resigned herself to another of Teddy's dry toast and icepack mornings. The lively atmosphere of the club was too much temptation for Teddy to resist.

When the Gemstones' saxophone player came over and asked Teddy to dance, she forgot all about her damaged lungs, too, and headed to the dance floor.

Opal and Lulu approached as Teddy disappeared into the crowd of dancing couples.

"You wanted to talk to me, Sugar?"

Cornelia looked up at the tall woman in white. The top hat added another six inches to a woman who was already at least six feet tall. Her smile was genuine, and broad. It created deep dimples in her cheeks and showed off teeth as white as her suit.

"Mind if I sit down? I wouldn't want you to strain your neck looking up at me."

Cornelia's throat was suddenly dry. She picked up her sweaty glass and took a deep drink of her ice water before speaking.

"I'm looking into the ...."

Opal finished the sentence for her. "The murder of Jaquinda Duarte for Mr. Wall. Nothing stays secret in the Scrub, Miss Pettijohn. Before you left her mother's house, everyone in the neighborhood knew Mr. Wall wanted to clear Chago's name."

"He asked me to find the truth," Cornelia said firmly. "If he is guilty, he'll get no help from me."

Their eyes met and locked into a test of wills as the two women sized each other up.

"I think you're on the square," Opal said. "What do you want from me?"

"How did Jackie come to record with your band instead of the one she is with now?"

"Shucks, that band thinks it's too good for her. Truth is, they aren't good enough for her. Jaquinda would have been a big name. Should have been. With her looks and voice, there's no tellin' how high she would go. It ain't right what happened to her. Mr. Wall should have left her here with us."

Clevon shifted in his seat.

"Just settle down, Clevon. I ain't said nothing about Mr. Wall that you can't repeat to him."

Clevon gave her a sheepish grin.

"Miss Jaquinda has been singing with my band since she was old enough to reach the microphone. Her momma cleaned offices at night and Lulu and I looked after her. We loved her like she was our own daughter."

"Were you angry that she started working with another band?"

"Mr. Wall saw her sing and offered her a job in his nightclub. He's not a man you can say 'no' to and stay healthy. Besides, it was a lot more money and a bigger audience than I could give her. The best I could do is keep an eye on her from a distance and finish the record."

She held her head higher. "I wrote 'Between the River and the Bay' for her. Made a deal for us with Black Swan records. Of course, she recorded it with us. We were family."

"Which member of your family wanted to get closer to Cousin Jackie?"

Lulu let out a laugh that bubbled across the room. "That would be the *cousin* out on the dance floor with Miss Lawless."

"Lulu, you know nothing ever came of that." Opal grumbled.

Lulu put her hand on top of Opal's and smiled. "But honey, it wasn't for lack of trying."

Cornelia made a mental note of Pearl's interest and tucked it away for when she and Teddy finished their dance. "What about the rest of your band? Is there anyone else we should question?"

Opal's brows wrinkled as she thought about what she should say. "Well, Diamond Fingers was carrying a torch. I don't think Jaquinda even noticed the way she watched her, but Pearl did. The two of them came to blows when we were in New York."

"I think you're looking at the wrong band," Lulu said defensively. "Our Jackie could handle harmless flirtation. She's had men and women falling at her feet since she was thirteen. Lately, she was different: quiet, and easily frightened. She had taken to propping a chair under the dressing room door between sets."

"Lulu's right. She was fretting over something. Since she started singing with that band, she was as skittish as a frightened kitten. Something was going on at that club. I tried to get her to tell me what it was. She'd just shrug and say it was nothing."

"Besides," Lulu said. "That band likes to claim they would have made her a recording star, but they know as well

75

as us, Jim Crow don't allow no Negro faces in their recording studios. They're jealous because we were willing to do what it took to get a record deal: go to Harlem."

Lulu might have said more, but she spotted Pearl parting the crowd carrying an unconscious Teddy toward them. She was instantly on her feet, waving the club bouncer over to their table.

When Cornelia saw Teddy, she reached for the smelling salts. "Don't be alarmed; Theodora loves to dance and refuses to recognize her limitations. Her lungs were severely burned in a German gas attack in the Great War. She was pensioned and sent home to recover. The poor dear was in and out of hospitals for years."

"I didn't know we had women on the front," Pearl said.

"Not many were, but at the time she and I were on ambulance duty. I was driving that day, and she was in the back with a couple of our boys. Two minutes later and we would have been clear. The gas didn't give us two minutes."

"Were you injured?" Clevon asked.

"I wore my gas mask. One of the soldiers didn't have his. Teddy decided her patient needed hers more than she did."

While she spoke, Cornelia waved the smelling salts under Teddy's nose.

The strong odor of ammonia made Pearl cough. She turned her head as far away from Cornelia as she could. That didn't stop tears from forming in her eyes.

Once the bouncer arrived, Lulu and Opal left her to deal with the ladies and fled to the back of the club, ending the interview.

Teddy roused and wrapped her arms around Pearl's neck. "Thanks for a lovely dance."

Cornelia frowned. "One of these days, Teddy, you are going to get yourself trampled by dancing until you swoon."

Teddy giggled.

Cornelia just shook her head and disentangled Teddy from Pearl's arms.

"Clevon, would you help Miss Lawless out? I don't think she can navigate alone." The old nurse paused for a second, and then added, "I'll be along in just a moment."

He looked delighted to have an excuse to escape the club and its clientele. In an instant, he was on his feet and steering the inebriated woman toward the exit.

Cornelia turned to Pearl and the bouncer. "Ladies, I would like to ask you both some questions about Miss Duarte's murder. Perhaps tomorrow, when you've had some rest, you could come to our hotel. Are you willing? I will send one of Mr. Wall's men to pick you up."

The bouncer's eyes opened wide at the mention of Charlie Wall. "I don't think we'd be welcome at your hotel, Miss."

Cornelia pulled a fountain pen from her purse and scribbled her name and her room number on a small slip of paper. "If anyone gives you any trouble, tell them to call me."

"Yes ma'am," the large woman replied as she tucked the paper into her vest pocket.

"Oh," Cornelia said, as she turned to leave, "Would you be kind enough to ask the drummer—Diamond Fingers, isn't it? Ask her to join us."

The two women stood open-mouthed and watched the strange white woman walk away.

Lobster didn't dare relax around the little old man he'd been ordered to keep an eye on. Small bits of plaster were still falling from the ceiling from the incident with Sal. He looked harmless enough, but was scary smart. Who knew what shenanigans he'd thought up since yesterday?

He lifted the telephone and ordered a pot of coffee from the dining room. "Do you want anything, Professor?"

The professor didn't look up from the magazine he was reading.

Lobster tried again, louder. "Professor, I'm ordering coffee. Would you like anything?"

The old guy picked up the earpiece to his hearing device. "Did you say coffee?"

"Yes." Lobster shouted. "Do you want some? The kitchen is closing soon."

"Not at this hour. I'd never get to sleep. Ask them if there are any more of those Plant City Strawberries. A bowl of those in cream would hit the spot."

Lobster made the request and added a slice of cake for himself. If he was going to be stuck here, he would make the most of it. The pastry chef at Tampa Bay Hotel baked the best lemon cake he had ever tasted.

The two of them were just finishing their bedtime snack when the ladies returned. Cornelia helped Teddy into the bedroom they shared, then returned to the sitting room where her uncle was regaling Clevon with details of his billiard games.

"It seems the one they call 'Rut' had planned to pluck a fat old goose and didn't realize geese are notoriously difficult creatures."

"So, you just walked out with Rut's money?" Clevon replied.

"As it happened, the young man didn't have the money he had wagered. Mr. Vacco paid his gambling debt. I suspect he is going to have to repay Mr. Vacco from his share of their illegal gains."

Clevon whistled. "Rut is not going to be happy with you, Professor. You might want to stay out of his way for the rest of your stay in Florida. He may be a foot shorter than his brother, but he has a mean temper."

"It was just a gentleman's wager."

"Professor," Clevon replied. "Gentlemen don't generally enter our line of work."

"He's right, Uncle," Cornelia added. "That young man was cheating, and you still beat him. He lost face and blames you. His boss's intervention is all that kept the situation from turning violent. The next time you run into him, he might take revenge."

She patted him on the shoulder. "Shouldn't you get some rest? You promised to escort Teddy to the concert tomorrow in the park. She will hold you to that promise."

"I doubt she will rouse early, but it has been a busy day."

Cornelia turned to their guide. "I'm going to turn in too, Clevon. I don't think we will be going out tomorrow, but a few of the ladies from the club are coming to talk to me. Would you be kind enough to bring them?"

Clevon jumped to his feet. "You invited those women here?"

"Considering Teddy's proclivity to pass out on dance floors, it seemed a better option than returning there. Besides, they are more likely to confide in me without all the extra ears in the room."

"Miss Pettijohn, that club is under Mr. Wall's protection. The hotel is not. In case you missed it, the Klan is active here. Bad things happen when you don't respect the race lines."

She sighed. "Clevon, I have had to deal with race issues all my life. If you can tell me a safer place than my hotel room to interview them, we can do that."

He started to say something, changed his mind, and sat back down. After a moment he stood up again. "I'll talk to the boss. Good night, ma'am."

Sunday Callers

The air was cool and heavy with moisture. Cornelia wrapped a warm shawl around her shoulders and settled into one of the rocking chairs lining the hotel veranda. Years of military life left her unable to lie abed in the morning. She normally used the time to work on a paper or catch up on her correspondence. Last week, she had finished the final draft of her research and submitted it the *American Journal of Nursing*. Today, she decided to just sit and enjoy the sunrise. The morning sun was spilling pastel shades of lavender, pink, and yellow over the silver dome of the casino and the city beyond.

She thought about taking the path along the river to do a little bird watching, but her field glasses were on their way to Colorado without her. She was half tempted to have Mr. Wall buy her another pair. It would serve him right for having her kidnapped. Being coerced into investigating this murder still sparked resentment. Of course, nobody was watching her now. She could slip away—no, the memory of those poor men being flogged would haunt her.

Florida was having a strange effect on her. Somehow, she had once again become embroiled in a murder investigation. Trying to help her family was one thing; working for a gangster in the seedy underbelly of Tampa was quite another. If the Army knew what she was doing, they would drum her out before she could retire. Besides, her poking around wasn't getting her any closer to knowing what happened to Miss Duarte. Despite what Mr. Wall thought, she wasn't a detective.

Clevon pulled into the closest empty space he could find for his Oldsmobile. No taking the circular drive to the hotel entrance today, no sir. "We're here, ladies," he announced. "Let me get the doors for you."

"That would be very gentlemanly of you," the large woman in the front passenger seat said. She was the club's bouncer, and Clevon had no trouble believing she could hoist an unruly patron out of the establishment by the seat of his pants. She was broad, muscular, and at least as tall as he was in stockinged feet. Last night, she'd worn a man's suit and a brilliant green tie. This morning, she was fresh from church. Fancy hat, modest dress, and heels. Oh, those heels.

He helped her exit the car, then assisted her companions. Pearl and Diamond Fingers also wore dresses and hats to conceal their short hair, but seemed more uncomfortable in women's clothing, especially the drummer. If he'd walked into any other bar last night, Clevon would have thought she was just a short guy. He wondered what her real name was, since he couldn't picture anyone naming their baby "Diamond Fingers." It was probably a stage name, since the band's name was The Gemstones.

There were employee entrances to the hotel, but *they* weren't employees. Clevon did what he'd done the past few days and went up the stairs to the main entrance, offering his arm to Fingers when she stumbled in her Mary Janes.

One of the doormen came down to meet them a few steps from the top. "Fella, you need to stop. Who are these ladies?"

"This is Miss Jackson," Clevon said, indicating the bouncer, who looked down and clasped her gloved hands. "These other two are her nieces. Miss Pettijohn asked them to come today. She's Mr. Wall's guest. Third floor?"

The doorman looked nonplussed. "This is very irregular. We can't have strangers just coming in and out as they please."

Clevon knew what *strangers* meant. It meant people who weren't white and rich. "I've come the past two days to assist *Mr. Wall's* guests. Today, they requested that I bring Miss Jackson and her nieces."

The goof wasn't taking the hint. Worse, the other doorman had come to stand behind him. "You squiring the old folks around is one thing. What will these ladies be doing while the guests are out?"

Clevon was trying to think of a good answer when the shadow of a large hat fell across his shoulder.

"Pardon me, sir," Miss Jackson said, "but Miss Pettijohn said that one of the clerks could call if there was any confusion." She offered the note. "Miss Cornelia Pettijohn. There's the room number."

There must have been something persuasive about the bouncer besides her build, because the second doorman took the note inside. After an uncomfortable wait, Miss Cornelia appeared at the door with her companion, Miss Teddy.

Miss Teddy cried out with delight and rushed to the three women. "There you are! I'm ready to get started."

"Get started?" the doorman asked.

"I'm getting married in a few weeks," Miss Teddy said, "and these ladies will be making my gown."

The doorman looked down at Teddy's hands, but she was wearing gloves that matched her hat. He shrugged. "Congratulations, ma'am. I apologize for the confusion."

As they crossed the lobby to the lift, Clevon heard a low chuckle and glanced around. The sound seemed to come from the direction of a man reading a newspaper. He couldn't see the face, but the seersucker trousers were just like a pair Mr. Wall had. He wondered if the boss was here for the amusement value, or to make sure Miss Pettijohn was able to ask her questions.

Cornelia stopped beside the polished brass elevator doors and glanced at the lavish carved banisters of the staircase. She had been seeking privacy for questioning the ladies when she should have been thinking about the logistics of inviting them to the hotel. Meeting someone in the elevator could cause trouble, but the burns on her legs made navigating the stairs problematic. Besides, the lift was faster than the stairs, which were just as segregated and more likely to bring them face to face with other guests. She pushed the call button and hoped nobody but the elevator boy would be in the car when it arrived.

She hadn't considered the expectations of her guests. They had been subdued, but were now keenly interested crossing the lobby with its ornate furniture and life-size statues. When she and Teddy stepped inside the elevator, they were met with blank stares from the other women. It took her a second to realize that none of them had ever been on an elevator before. Businesses near The Scrub were older and smaller than those in the white business district. If they were equipped with a lift, it was probably for freight, not people.

The operator started to protest when Clevon stepped inside, but Cornelia gave him a look that made him swallow his words. He stared at her, waiting for an explanation.

"Third floor, please," was all she offered.

He turned his face to the elevator controls and said nothing.

The brash drummer's face drained of color as the elevator began to move.

Pearl flinched when the elevator dropped a few inches before settling into its climb.

Only CJ seemed comfortable with being carried up and down a large shaft in a box. Both her friends looked relieved when the doors opened again, and they could escape.

Clevon led them down the corridor to the suite. He was startled when Sal answered it.

"Boss! Is there something I should know?"

Sal grunted and waved him in. He was more discomfited by the new visitors. "This is getting to be a big crowd up here. Someone's gonna say something."

"It's a little late for that," Cornelia said, closing the door behind them. "I didn't realize the amount of trouble it would cause to have the meeting here. The Army is more practical about such things."

"The hotel guests should have something new to talk about this afternoon; it should make them happy," Teddy said, seating the three women on the sofa. "I'm sorry there's not more room. Percival and I will be leaving shortly to hear the Bachman Million Dollar Band play in the park; there will be more space then." She left them and went into the bedroom.

"I'll be going with them, although I got a tin ear," Sal said. "You need to keep things low-key here, Clevon."

The young man nodded, then leaned closer to the Cuban. "I think Mr. Wall was downstairs, boss. In the lobby, watching things," he whispered.

"I wouldn't put it past him," Sal murmured back. "He seemed plenty interested about this meeting last night."

Cornelia set a tray on the table and lifted the lid. "I had Room Service deliver sandwiches and cakes. I wasn't sure if you would have time to eat."

"That was very thoughtful of you, ma'am," the bouncer said. "I can't speak for these two, but I came directly from church."

The way Miss Jackson looked at Diamond Fingers made Cornelia think the drummer never attended church.

Teddy returned with her own tray, bearing glasses and two of the Ball jars from her stash. "I've brought some extra refreshments," she said.

"Of course you have," Cornelia replied.

Teddy gave her a sheepish smile.

Cornelia took a sandwich from the tray and placed it on one of the small plates. She wasn't especially hungry, but she could tell that her guests weren't about to eat anything until she did. There was nothing she found more unnatural than segregation; it created an awkwardness where there shouldn't be any.

"These fancy hotels are more interested in how the food looks on the plate than they are in filling an empty stomach, so I ordered plenty. Ladies, help yourselves. Clevon, if you and Sal would like to have a bite to eat, just grab a plate," she added.

Sal declined. "That show is going to start soon. We'll blouse and let you ladies get to talking."

Cornelia nodded. It was probably best if her uncle weren't in the room. The presence of an elderly man might discourage openness. Sal escorted Teddy and the professor out of the suite.

When her guests had devoured the sandwiches and moved on to cake, Cornelia decided it was time to see what they knew about Jackie's life in the days leading up to her demise. "Miss Jackson, you have a different view of what goes on in the club than the band. Did you notice anything different about Miss Duarte?"

"She wasn't all that keen about the new gawkers hanging around, if that's what you mean."

"Gawkers?" Clevon asked.

The big woman shrugged. "You know how it is. Menfolk come into the club 'cause they get a charge from watching women dancing together."

Diamond Fingers rolled her eyes. "Then there's the other kind. The tough guys who get excited watching the boys then lurk in the ally to beat them up. They're the worst."

"Those don't have no truck with Jackie," CJ replied. "That bunch from Ybor that took to following her are the ones that scared her."

"Do you know their names?" Cornelia asked.

"No," CJ said, a little too fast.

Cornelia waited, giving her time to collect her thoughts.

The bouncer let out a heavy sigh. "The ringleader is that club manager from that other place she worked at. They're all buddies of his. None of them did anything that could give me an excuse to throw them out. But the way he looked at her gave me the shivers."

Pearl nodded agreement. "He's the reason she took to looking over her shoulder and being afraid to be alone. I saw him back in her dressing room a week or so ago. He said he was lost. I didn't believe him for a fat minute. Ain't no wonder she was ready to jump out of her skin. That man ain't right in the head."

"What was the name and location of this other place?"

"Club Tropical in Tampa," CJ said. "That's where she and the Mojos usually play."

"And this unsavory gentleman's name?"

"Lester Baldwin."

Cornelia made a note. "Thank you. We haven't been there yet, so now I know where to start."

Diamond Fingers, who had been shuffling her feet, spoke up. "I know the boss told you about me and Pearl getting into a scuffle when we were all in New York. I'm not denying my interest. But that's as far as it went. Jaquinda wasn't interested in women, if you know what I mean."

Clevon aspirated the cake he was eating and broke into a fit of coughing.

Plant Park, close to the hotel, was already filled with people waiting for the concert. Women in fashionable dresses chatted on benches circling a rock garden fountain while men smoked nearby under the palms. Teddy couldn't see the band *per se*, but she knew where they had set up. A giant figure of the conductor towered over the crowd. Harold Bachman didn't look much older than he had when he was entertaining doughboys in France with his original military band. She plucked her opera glasses out of her purse and tried to get a better view.

"You wanna get closer?" Sal said. "I can get you closer." He began pushing other patrons aside, opening a path for them.

"Oh, Sal, please don't bother." They were receiving glares from people who were much further up the social echelon than she would ever be. "No, a good spot would be over there, near the hibiscus bushes. Cornelia wouldn't want us to draw attention."

Dropping Cornelia's name did the trick. Sal headed off to clear a bench. At least it would only be a few people he offended now. Teddy sat down on one of the ceramic garden seats scattered throughout the park. This one was a lovely blue and white, and meant for women or children. Most men would think it too dainty—at least American men would.

"That was a splendid live oak we passed," the professor said, leaning on his cane. "I daresay it is well over five hundred years old."

"Oh, yes. Did you notice that they'd placed a bronze squirrel in the tree for the dog statues to look at?"

"Indeed?" Percival closed his eyes. "Oh, yes, there it is. I remember now. I was busy estimating the circumference."

Percival did have a remarkable memory. She thought Cornelia had a touch of it; she remembered conversations word-for-word and had often known the way back to the Army Hospital when Teddy got lost shopping in Paris.

Cornelia was upset with her over the engagement. She was angry with her uncle, who had used the idea as a quick dodge with the authorities in Saint Petersburg, but far more dismayed that Teddy had continued the farce. Unfortunately, the lie had proved useful to them in too many ways ... until Teddy's mother read about it in the paper and invited herself to the wedding. After that, she and the professor had a long chat about what they should do. He believed they should go through with the wedding.

Her shock made him chuckle.

"My dear, I have no amorous intentions." He'd assured her.

They talked about the photograph on his nightstand and how he lost the only woman he'd ever been in love with to another man. They had the most extraordinary conversation about Cornelia, and she realized how much he loved his niece.

The music began with a flourish of notes, and brass instruments stridently began playing "Over There." Well, that was traditional. Teddy stood and tried to see over the crowd. Oh, if only she were as tall as Cornelia. She put a foot on the ceramic stool, testing its strength.

Two men rushed past her, knocking her to the well-trimmed grass.

"Got you now, old man!"

Teddy rolled over and saw that the men had flanked Percival. She recognized the one who had cheated at pool immediately. The other was like a larger version of the same man, much taller and with a bit more red in his hair.

"Sal!" she shouted, fumbling in her bag. "Sal! Help!"

The professor blocked a punch from the cheater and swatted at his assailant's knee with the silver head of his cane.

Teddy sent him tumbling to the ground with a well-aimed rock from the slingshot the Professor had made for her. She hadn't had much practice shooting rats since the Philippines. It was nice to know she could still hit her target.

She whizzed a couple more rocks at him to keep him pinned down while Sal took care of his companion.

Her arm wasn't strong enough to do any real damage to the scoundrel. The professor was doing more harm with his cane. Still, between the two of them, they did a respectable job of preventing him from getting away.

Sal stuffed his handkerchief into the mouth of his now barely conscious captive. Then he used his necktie to restrain the young man.

He pointed his revolver at the one still trying to get away from the professor. "Stop squirming like the snake in the grass you are, and get up."

The would-be attacker wriggled away from the professor's cane. "Call these two off."

Sal chuckled. "Your name is going to be mud when word gets around that you were bested by these two."

The ruffian sat up and rubbed the red lump under his left ear where Teddy's last rock struck. Then he noticed Rut, face down in the grass. "What did you do to him?"

"Relax," Sal said. "Your brother had a little too much sun. He's going to need help getting home."

His eyes widened. "You're letting us go?"

A wicked grin spread across Sal's face. "I know where to find you."

The young man swallowed hard.

"Take your brother and get out of here before I change my mind."

"Yes, sir," he said as he pushed himself up from the ground.

"One more thing," Sal said as he picked up Rut's hat and handed it to his brother. "I am assuming that you two weren't smart enough to clear it with your boss before coming into Mr. Wall's front yard and attacking his guests. That sort of mistake is bad for your health. If you've got any smarts at all you'll head north and keep going until Florida is just a memory."

They watched the one brother shake his shorter sibling awake, then help him to his feet. They tottered away through the gawking crowd.

"Do you think they will take your advice?" Professor Pettijohn asked.

Sal shrugged. "It's their funeral."

That evening, they ate in the grand dining room. Keyhole arches, indoor palm trees, and tall windows with curtains accentuated the Moorish theme of the hotel, but the real showstopper was the great dome overhead, painted to resemble the sky. It was a place where one dressed for dinner, so Cornelia wore the deep blue gown she'd purchased Friday—had it only been two days ago?—and a fan-shaped hair comb Teddy had loaned her. The Tampa Bay Hotel had its own china and silverware embossed with its name. The white linens on the table and dark studded leather chairs reminded her of the white tablecloths and black chairs of The Black Opal—but the music was less lively, and she couldn't picture any of the seated gentlemen in this room or their powdered wives ordering fried chicken.

"Is Sal gone for the night?" Teddy asked.

"Yes. I think he's decided that I'm not going to run away after all."

"I seem to have lost my babysitter," the professor commented. "I'm sure I've provided them with plenty of

90

excitement today. Perhaps they think I will behave better since I was accosted."

"I think Sal needed some rest and turned you over to the experts." Cornelia said, taking another spoonful of her Charlotte Russe. The layers of ladyfingers made her feel slightly spoiled. She should be working on the case. But, just one more bite first ...

"When we go back upstairs, I want to see those photographs again," Teddy said. "I think one of Jaquinda's rings might have been on the hand in my vision."

Teddy wouldn't let go of the idea that she'd had a real psychic experience, rather than a dream born of oxygen deprivation and Cuban rum. Cornelia remembered when they were in the Philippines and Teddy kept dreaming about a headless priest walking the grounds around the hospital. The local *tubâ* she'd grown fond of was a more likely source of the dreams. At least this was a less gory vision.

"So, what will that tell us?"

"We can find out who wears—or used to wear—the ring, and we catch our murderer."

"I don't think the court will accept spectral evidence."

Teddy waved her own spoon. "Ah, but once we know who it is, getting the evidence will be much quicker."

"Really? Don't you think that's exactly what the police did with Chago? Decided who most likely committed the crime, and then found evidence to back up the circumstances?"

"We're already acting on the premise that he *didn't* do it. We're not outside investigators."

"I told Mr.—" Cornelia realized her voice was rising, and leaned closer. "—our employer that if I found proof of Chago's guilt, I expected justice to be done then, too."

The professor interrupted them. "I suggest that we check the photographs first and then ask the family or friends if all of the jewelry was Miss Duarte's. If one of the rings is unfamiliar and matches one a suspect was known to wear, it would be a strong indicator of a connection."

It sounded sensible and was less blunt than Cornelia's opinion had been. "That is an excellent suggestion. I'll take the photographs out when we return to the room."

Her uncle smiled. "Speaking of rings, Theodora, I think we should look for an engagement ring tomorrow morning. I've spoken to the concierge, and there is an excellent jeweler near the courthouse."

The ladyfingers turned to mush in Cornelia's mouth.

Teddy was delighted. "Yes, that would be marvelous! What sort of gemstone are you thinking of? I'll need to buy a trousseau to suit. Are you going with the traditional diamond, or an emerald or ruby?"

"Are you both crackers?" Cornelia spluttered. She coughed into her napkin.

They both stared at her with confused expressions.

The couple at the next table turned to look. She leaned forward and hissed, "You don't need to look at rings. The two of you are not engaged. This whole mess started as a ruse to explain our living arrangements to the police."

"It's more respectable than my living alone with him," Teddy said. "You're leaving after you crack the case."

Cornelia planted her face in her palms and muttered something unintelligible except for the word "insane." After a long moment of silence, she lifted her head and looked at Teddy. She drew in a breath and let it out slowly before speaking. "Teddy, we are talking about marriage. You would be my uncle's wife."

Teddy enunciated her reply slowly. "Yes, being the wife is the usual role of marriage for a woman."

"Do you really want to be my *Aunt Teddy*?"

Her companion giggled. "I hadn't thought of it, but that's what I would be ... technically, of course. You don't have to call me Auntie if you don't want to. It's socially acceptable for you to call me by my first name, since we've been friends a long time."

"*Friends?*" Cornelia exploded, and stood. She threw her soiled napkin on the table, shoved her chair in, and charged out of the room, eyes burning.

Cornelia reached the palm-lined walk by the river before she ran out of steam. How had this happened? No, she knew how it had started—with a lie to make their traveling together socially acceptable. Why were they continuing this farce, though? Her uncle had become friends with Teddy, but that was it. His great love had always been Mildred Hamm. And Teddy had always loved Cornelia ... or so she had thought.

She found an empty bench and sat. Couples passed her, some holding hands. More salt in the wound; something so simple, denied to her. The women she'd met today were in the same situation. At least they had The Black Opal, a place where they could be more open, but the police would eventually shut it down. When they had time.

The water flowed by, oblivious to her pained thoughts. Why couldn't people be more like the river, following its own course instead of making others miserable?

With a ruffle of fringed skirts, someone sat down beside her. "There you are." Teddy said. Her cool hand rested on Cornelia's, which was still balled in a fist.

Cornelia jerked her hand back. "We can't do that."

"We're old ladies. They're unlikely to even pay attention."

"You're not old. You're eight months younger than I am."

Teddy laughed and moved closer, patting her arm. "My hair is whiter than yours."

"That doesn't dispel my illusions."

"I'm so sorry we upset you. That *I* upset you. I can be so thoughtless."

"With a friend?" Cornelia pulled away.

"With someone I love dearly."

"Then why don't you stop?" Cornelia spat. A couple strolling by slowed briefly, then hastened their pace.

She lowered her voice. "How far are you willing to go for appearances? Will you really marry my uncle so your mother can be pleased at last?"

Teddy looked down at her hands, still ringless. "I've lived a long time without her being pleased with me. If I must, I can continue to do without."

Cornelia glared. "If you *have* to?"

"To keep you. Percival used the engagement as a quick excuse, but I knew it would make so many parts of our lives easier."

The looks. The whispers. The time their Commander wanted to assign Teddy to another unit to split them up instead of discharging them because he considered Cornelia indispensable.

The faces of Opal, CJ, and Pearl replaced the memories. Despite all the persecution those women had had to endure, they had found a place where they could be themselves. No, they had *created* it, and Charlie Wall was their buffer from the police. Teddy saw Uncle Percival as *their* buffer.

She softened her face with effort; a frown was the expression she used the most. "So you don't love Uncle Percival, but want to marry him for convenience? What if he's in love with you?"

"I love him as family," Teddy said, "but not in that way. I see so much of you in him. What's more, he loves you too."

"He has hit upon a strange way of showing it."

Teddy reached out and put her hand on top of Cornelia's.

This time she didn't pull away.

"Cornelia, your uncle doesn't want to die alone."

"It was a game," Cornelia said, "but, like poker, someone has called your bluff."

"It is not a game to him. Percival may pretend to be seventy-five, but the bout of pneumonia really scared him. Marriage would let him keep us around all the time without making him feel like an invalid."

"How can you be so sure that's what he's thinking? Has he told you any of this?"

"No, but he has told me about losing the woman he loved. Your uncle keeps Mildred's picture on his dressing table. We've both seen how he looks at it. I have not replaced her in his dreams or his heart. He also told me how much he loves you and how important I am to your happiness. All your uncle wants is to protect you. But it is such fun to play the devoted couple."

Teddy coaxed Cornelia to return to their suite. The professor had beaten them there and was reading the newspaper. "Ah, you're back, ladies. I'm afraid that while we were busy in Saint Petersburg yesterday, Tampa Downs hosted the first Florida Derby. On the same page, there is an article about the alliance between the gangsters of Chicago and enforcement officials. They really are importing all the elements of the North here."

No reference to Cornelia's abrupt departure from the table. Very well, she could handle that. "I could do without a few of them."

"We need to have another look at the evidence before I turn in. Sit down, Teddy, while I get the file."

She opened the pouch with the police report and photos of the Duarte murder and spread the pictures of Jaquinda's body on the table for Teddy. She didn't include the closeup of the disfigured head and face, which were utterly horrid.

Cornelia predicted that her companion would fixate on one of the rings, and hunting for the owner would satisfy her. Meanwhile, she was going to have to do the real work of the investigation. She was a nurse, not a detective, so she would need to figure out their next move. Her uncle's suggestion about showing the rings to the family wasn't a bad one, though. Which photos would be the least upsetting to Mother Duarte?

"That one," Teddy said, pointing to a heavy ring in one of the photos. "That's the ring I saw on the man's hand. And look, it's on her left hand."

Despite herself, Cornelia looked. It was thicker than the other rings on Jaquinda's slender fingers, and a different shade—perhaps gold, although that was just a guess with the gray, grainy pictures. And, indeed, it was on the third finger of the left hand.

"I told you!" Teddy crowed. "I told you I'd seen a ghost."

"In the bottom of a bottle," she replied, "but you did find an outlier."

Some Light Shopping

Monday and March began early. It was the day Cornelia had been due back in Colorado, and she resented Charlie Wall's overestimation of her skills. Instead of reviewing patient reports from her staff and updates on supplies, she would be bothering a grieving mother again.

She sipped her morning coffee. At least it was of good quality, and strong; it should bolster her energy today.

Uncle Percival had his nose in the papers. "The police department is hosting a benefit for officers disabled in the line of duty," he said.

It was disappointing, but not unexpected. With the amount of crime in the city, anyone who did their duty was going to get hurt.

Teddy came to his side and peered at the article with her spectacles. "Makes me think of the benefits the Auxiliary hosted for the doughboys," Teddy said. "Will we still be in Tampa on the 22nd?"

"Lord, I hope not." Cornelia hoped Clevon would be their escort, although she wondered how much more broadening of his horizons he could take. Sal might want to escort them himself after the trouble yesterday afternoon. Who knew how many brothers 'Rut' had?

Either way, they had nowhere to go immediately. It wouldn't do to wake up Mrs. Duarte, who had enough problems.

She was wrong.

"The concierge has arranged an appointment for 9 AM at WH Beckwith Jewelers," Uncle Percival said at breakfast. "I requested that they show us a wide variety of rings."

Teddy directed her eyes towards Cornelia. "Are you sure we should do that mid-investigation, Percival?"

"We could be in the Pennsylvania papers again before this is all over," the professor said, ignoring the hint. "You could be excused for leaving your ring at home during your arraignment, but your mother will be checking all future photographs."

Teddy continued to look at Cornelia. "Do we have the time?"

The older woman sighed loudly. "To not add more fuel to her next call? Yes, although I hope there is no need for press coverage."

"I'm sure Mr. Wall would want us to keep a low profile," Teddy said, spearing the last segment of her sliced orange. "Should I wear the hat with the feathers, or the red silk flowers?"

Cornelia thought of Clevon, who had been sent to escort them to The Scrub. He was already waiting outside for them to finish their breakfast; there would be more waiting coming his way.

The owner of WH Beckwith Jewelers had taken the professor at his word. A young man ushered the trio from the door to comfortable seats in the rear of the shop. The proprietor, who introduced himself as Wilson Beckwith, inquired if Mademoiselle preferred sapphires, diamonds, emeralds, or Burmese rubies. Teddy professed a fondness for all of them.

Very good. Would Mademoiselle prefer a setting of yellow gold, rose gold, or perhaps white gold, which was *de rigueur* these days? Naturally, she was interested in seeing the latest fashions, although it should be elegant enough to pass on as a family heirloom.

The bride-to-be was nearly sixty years old, and Cornelia estimated that her uncle was somewhere around ninety. The jeweler didn't bat an eye or crack a smile.

The parade of rings began. Mr. Beckwith set tray after tray in front of Teddy, allowing her to try on rings to her heart's content, which took a while. The sapphire in this one was lovely, but a little too large for her delicate fingers. The ruby in that one was too small, and the setting too angular. The clarity of this diamond was lovely, but Teddy didn't care for the baguette cut, which she claimed would fall out of fashion as quickly as it had entered. She waved away the suggestion of topaz. It was her birthstone; she already had too many pieces of topaz jewelry.

Cornelia was thinking about lunch by the time the choice was made: a hexagonal diamond, surrounded by caliber-cut emeralds. The setting: white gold. Her fiancé, leaning forward on his cane, complimented her taste and the perfect way the emeralds fit together.

"The precision of the cut on the stones is remarkable," he said. "Excellent craftsmanship."

Mr. Beckwith accepted the compliment on behalf of the store, and also accepted a check for an eye-popping amount of money from the would-be bridegroom. They exited into the noonday sun, Teddy holding her hand up to better see the flash of light surrounded in a hedge of green.

Clevon spotted them and got out of the car, tossing the remnants of a sandwich into the gutter. Good; she wouldn't be starving him like she did Sal. The young man opened the doors for them. "Did you find what you wanted?"

Teddy showed him her new acquisition and he smiled. "That's pretty. It suits you."

The compliment stung, but Cornelia thought she'd better get used to it. Everyone wanted to see a new engagement ring, and this was a beautiful one. Her great-grandmother had offered to give hers to Percival when he was courting Mildred, but it had passed to Cornelia's mother instead. Dovie's ring sat in Cornelia's jewelry box now, reserved for special occasions. The wedding would count as one, but the ring should have just arrived in Colorado.

After a quick lunch at a café near the courthouse, they returned to The Scrub. The neighbors stopped to watch as the four climbed the stairs to the Duarte home again, Teddy especially conspicuous in her finery, even though she had switched her hat and jacket again. She had looked perfectly at home among the tropical plants and gilded glass cases of the jewelry store. It was embarrassing in the Scrub.

Cornelia showed Mrs. Duarte the picture of Jaquinda's hand, carefully cut away from the original photograph. There was no need for the poor woman to see more of her dead daughter's body. "Was this one of her rings?"

Clevon translated the question into Spanish, and the mother shook her head no. She didn't remember the ring, although Jaquinda received many gifts from her suitors. However, she would definitely remember her daughter getting engaged, and it hadn't happened.

Bembe popped up by her side. "*Déjame verlo!*"

Mrs. Duarte snatched the cutout away from the small fingers. No, he could not see it. He was too young for such things.

Shortly thereafter, the group left The Scrub and returned to the El Dorado. It was time for a changing of the guard; the same segregation laws that made Clevon an acceptable escort for one section of town made him unsuitable for others.

Their new companion was Eddie the Hat. He was taller and thinner than Clevon, which made his large white fedora, curled up on the sides, almost comical. The muscles under his jacket, though, discouraged any open disrespect.

"I hear you were getting some handcuffs," he said to the professor.

"You'll never see a prettier manacle," Teddy said, holding up her hand.

The man goggled. "Must be love."

Cornelia grumbled and tapped her shoe.

100

It got Eddie's attention. "We meet again, ma'am," he said to Cornelia. "I hope it's on better terms this time."

"If you behave yourself, there should be no problems," she replied.

"I share that sentiment," he responded. "Are we still going to Club Tropical?"

The club's name was painted in bright yellow on a barrel outside the club with palm fronds and flowers surrounding the name. Eddie poked his head inside and shouted for someone to find Baldwin. "Tell him he has guests." Then he stepped back and held the door open.

Cornelia remembered what Lulu had said about the manager of Club Tropical. If this "Baldwin" was the manager, it would be an especially unpleasant conversation.

The club itself, however, was gorgeous. Instead of dust or planking, the floor was concrete tiled with barrel tops. The booths were made of bamboo and lit by stained-glass lamps in bright floral colors. Eddie indicated one of the booths for the trio and pulled a seat, one carved from a rum barrel, over for himself.

Cornelia rested her arms on the cool glass tabletop and took the opportunity to further observe her surroundings. It looked like the Mojos would be playing there tonight; the Garcias were setting up their stands, and Lefty was arranging his drums. Live palm trees flanked the stage, and the space behind the band was filled with bromeliads and dumb cane.

Nearby, a curly-headed man polished the glass of the bar. Occasionally, he would sneak a glance at them. Word had traveled fast. It might be worth speaking to the bartender separately; they often provided an open ear to distressed patrons—or performers.

"Eddie." A squat middle-aged man in a dark suit stood at the edge of the booth. He had a receding hairline, except for one strand in the front that made his face look like the back end of a bulldog. "What brings you here on a Monday night?"

Eddie stood, and they all followed suit. "Mr. Wall has guests that need to speak to you. Jerry, too."

Introductions were made and they sat again, Baldwin pulling up another of the barrel chairs for himself.

"So, you're here about the girl. The one who did the torch songs. Not much I can tell you. I don't take much interest in the performers, as long as they bring in the clientele."

He'd begun with a lie; Cornelia treated him like she had Vacco. "Really? I've heard the opposite. I've heard you followed her to other bars, including ones where you caused trouble."

Baldwin sniggered. "Oh, you've been to *that* joint. If you ask me, they're looking for trouble. No one wants a place like that in their neighborhood."

"*You* do. Ybor City is hardly in your neighborhood, but you've been making more appearances at the Black Opal than a pop fly in Yankee Stadium."

"Maybe I like the fried chicken."

Cornelia snorted. "No, you find the sights there titillating. It's unseemly."

The manager scowled. "If it's unseemly for me, I don't wanna think about what it is for you, sister. Were you dancing, too?"

"Please. Do I look like a dancer?"

"More like a fire plug."

Teddy, who was doodling on a sheet from her notepad, muffled a snort.

"I wasn't there to leer, unlike you," Cornelia replied tartly. "There are men who were harassing Jaquinda Duarte before her murder. You were one of them. Did she refuse your advances one too many times?"

"I don't gotta take this in my own place, lady." Baldwin stood, but Eddie shoved him back down.

"Mr. Wall has taken a personal interest in finding Jackie's killer," their escort said. "Stop yapping about fireplugs and answer the question."

"I was interested, sure, but I didn't hurt her. That would have been killing the goose that laid the golden eggs. She brought a lot of traffic in here."

"What about the disc she recorded with the Gemstones? Wouldn't that be where the traffic started heading?"

"Nah. The Black Opal don't attract the same people we do. Our patrons can pass the paper bag test."

The professor made a harumph, but said nothing.

"You've made your point," Cornelia said. Distaste filled her. "Where were you Wednesday night?"

Baldwin waved around him. "Where d'ya think? I was working. I got dozens of witnesses. Everyone knows Jackie was playing the Cuban Club that night. You don't think I'd stand out like a sore thumb?"

"You have a point."

She paused, thinking of what she should ask next, but Teddy cut in.

"When they found Jaquinda, she was wearing a ring that her family didn't recognize." She held out the slip of paper to their ex-suspect. "Have you seen her wear it?"

Cornelia leaned over to see, too. Teddy had done a sketch of the ring, which was an excellent idea. Showing a picture of a dead woman's hand to strangers was gruesome; she wished Teddy had thought of it before they visited the family.

"Huh," the bulldog said, studying the drawing. "I'm not sure. She wore a lot of rings; some of them were probably gifts from admirers."

"This was a new acquisition," Teddy said, stretching what they really knew. "When did you last see her perform?"

"Last Tuesday. She was supposed to be here on Saturday, but she canceled. Her brother got killed. That family's had a lotta bad luck."

"Yes, it's terrible." Cornelia leaned forward. "Think hard, Mr. Baldwin. Was she wearing the ring then?"

"No."

"Did anyone else around her have a ring like this? It's very heavy for a lady's ring."

"I wouldn't know." Baldwin set the picture down. "I don't pay much attention to men's jewelry. Besides, you're one to talk about heavy jewelry." He pointed at Teddy's emerald. "Guy who bought you *that* must've spent a wheelbarrow of cash."

The trio could do nothing but agree.

Next, they spoke to Geraldo Zayas, Charlie Wall's man and protector of the dressing room. Cornelia was becoming familiar with Wall's taste in muscular employees, although this one was closer to Sal's age. His deeply tanned face was well-lined.

"The Duarte girl had many followers," he told them. His accent was different from Wall's other men; not Cuban, not Panamanian, not Mexican. "She knew how to play to an audience, focusing on one man at a time and drawing them in with her charm. Some of them hoped it was more than a performance."

Cornelia forced an ugly emotion back down her gullet. "Are you saying that she brought this on herself?"

"Do *sequillos* demand to be eaten simply because they smell good? Some men have no sense."

"*Sequillos?*"

"Cookies. From Spain."

Ah. "I thought your accent sounded more ... European."

"I came here as a young man to seek my fortune. Then the war with Spain happened." His mouth quirked. "Bad timing."

"I can see why. Were any of Jaquinda's admirers particularly persistent? I understand that a mystery man was leaving gifts in her dressing room."

"Many men sent flowers or candy, but going backstage crossed a line. After the first time, I asked Mr. Wall to give me an extra man for the nights she played. He watched the crowd, and I stationed myself by the stage. I rebuffed those that got too close."

"She still received gifts."

104

His lips twisted into a frown. "*Sí*. I believe someone bribed one of the dancers or waitresses. Or it could have been a member of the band. Garcia and Fernandez both wanted that girl."

Cornelia wondered how Jaquinda would have responded to the advances of a man like Lefty. Roberto's jab about his looks hurt because it was true. "Let me ask you something else, since you're a keen judge of nature. Do you think Santiago Aldama could have killed Jaquinda?"

He shrugged. "I know the Boss doesn't think so, but love can drive a man crazy."

"So it can. My next question is rude, but I must ask it. Where were you Wednesday night?"

His gesture around the room was identical to the manager's. "I was here, keeping the peace."

"Was Mr. Baldwin here the entire time?"

"Yes, it was very busy. There was a bachelor party."

Teddy tapped Cornelia's shoulder and handed her the drawing. She showed it to Zayas. "Do you recognize this ring? Miss Duarte was wearing it when she died, but the family doesn't remember it."

The man looked at it briefly, then handed it back. "No, ma'am, I don't recognize it." He closed his eyes and rubbed the bridge of his nose. "But I'll think back, see if I can remember something. This is a bad business."

Cornelia was reluctant to accept his answer. She wasn't sure that any of the men in Jacky's life were telling her the whole truth. There was too much that couldn't be pinned down. She put the photograph away and stood up. "I would like to have a look at the dressing room before interviewing the band."

Eddie led them through a hallway cluttered with stage equipment to the small back room that served as a dressing room for the ladies. "I'll wait here," he said, "keep an eye out."

"Splendid," Professor Pettijohn said. "You can keep me company."

105

Eddie's face fell. He glanced at Cornelia with eyes that pleaded for rescue.

It was clear that the professor's reputation had spread through the ranks of Mr. Wall's organization. Cornelia didn't have much sympathy for Eddie. She was still peeved at his part in abducting her from the train. She secretly hoped he said something that got her uncle started on one of his long-winded mechanical explanations.

She didn't know where to begin in her examination of the dressing room. It wasn't much to look at. A metal rod with a wood shelf above lined one wall. It was divided into half a dozen sections, each labeled with initials. Identical dresses hung in three sections of the makeshift closet. The opposite wall consisted of a long counter and six wooden chairs. Mirrors of varying sizes and shapes sat on the counter. A screen spread at the far end of the room allowed privacy for the girls as they changed. Cornelia doubted that it was large enough for more than one or two people to use at once. She cringed at the thought that between acts the dancers would be rushing about in the unlocked room in their unmentionables.

Teddy seemed unconcerned with anything except the display of makeup.

Cornelia didn't know one shade of lip rouge from another. She left her companion to ponder the contents of various compacts and eyeshadows while she examined the room.

It was noteworthy that there were no windows. The only way in or out of the room was through the door. Whoever the mystery admirer was, he had to enter and leave in full view of anyone in the hallway. This added to her doubts about Mr. Zayas' claim that he didn't know the identity of Jackie's mystery admirer. Was he protecting someone? Could he be the admirer himself? He wouldn't be the first older man attracted to a much younger woman.

At the edge of her peripheral vision Cornelia saw Teddy move away from the cosmetics she was examining and take a position near one of the larger mirrors.

Teddy reached out toward the empty chair.

106

"Theodora, what are you doing?" Cornelia demanded.

Teddy didn't answer. In fact, she didn't appear to hear Cornelia. She pulled the chair out and knelt beside it. Before Cornelia could cross the small room, Teddy had crawled under the table.

"Tu eres mia," Teddy said.

Cornelia bent over and peered under the table. "Of course, I am. But what are you going on about, you silly goose?"

Teddy giggled. "That wasn't a question. It's what the note says."

"What note?"

She scooted out from under the counter and handed Cornelia the torn slip of paper she was holding. "The note the killer sent to Jackie."

The words were scrawled under "Jaquinda" and were slightly smudged. "Don't let your imagination run away with you Teddy. There's nothing on this scrap of paper to indicate who the sender or the recipient were. There's not even a way to tell how old it is."

"It is from the killer. I'll bet it was on one of the mystery gifts he left for her. See how it's torn? She must have ripped the note to pieces and thrown it away. This piece escaped. Now that she's dead, she wanted me to find it. That's why she pointed it out to me. There must be a way to use it to identify him."

Cornelia rubbed her forehead. It was too early in the day for Teddy to be in her cups. What other explanation was there for thinking the spirit of the Duarte girl lingered around Ybor City to help find her killer?

"So, Miss Duarte is talking to you now? Why don't you just ask her to identify the killer, and I'll be on the next train to Colorado?"

Teddy's eyes narrowed into slits. She used the chair to pull herself up. Once she retrieved her cane, she grabbed the slip of paper from Cornelia's hand and marched out without saying another word.

107

Cornelia groaned and chased after her, nearly knocking Eddie to the floor in her haste. "I'm sorry. Really. I was flippant. If the note was from her admirer, the handwriting could help us identify him."

Teddy stopped. "Apology accepted if you promise to listen. Oh, I also need your word of honor that you will not dismiss what you don't understand."

The thought of having to take spectral evidence seriously was hard for Cornelia. She looked Teddy over carefully, trying to determine if the spirit world she was seeing came from a bottle of Mr. Scroggins' hooch. None of the usual signs of drinking were present. She was going to have to take Teddy's new ghost encounters seriously, whether she believed in Spiritualism or not. It was clear that Teddy believed she was communing with the dead singer.

She put an arm around Teddy's waist as they walked back to the main room of the establishment. "Tell me exactly what happened," she said. "I'm ready to listen."

"I had this strange feeling when I was looking at the cosmetics the dancers were using. It was as if I were being drawn to the empty chair where Jackie used to sit."

Cornelia's heavy brows drew together, creasing her forehead. "How did you know it was Jackie's chair? I saw labels on the clothes racks, but nothing at the table."

"I just knew. You can ask Mr. Zayas if you wish, but I am certain he will confirm that she used that spot. I sensed her there, but all I saw were her feet in those sparkly red heels. Her toe pointed out the paper under the counter. I knew it was important."

She gave Cornelia a smile that lit up the room. "Checking handwriting is an excellent idea, Cornelia. We'll need to collect samples without alerting our suspects."

Her companion was less certain of the value Teddy's scrap of paper held, although a smiling Teddy was infinitely preferable to more fighting. This trip had put a strain on their relationship.

The band was in the middle of a rehearsal by the time Teddy calmed down.

Mr. Zayas shrugged when Cornelia asked when they would take a break.

"It is hard to say. Sometimes rehearsals go well, others are a struggle. I've seen them work on a new tune until the club is ready to open."

Cornelia knew how frustrating it was to be interrupted when trying to learn a new piece of music. She had missed having her fiddle with her on this trip. "Thank you for your time, Mr. Zayas. Please let them know that I'll be back this evening. I will plan to interview them between sets."

Eddie the Hat held the door for the trio, then rushed ahead to open the doors of the Oldsmobile. He waited until Cornelia had settled into the front seat. "Where to now, Miss Pettijohn?" he asked as he closed the door.

"I need to have a word with Mr. Wall. Do you think he could see me this afternoon?"

Cornelia's voice was calm, but her mind raced over questions about Miss Duarte's older brother. The deaths were too close together for her to believe there was no connection. She needed to know more about what happened to Renzo.

Bolita tickets were everywhere in Ybor City. There were games in every club. Boys sold tickets on the street corners. Housewives bought tickets at the local grocery. Cigar workers could purchase them in the factories. Wagers went from a nickel to several dollars, and jackpots could be more than a year's wages.

It seemed fitting that Charlie Wall had named his casino the "El Dorado." *Bolita* had lined his pockets with gold. The game that was the foundation of his business had spread like wildfire through the state. So much money flowed from *bolita* tickets that mobs from the north and Chicago were trying to muscle in on the action. It was no wonder people were dying. The question that troubled her was how the game might have led to a young singer's brutal murder. So far, the only connection she saw was that other members of her family were involved in the gambling racket.

The young man with the scar was standing in the café when the Oldsmobile pulled up in front of the building.

"Wait here," Eddie the Hat ordered.

He got out of the automobile and hurried inside.

"There's trouble," Cornelia's uncle said.

"What kind of trouble?" Teddy asked.

The professor's dark blue eyes studied the two men. "They're turned the wrong way for me to get a good look at their lips. There's been a shooting, that part was clear. I'm not certain what was said after that. They turned the wrong way. I am sure the last part was that their boss wants Eddie to take us back to the hotel."

"Oh, I wish I could see, too." Teddy was on the wrong side of the car for an unobstructed view.

Cornelia leaned closer to the window to get a better look at the two men inside the diner. Eddie's broad-brimmed hat was clenched in his hands in a way that made her think he was going to ruin the brim. She wished she had her uncle's ability to read lips. Whatever was said had him agitated. His cheeks were flame red as was his neck.

Eddie shoved the diner door open and walked out.

Cornelia hadn't seen anyone this mad since Corporal Harris had his ear bit off by a trench rat. She half-expected Eddie's temporal arteries to explode as she watched him walk back to the car. The way they stood out from his head made him appear close to having a stroke.

He flopped into the seat and started the engine. "Sorry, ma'am. The boss sends his regrets. He has business to attend to this afternoon."

The words didn't sound like Eddie. He must be repeating what the other man told him. Not that it mattered; Eddie wasn't waiting for an answer. They were already moving by the time he finished his short speech.

Cornelia bit back the urge to question him. The set of his jaw made it clear that he was not going to be forthcoming with further information. All the way back to the hotel, he gripped the wheel as if it would fly off any second.

The hotel grounds were lovely this time of year. If they were going to be stuck at the hotel, Cornelia would have preferred to find out what books the reading room had available. An afternoon where she could settle down in one of the rocking chairs lining the veranda was her idea of perfection.

Eddie the Hat wouldn't hear of it. He unfastened the leather strap holding his gun in its holster before they got out of the car. Then he took them to their rooms and insisted they stay put.

Splendid weather, and she was stuck in the hotel room with nothing to read but Teddy's Gertrude Stein book. She had a seat by the window and tried to read the tome again. It was no use. The stream of consciousness writing, and lack of proper punctuation, grated on her. Cornelia set the book on her nightstand and went to find Teddy's packet of BC Headache Powders.

Teddy and the professor were both huddled near the door to the suite when she walked into the sitting room. "What are you doing?"

"Shush," Teddy ordered from her spot near the floor.

Cornelia raised an eyebrow. "Theodora?"

Teddy turned just enough for her to see the slender black wires of her uncle's hearing device hanging from her hand.

"Are you two eavesdropping again?"

"Mr. Zayas has been murdered." Teddy said. "Now, do be quiet."

Cornelia's knees went weak. They had only left Club Tropical two hours ago. How could the man be dead?

It was a stupid question. She knew all too well how quickly a life could be snuffed out.

She found the nearest chair and sat down to gather her thoughts. Zayas had denied recognizing the ring, but had he remembered something after they left? He'd promised to think about it. Was that what got him killed? Had the killer been in the club when they were asking questions?

Her next thought was more chilling. Was the killer now after them?

111

She glanced toward the door where Teddy and her uncle were huddled like schoolchildren listening. Did they even realize the implications of Mr. Zayas being murdered? Were they aware that they could be next?

Maybe they deserved to be next. Working for Charlie Wall gave her a bad feeling. Murder was an everyday occurrence in his business. Teddy seemed perfectly fine working for a gangster. Chasing after a killer in a world of crime was a bit of excitement to her. Cornelia was repulsed by the underworld they were entangled in. She wanted no part of Charlie Wall's world. Fine suits and fancy clubs didn't make up for the sinister underside of the rackets. Life was cheap in Ybor City.

Wall's town was full of dark secrets crisscrossed by half a dozen different cultures clashing in a fight for power. Cuban, German, Italian, Chinese, Spanish, and English were spoken on the streets and every color of the human rainbow was represented. The port of Tampa could stop every ship, examine every crate unloaded, and still not make a dent in the flow of booze and drugs smuggled into Tampa. There were hundreds of inlets where small boats could offload cargo undetected. Local moonshiners vied for a piece of the trade, as did the brewers. The Volstead Act meant nothing to these men or Ybor City's brewers. It was an open secret that more beer than soda pop was bottled downtown. Crime was a much bigger slice of the local economy than cigar making.

There were even rumors that Charlie Wall's control of the gambling rackets was a front for the more legitimate family members who didn't want the *Bolita* profits siphoned off to Cuba. With the games safely in his hands they were assured that Tampa dollars stayed in Tampa. The White Shadow, as the locals called him, had his fingers in every pie.

Of all the rackets, prostitution bothered her most. The human trafficking went against everything she believed. Working for Mr. Wall made her feel dirty every time she thought of those girls purchased in the Orient and imported from Cuba to the Tampa brothels had no choice in what happened to them.

112

She forced her attention back on the murders. The sooner she figured this out, the sooner she could begin washing away the stench of Tampa's criminal underworld. Geraldo Zayas was dead because a murderer was hiding in plain sight. At some point during her interview with Zayas, the killer was within earshot. A shiver ran the length of her spine at the thought that she and the killer were in Club Tropical and probably only a few feet apart. Mr. Zayas wouldn't be dead if it weren't for her questions. She had to figure out who was in the room.

Baldwin, the club manager was there, as was the bartender. Either of them could have overheard their conversation. Two of the women from the band were there, but they were nowhere near the table when Mr. Zayas was trying to remember where he saw the ring. What about the rest of the band? There was so much milling about as they set up equipment and turned instruments. She couldn't rule anyone at the club out. Dancers, waiters, and even the kitchen staff needed to be accounted for, although they were less able to afford expensive jewelry.

Her train of thought was shattered by the sudden scramble when someone knocked on the door. Teddy fell flat on her backside attempting to get out of the way. She was unperturbed by the fall.

"Who is it?" she called.

Her uncle wasn't crouched as low. He stashed his hearing device in his pocket, then helped Teddy to her feet. His earlier antics with the pipe gun had made the gangsters wary of his shenanigans. The advantage wasn't wasted. By the time they answered, he was in full manure-spreading mode.

"Who do you think it is?" Eddie snapped.

Professor Pettijohn opened the door. "Mr. Hat, what can we do for you?"

Cornelia almost laughed.

Eddie's brows drew together as he stared at the professor.

Sal slapped him on the back. "Mr. Hat! Wait until the boss hears that moniker. He could use a laugh today."

Eddie the Hat wasn't amused. "Don't you dare."

Sal rubbed his fingers together. "Oh, don't worry, Eddie. I can be reached."

"I hate to break up your shakedown, Mr. Borrero," Cornelia interjected, "but how long are we going to be detained? I have a job to finish."

"My apologies, Miss Pettijohn. There was a shooting at Club Tropical. The boss wants you out of harm's way."

"Mr. Borrero, if he wanted me out of harm's way, the Denver train would have accomplished that."

Sal grinned despite himself. "Point made, Miss Pettijohn. There are risks in what he has asked of you. However, we needed to determine if our competitors were involved."

"Have you succeeded?"

"No."

Cornelia waited for Sal to elaborate.

The gangster studied her for a long moment. "You haven't asked the identity of the victim."

She glanced at Teddy who was carefully avoiding her gaze. Cornelia wasn't about to tell Sal Borrero that she knew who had been murdered because her uncle had been eavesdropping at the door. "I have heard that it is unhealthy to ask questions about Mr. Wall's business. In this instance, I'm relieved it wasn't one of us on the receiving end of that bullet."

"Miss Pettijohn, you're a lousy liar."

Cornelia turned the face she usually reserved for impertinent medics on him. Her heavy brows, the color of iron, accented penetrating blue eyes. She neither blinked nor looked away when Sal attempted to stare her down.

The battle of wills lasted only a few seconds. Nobody in the room so much as breathed.

In the end, it was Sal who lowered his gaze.

"My apologies, ma'am," he said. "The boss wanted me to let you know that Geraldo Zayas was shot not more than half an hour after you spoke to him. Emotions are running high. He wants you to stay in tonight. Eddie and I are to guard the door."

He paused for a second. "I don't believe anyone would be foolish enough to attempt harm on Mr. Wall's personal guests, but precautions are necessary."

Backtracking

Professor Pettijohn slammed the evening paper down on the table. "I don't understand these Tampa editors. They give most of the front-page to the Congressional hearings on the supernatural and bury details of the murder on page seven."

"Congress is having hearings on the supernatural. How intriguing!" Teddy snatched up the paper and began reading an article titled *"Lawmakers Consult Mediums"* aloud.

"For goodness' sake, Theodora, we have craziness to deal with in Ybor City, without delving into Washington's obsession with mediums advising government officials." Cornelia groused. "I don't care if Mrs. Harding holds seances at the Whitehouse or whether Harry Houdini gets his bill through Congress. We have armed guards outside our door. Two people have been murdered."

"Corny, don't get all worked up," her uncle chided. "The paper blames Mr. Zayas' death on his involvement in rum running."

Cornelia reached for the paper. "Let me see that."

She read the short article. It detailed Geraldo Zayas' previous arrests but gave little information about his murder. "He was found dead in his backstage office with a single gunshot wound to his back."

Teddy peered over her shoulder. "The newspaper says that there were no witnesses. That's the bunk. We were gone less than an hour before he was shot."

"There must have been two dozen people milling around in the club when we were there," Cornelia said. "More were coming in. Somebody was backstage when it happened. They're either too scared to come forward or are saving their story for Mr. Wall. I don't imagine his employees are keen on talking to the press or the police."

"Do you think they'll talk to us?" the professor asked.

Cornelia's eyes narrowed. "I'm not even sure that Mr. Wall's men are going to let us continue investigating. Whoever shot Mr. Zayas had a reason to be inside the club while it was closed. Having one of his henchmen gunned down inside his own club must worry him."

"We can't just sit here and do nothing."

Cornelia picked up the room service menu. "Teddy, Sal isn't just any of Mr. Wall's men. He's trusted. He was sent to make sure that we're safe and to see that we stay put. The best thing I can do is see if our guards would like to join us for dinner. They would be less conspicuous in here than loitering in the hallway."

"Dinner sounds like an excellent idea," the professor said. "I hope they have more of those Plant City strawberries."

Cornelia held off on asking questions until the gangsters finished their steaks. "The newspaper claims that there were no witnesses to Geraldo Zayas' murder. How could a shot be unheard in the club? Was the band rehearsing at the time?"

"Miss Pettijohn, you are supposed to be looking into Miss Duarte's murder. It would be best if you confined your questions to that."

He was polite about telling her to mind her own business, but she got the point. In her mind, though, the two murders were inextricably linked. It would be impossible for her to investigate further without understanding the connections. There was, however, no point in pressing the issue with Mr. Wall's lieutenant.

Teddy wasn't about to let the subject go that easily. "The cases must be connected. Less than an hour after he told us he would think about the ring, he was dead."

Eddie looked up from the slice of cake he was devouring. "Geraldo said he didn't recognize that ring. Why would anyone think he was a threat?"

"Mr. Hat, has it occurred to you that your associate lied? I knew he recognized the ring the moment he looked at the sketch. He didn't have much of a poker face," the professor said. "What matters is why he lied. I suspect that when we have the answer to that, we will know why he was shot."

The remark about his lack of a poker face caught Cornelia by surprise. She was beginning to think her uncle was more of a gambler than she realized. He'd always seemed so responsible with money, but since arriving in this notorious city he had indulged in illicit games of chance more than once. Now that he mentioned poker, she remembered that in his younger days he had participated in a weekly poker game with the local medical examiner and a detective friend. A real detective would be useful now.

Eddie and Sal stared at the professor in dead silence. Nobody else, not even Teddy, spoke as the importance of his observation sank into their consciousness.

Sal's dark eyes studied the professor's face thoughtfully before nodding agreement. "A man lies when he has something to fear or something to gain. Which drove Zayas, Professor?"

The professor stroked his snowy beard as he considered the question. "I believe it was the latter. Mr. Zayas was not a man to frighten easily."

Sal nodded again and stood up. "Excuse me sir, ladies, I need to make a call."

He picked up the candlestick phone and turned his back to the group. His voice was too low for any of them to understand what he said. His expression was grim when he placed the earpiece back on the hook and turned around. "Mr. Baldwin will have your list of names tomorrow, Miss

119

Pettijohn. He should be able to tell you where his employees were at the time of the shooting."

"Are the dancers employees? I know the band works in other venues."

"That's a question for Mr. Baldwin," Sal said. "My job is to protect you, ma'am."

"Are you able to get the police photos and statements like the ones Mr. Wall gave me from Miss Duarte's murder?"

"I will ask," Sal replied.

There was a war brewing in Ybor City, a war between rival mobsters wanting to control the rackets. She was getting pulled deeper into the slimy underbelly of these criminal enterprises with every passing hour. Her only way out was to find a killer before he killed again.

Today at the club she had crossed paths with the murderer. If Mr. Zayas had been honest with her, he might still be alive. Whatever secret he was keeping got him killed. The trouble was, she didn't have any idea of what he held back. Without knowing what he lied about, it was impossible to see how Mr. Zayas' murder was connected to that of the young singer. She looked through the police file again. There wasn't much.

Their efforts had produced little: a cigar band, some loose beads, a sketch of a ring, and a scrap of paper. Teddy swore that the latter two items were the results of her encounters with the dead singer.

She grimaced at the thought of a ghost helping to solve her own murder.

Worse, she was going to have to impose on Jaquinda's mother again; amid the discomfort of assuming authority she had no right to, she'd forgotten to ask to search the singer's room. She was definitely no detective.

"I'm going to bed," she said to nobody in particular.

"Good night, Corny," her uncle replied.

Cornelia cringed but resisted the urge to say "don't call me Corny" again. He was never going to stop no matter how much she detested the nickname.

Cornelia changed into her nightdress before carefully cleaning the burns on her legs. She winced each time she pulled a bandage away from burned flesh. There was nothing to do but press on with washing each open sore. The pain eased slightly when she applied fresh ointment.

Perhaps the daily torture of redressing her wounds was a just punishment for letting the two crazy people in the next room drag her to Florida.

This trip had been nothing but trouble from the beginning. Teddy's drinking and her uncle's secrets had landed her in one nightmare scenario after another. St. Petersburg had been the worst. She had never been fond of beauty salons. After her adventure with the permanent wave machine, she would never set foot in one again.

She put away the medical supplies and then laid out the clothing she would wear the next morning before climbing into bed. It would have been nice to have a good book to read. Her mind was too full of those ghastly images to sleep. Who was she kidding? It wasn't the murder keeping her awake. Her thoughts were dominated by this insane marriage plan Teddy and her uncle had cooked up. Compounding a lie never helped anyone.

The youngest, greenest, recruits ever drafted into the Army had more common sense than those two put together.

That unscrupulous jeweler had pegged her uncle as a rich old fool the minute they walked into his store. He had brought out tray after tray of his most expensive wares.

She still couldn't believe how much money her uncle had spent on that ring. And for what? To impress Teddy's mother? After the way she treated Teddy, that woman had some nerve demanding to be at her wedding. If she had been in Theodora's shoes, she would have hung up the phone. No. If she had been Teddy, she wouldn't have returned her call, not after the way she'd turned her back on her daughter.

The very thought of having to spend time with Theodora's mother made her blood boil.

Cornelia was still brooding about the prospect when Teddy came to bed. Pretending to be asleep made her feel childish, but she didn't want to talk about the situation

121

anymore. There was a certain logic to their getting married. Cornelia didn't think being seen as a gold digger was much more respectable than a mistress, but from a social standpoint marriage was the difference between being invited in and being a social outcast.

Mrs. Lawless would have married Teddy off to that brute, Ansel Stevens, for the sake of her social standing.

That thought was going to give her plenty of sleepless nights. A truckload of gangsters didn't worry her half as much as the prospect of Mrs. Lawless and her daughter under the same roof. The woman was relentless in her pursuit of social advantage and Teddy would never be good enough for her mother.

Sal pulled the Oldsmobile into the open space outside the El Dorado. Instantly, the door to the café swung open and Lobster came out.

"Boss says get some sleep. I'll take over babysitting the geezers."

"Geezers indeed," Teddy snapped. "That young man had better learn some respect."

Sal grinned. "Don't take it personally, Miss Lawless. At his age, anyone over thirty is ancient. He'll learn."

Ice cracked in her tone. "He certainly will."

Cornelia knew that tone well. Lobster was in for the worst day of his life.

The grin disappeared from Sal's face as his eyes met Cornelia's.

Neither spoke.

Sal gave her an almost imperceptible nod before opening the car door.

"Hang on a minute, Lobster. I'll be right back." He didn't wait for an answer. The kid knew better than to challenge his orders without the boss's say-so.

In less than a minute Clevon was walking out of the café.

He said something to Lobster.

The redhead glared at the Oldsmobile before turning and going back into the café.

"Change of plans," Clevon said, as he climbed into the driver's seat. "I'll be your driver today. Mr. Wall wants Lobster to take care of some other business."

"He didn't look happy about his new assignment," Cornelia said. "Do you think he would be less angry if he realized that his boss had just rescued him from the wrath of Theodora Lawless? At least he is safe for now. She's been known to nurse a grudge for quite some time."

Clevon sneaked a peek at Teddy in the rearview mirror and chuckled. "I'll let him know he dodged a bullet today."

Cornelia's sighed. "But *you* haven't. We need to go back to The Scrub."

She felt terrible. The devastated Duarte family should be left alone to mourn in privacy, but she needed to see the room or rooms where Jaquinda lived. She felt like a horrible intruder with no good reason to trouble the grieving mother again.

In the last few days, though, she'd grilled a gangster, stared down a lecher, and visited a club no respectable woman of her age would be caught dead in. Her sense of shame had died a painful death.

"*Senora* Duarte, I apologize for troubling you again. We're still investigating. Would it be possible for me to see Jaquinda's room?"

The woman's eyes went from sorrowful to flat. She grimaced and lowered her face. "Must you?"

Cornelia sighed. "Yes, I believe I must. Your daughter had many admirers who were not as successful as Chago. She may have received a gift or a note that will help us find her killer."

The woman's hands balled up. She had lines of strain on her face that had come from loss after loss. This time, it wasn't just her daughter, it was her daughter's dignity.

"You can come with me," Cornelia said gently. "To ensure I pay proper respect. And my friends can wait outside."

Mrs. Duarte nodded. "If they leave. Bembe, go keep them company."

"Miss Pettijohn," Clevon said, "I'm supposed to stay with you."

"Tell Mr. Wall you were guarding the door."

Once the others were outside, Mrs. Duarte led Cornelia to a small room at the back of the house. Outside of the dress and shoes on the bed, selected for the burial, the room seemed untouched. Several photographs of singers were pinned to the wall, labeled with their names— mostly Bessie Smith and "Ma" Rainey. Flyers advertising Alligator Mojo, starring Jackie Dart, were pinned up as well. A feathered headdress sat next to a small mirror on the dresser. On the other side of the mirror was a framed photo of Jaquinda with her family.

Caridad Duarte had been happier in those days, content and looking directly into the camera. Her husband stood beside her. Jaquinda, barely into her teens from the look of it, was slender, mischievous, with dancing eyes and a smile she'd inherited from her father. Bembe grinned, bold; he had likely been a little stinker at that age.

The oldest son, as Sal said, was darker than the rest of the family. He stood on the edge of the family. His face was more solemn. Already a young man, he had discovered that life had a number of doors that were closed to him.

The old nurse slid the top drawer open, revealing an assortment of lipsticks and other cosmetics. A small photograph, face down, was in one corner. She quietly lifted it and saw it was Chago.

"I put that in there," Mrs. Duarte said. "I couldn't bear to see it while I looked for the dress."

"I understand."

Another drawer contained several strands of beads and pearls, a third held bracelets and costume jewelry.

The fourth drawer had a couple of envelopes with a New York address on them. Inside were several professional photographs—probably taken during Jaquinda's visit to Harlem. The young woman had been extraordinarily

124

beautiful: large dark eyes, plush lips, and a glint of sassiness in her expression. She posed in different gowns and jewelry in each, although the gowns were always white. Cornelia studied Jaquinda's hands in the shots. None of them contained the heavy ring.

"She was a lovely girl," she murmured, and carefully replaced the items.

The fifth drawer contained stacks of notes in varying sizes and handwriting styles. They were from admirers, praising her singing, her beauty. Calling her a goddess. Begging for a crumb of her attention, demanding to take her to dinner, promising to treat her like a queen.

Most of them addressed her as "Jackie;" the author of the torn note had used her given name. Someone who knew her better, then.

"I'm going to take a closer look at these," she said to Mrs. Duarte. "We found a torn piece of a note in her dressing room."

The woman nodded.

Cornelia placed the notes atop the dresser and sat to examine them. Her burned legs protested, but it would hurt less than shifting around.

She skipped over notes to "Jackie" and spent extra time with the notes in Spanish.

One drew her attention; it was smudged like the scrap Teddy had found, and was on similar paper. It had apparently arrived with flowers; a portion translated as "flowers today, my ring tomorrow." A shiver ran down her body.

"Do you know who sent this, *Senora* Duarte?" She held it up.

Jaquinda's mother studied the note. "No. He seems very confident."

Like someone who wouldn't take no for an answer.

After persuading Caridad Duarte to let her take the note, she joined her friends outside the house. Two girls slightly older than Bembe were teaching Teddy one of the

125

local dances. Because she hadn't killed herself yet with the ones she already knew!

By the time they reached Club Tropical, Cornelia's mind was back to thinking of Mr. Zayas. It had been less than a day since she had sat across the table questioning him about the murder of Jackie Dart. Now he was dead—murdered. The only thing she was certain of was that this time Chago could not have been the killer. His alibi came with iron bars and a locked door. That didn't eliminate him as a suspect in his girlfriend's murder, but it did make his story more probable.

Clevon pulled into the near-empty parking lot outside Club Tropical and chose a spot near the back door.

The club manager, Mr. Baldwin, was waiting for them. On the first knock the door swung open.

Baldwin led them down the dingy back hallway to his office. Once inside, he handed her the list of names and addresses of everyone who was on the premises when they were here the previous day.

Cornelia read the list before tucking it into her handbag. There were no surprises.

"Is there anything else I can do for you?"

Teddy didn't give Cornelia a chance to answer. "Was that one of the dancers I saw go into the ladies' dressing room?"

"Yes, Liza. She's just dropping off some dry cleaning."

"None of the dancers were here yesterday," Cornelia commented. "Do they work for the club or are they contracted like the band?"

"Contracted."

"We would like to speak with her," Teddy said.

Cornelia started to say something, but movement near the wall caught her attention. Professor Pettijohn had wandered off in the brief time they were talking. He was crawling around behind Mr. Baldwin's desk, examining the floor.

She resisted the urge to plant her face in her palm. "Clevon, would you please help my uncle to his feet and get

126

him out of Mr. Baldwin's office? Get him out of the building. He can wait for us in the car."

"My apologies, Mr. Baldwin." She didn't take her eyes off the professor as he was escorted to the hallway by their bodyguard of the day. "One more thing; what can you tell me about Mr. Zayas?"

"I didn't know him well. He worked for Mr. Wall, not the club."

She frowned at the non-answer. "Mr. Zayas was in your club every night. You must know something about his life outside of work. Did he have a family? Was he part of one of the social clubs?"

"Ah, yes. I see what you mean. He had no family that I know about. His wife died around the end of the Great War. They had no children."

Cornelia nodded. "We've taken enough of your time. Thank you for your assistance. I would like to have a few words with Liza. We'll be on our way after that."

Teddy was already in the dressing room chatting with the young dancer as if they were old friends. Cornelia joined them in time to hear Liza confess to being the confederate of Jackie's mystery admirer.

"He gave me a fiver every time I put one of his gifts on her dressing table. I stopped though, as soon as I realized the gifts were unwanted. He was frightening Jackie." She looked from one woman to the other, frantic to find a sign that they believed her. "I liked Jackie. I would never hurt her."

"Who was her admirer?" Cornelia demanded.

Liza's dark eyes opened wide as all the color drained from her face. In that instant, the distinct sound of a gunshot stopped the conversation.

Cornelia and Teddy instinctively dived for cover.

There was no need. The gunman was already running away. His heavy footsteps pounded in Cornelia's ears, nearly as loud as her own heartbeat.

Neither she nor Teddy tried to help Liza. There was no need. The beautiful young woman they were talking to less than a minute ago was dead before her body hit the dusty dressing room floor. The bullet had struck above her brows and cut a deadly trail through her brain.

On some level Cornelia was aware of doors opening, a trio of male voices calling her name, the click of her uncle's cane on the floor. Mr. Baldwin shouting for help. On some level she was aware of Teddy squeezing her hand, softly sobbing.

Clevon helped them up from the floor and ushered them into Mr. Baldwin's office.

The drive back to the hotel was made in silence, despite the long wait to cross the bridge. Baldwin's first call had been to Charlie Wall. His second was to the police. In the minutes between those two calls, Baldwin and Clevon made every drop of alcohol in the club disappear. Officers arrived at a magically dry Club Tropical. Baldwin escorted them to the ladies' dressing room. Shortly thereafter, police questioning began. It didn't stop until Mr. Wall's attorney arrived. By the time the four of them were allowed to leave, they were exhausted. None of them had anything left to say.

Clevon glanced at his backseat passengers in the rearview mirror now and then.

Cornelia didn't dare look at either of them. One look and her resolve to hold herself together would vanish. It could just as easily have been one of them the gunman targeted. She bit down on her lower lip to stop it from quivering. The salty taste of her own blood oozed over her tongue, reminding her of the bloody scene they had just left.

She forced her mind back to the case. Solve the murder and she could go back to clean white Colorado snow, orderly wards, and an ordinary life. The thought of an ordinary life comforted her. She closed her eyes and leaned back in the seat. Traffic noises, the hum of the engine, and even the sound of others' breathing drifted away.

In her mind, she spread her notes on an imaginary table and went over every detail of her interview with Zayas. Somewhere in the interview was a bit of information that had marked him for murder. Otherwise, he would not have been killed within an hour of their meeting. That was too much of a coincidence.

After much deliberation, she had no definitive answer. All she had come up with were three possible reasons the murders were connected.

Her interview with Zayas may have revealed information she didn't recognize as significant. In that case, the killer realized that Mr. Zayas knew too much. He could have known the killer was watching and lied to protect himself. Was he eliminated because something he knew could identify the killer? Self-preservation was a powerful motive.

Was Zayas himself the murderer? Life was cheap in Ybor City. Jackie was a beautiful woman with a voice that had provoked strong emotions in several dangerous men. She didn't see anything resembling a confession in her notes, but had he inadvertently said something that gave his guilt away? In that scenario, his murder was revenge for hers.

Her final, and in her mind, most likely scenario in this hotbed of crime, was that Zayas had something to gain by lying to her. He knew, or thought he knew, the killer and could leverage that knowledge for money, power, or maybe both. In that case, greed got him killed.

There could be other motives, ones she hadn't thought of yet, but greed, revenge, and self-preservation all struck her as deadly possibilities that fit with the facts they knew.

Holding a Full House

Cornella thought the day couldn't possibly get any worse, right up to the moment she stepped through the ornate double doors of the Tampa Bay Hotel.

Beside her, Teddy swooned.

Clevon's quick reflexes saved her from hitting the floor. The young man swept his silver-haired charge into his arms and carried her to the nearest round sofa.

Cornelia and the professor hurried to her side.

The bottle of smelling salts she always carried was in her hand by the time Cornelia reached the sofa.

Her companions were so busy tending to Teddy, that they didn't notice that the white-haired reason she fainted was rapidly approaching.

Teddy coughed and pushed the ammonia bottle aside. She opened her eyes and what little color remained in her face drained away. "Mother?"

Julia Lawless stopped inches from where Cornelia was kneeling beside Teddy. One finger of her gloved hand rested delicately under her nose as if it could block the overpowering scent of ammonia permeating the air.

"Really, Miss Pettijohn! Put that awful concoction away. The last thing Theodora needs is someone indulging her dramatics."

Cornelia's first thought was unkind. *What would you know about what Teddy needs? You haven't been in the same room as her for more than half her life.*

Fortunately, she had the good sense to keep the thought to herself.

Her uncle stepped in to rescue them from the old bat's clutches. Cornelia had neither the patience nor tact to deal with the woman who treated Teddy like property to be sold off to the richest suitor.

The professor instantly assessed the situation and turned his full attention to the willowy matriarch who had chosen the worst possible moment to arrive unannounced. "Mrs. Lawless! How intrepid of you to make such a rapid journey. You must have been incredibly anxious to see dear Teddy again."

As the professor smiled and chatted, he kept inching away from Teddy's line of sight and pulling her mother's attention away from the ladies.

"I hope you don't mind my being so forward as to introduce myself, dear lady. I'm Professor Percival Pettijohn, professor emeritus, to be precise. I retired a few years ago. It is easy to see where Theodora gets her zest for life. And, if you'll forgive me for saying so, her good looks as well."

"Yes, well, thank you, Mr. Pettijohn," she replied.

"Oh please, do call me Percival," the professor said, a broad smile spread across his face and his deep blue eyes crinkling at the corners. "After all, you are practically family."

Mrs. Lawless was at a loss for words. Her daughter had said that the photograph in the paper didn't do him justice, which was true. From the shine on his oxfords to the snow-white beard, Percival Pettijohn looked like a man of distinction. She could see why her daughter liked him. But he looked even older in person than he had in the papers. If he had just turned seventy-five, he hadn't aged well. The man looked a decade older.

He was built much like his niece, square-jawed and broad shoulders. On a man, the look was much more attractive.

It would have helped if Cornelia had inherited his sense of style. His suit was impeccably tailored by someone who knew his craft and kept up with the latest trends. His gold pocket watch and matching fob bore the logo of the United States Military Academy. It seemed well-worn, but she couldn't help wondering if the timepiece worked. He had another on his wrist, a Rolex Oyster like the one she'd given Tommy for Christmas.

Her prospective new in-law had taste. She'd give him that. He must have been striking in his youth. The sunlight filtering through the windows gave his whole demeanor a warm glow. Julia Lawless found herself smiling back at him despite her intention to remain aloof.

Tommy Lawless was shocked to see his baby sister collapse. He knew it was his mother's fault. She had no idea of how badly Teddy was injured in France. She had chosen to remain willfully ignorant because she didn't want to face the result of driving his sister away.

Now, she was up to her old tricks. She'd posed herself in front of a mountain of luggage to stake out her territory. They had been waiting for Teddy to arrive for two hours, but she wouldn't hear of having the bellhop take her things to her room. It would ruin the tableau.

Thank God he was staying on his yacht. He had joined the Navy to get away from the family drama. He chose to stay in Florida after he retired for the same reason. Having a thousand or so miles between him and the rest of the family kept him on better terms with all of them.

While his mother trotted off to annoy Teddy, he waved a bellhop over and tipped him to fetch a glass of ice water for his sister. She still looked like he remembered, except for the silver hair. Nurse Pettijohn had written to him about his sister's selfless actions in Verdun. She told him then that her hair had turned silver overnight. Other letters followed, one or two a week, for months while his sister was in France. Once she was sent stateside, he still corresponded with Cornelia. Her insight into the complicated nature of war and her keen intellect made him value her opinions. But

133

her iron will and determination to do whatever needed to be done were the qualities he admired most.

It didn't surprise him at all to see Nurse Pettijohn on her knees tending to Teddy. Nor was he surprised when she looked up and mouthed the words "thank you" when the bellhop arrived with the water he'd requested.

He hoped that he could get a private word with her about this wedding. She was the only person he knew that could be relied upon to always tell him the truth. Sometimes that truth was a little hard to take. She was brutally blunt.

Clevon found a pay phone within sight of the Pettijohns and called his boss. Mr. Wall needed to know about this new pair of old people that had arrived. Three old coots were hard enough to keep out of trouble. What was he supposed to do with five? The way this day was going he was going to have white hair, too, by the end of it.

He could hear Mr. Wall's fingers tapping on the desk while they talked. Every tap made him twitch. The last time he'd heard that sound was when Wall learned that the Chicago boss had his Jew buying up land on Lido Beach.

Clevon swallowed hard. "Right, boss, I'll let Miss Pettijohn know. Yes, sir. You can depend on me."

He hung up the phone and returned to his charges. With every step, he reminded himself that help was on the way. This time of day it would take a couple of hours to get across the bridge. He could do two hours alone with this bunch to help Chago.

A Family Meal

"If you aren't up to this, I will tell your mother that you're resting and not to be disturbed."

Teddy grinned, mischief dancing in her eyes. "That's so sweet of you Cornelia, but I'll be fine. If Mother starts trouble, I'll have Clevon bump her off."

"That's not funny. Your family has no idea of what they've barged into."

"Well, over dinner you could explain it to them."

Cornelia glared at her.

"I would do it myself, but Mother would just accuse me of being dramatic." She chuckled. "Wouldn't you just love to see her face if you pointed out the gun under Clevon's left shoulder? Sal hides his well, but Clevon and Eddie the Hat are too skinny. Their guns are easy to spot."

"Teddy, you are incorrigible. There are three dead people. Three murders. I know your mother is a royal pain in the backside, but do you really want her dragged into this?"

Teddy sighed. "I suppose not. What are we going to do with them? I'm sure Tommy could handle himself, but a ninety-one-year-old socialite is another matter. Mother isn't half so strong as she pretends."

"Look who's talking," Cornelia put a hand on Teddy's shoulder. "I am worried about you. There have been far too many shocks lately."

"I'm not the one who was dragged off a train at gunpoint."

Cornelia shook her head. "No, dear. You are the one who hangs out with gangsters to get invited to swell parties where you dance until you drop and have way more booze than you should. Do you really think that Charlie Wall would know me if it were not for you?"

A single tear rolled down Teddy's face. "I am sorry, Cornelia. I didn't mean to get you into all this trouble."

Cornelia sat down beside her on the bed and wrapped her arms around Teddy. "I know you didn't. Now dry your eyes. Put on your best dress, and we will go have dinner with the dragon lady who whelped you."

"I dare you to say that to Mother's face."

Cornelia gave her another squeeze. "Theodora Lawless, you are incorrigible."

While she waited for Teddy and her uncle to dress for dinner, Cornelia called Room Service and ordered a steak dinner for her young bodyguard. She knew the young man couldn't have eaten since breakfast.

She should have told him what she'd done. The instant the elevator bell sounded his pistol was in his hand and he was motioning her away from the door.

"Clevon, put that thing away," she ordered. "One bullet hole in the suite is quite enough."

"Sorry," he said, "the boss will have my hide if anything happens to you."

The conversation was interrupted by a knock at the door. "Room Service."

"Your dinner is here," Cornelia said.

Clevon still checked the peephole before allowing the professor to open the door.

"Leave the cart," he said, pressing a coin into the waiter's hand. We'll serve ourselves."

Clevon's eyes widened at the sight of the enormous steak the professor put in front of him. "Thanks for the grub, Miss Pettijohn. I'll eat quickly. I can't let you go downstairs without me."

"At least take time to taste the food," Cornelia told him. Large chunks of steak were disappearing into his mouth in rapid succession.

He gave her a sheepish grin and slowed down long enough to have a sip of the iced tea she'd ordered for him. "I haven't eaten all day. It's good, too."

"I'm sure you have time to finish. Neither of my companions will set foot outside the suite anytime soon. They're a bit fussier about their appearance than most."

That made the young man laugh out loud.

Professor Pettijohn stood up when he saw Teddy's mother enter the grand dining room on her son's arm. It was easy to see where Teddy got her sense of style. Her mother's gown was silver-gray silk with a black mesh overlay in an Art Deco design. A long strand of black pearls, black opera gloves, and an Art Deco headband set with black pearls accessorized a dress designed to turn heads. On the willowy Mrs. Lawless, it succeeded magnificently. All eyes were on her as she crossed the room.

The professor bowed slightly when they reached the table. "You look lovely this evening, Mrs. Lawless."

She sat down in the seat Tommy was holding for her. "Thank you, sir."

"How are you, Teddy dear? Feeling better?" Her mother asked, looking across the table at her youngest child.

Their waiter was just putting a glass of lemonade in front of her.

"Much better, now," she said, reaching for the glass.

Cornelia eyed her. "Juiced?"

Teddy smiled.

"Order another," Cornelia said.

Teddy waved the waiter over and asked him to bring a glass for her friend.

"Is that your engagement ring?" Her mother asked as the light sparkled off the jewels adorning Teddy's left hand.

Teddy held her hand out so her mother could see it better. "Isn't it the most beautiful ring you've ever seen?"

Tommy let out a low whistle. "That must have set you back. Is that why you have a bodyguard at the door, Professor?"

His mother's face blanched.

"Oh, Clevon's here for Cornelia," the professor said.

The statement was followed by a loud "Ouch!" as Cornelia kicked him in the shin.

It was at that moment that Sal walked in with Lobster and Eddie the Hat.

Cornelia picked up her lemonade and drained the glass. She grabbed her bag and marched over to where the gangsters were gathered. She caught Sal by the sleeve, guiding him out of the dining room.

The others followed.

A few seconds later, Clevon returned to his position by the entrance.

The professor looked at him for a second, then said. "Huh, I guess I was wrong. Clevon is our bodyguard after all."

Tommy looked at his mother, then at Teddy. "Explain," he ordered.

Teddy shook her head. "I'm sorry, Tommy. The less you know, the safer it is for everyone."

Tommy threw his napkin on the table and stood up. "I'm going to go ask Cornelia. She certainly got those others out of here in a hurry."

The professor spoke quietly but the tone brooked no disagreement. "Lower your voice and sit down, Mr. Lawless. That young man may look like a farm boy, but the bulge under his left shoulder is a pistol and he won't hesitate to use it."

Tommy sat.

"Very good," the professor said. "Now pick up your menu and order dinner as if having a gangster watching your back was not at all unusual."

Teddy glanced at her menu. "I think I'll start with the shrimp cocktail. You should try it, Mother. The shrimp here are always fresh and succulent."

Tommy's eyes narrowed. "Do you not realize how much danger your niece is in with those hoodlums? How can you just sit here and do nothing?"

Professor Pettijohn's smile belied the intensity with which his gaze met and held the younger man's. "Mr. Lawless, you chose to barge into a situation you don't comprehend, involving yourself and your mother in Charlie Wall's business. The man is both dangerous and well-connected. He wanted Cornelia here enough to have her kidnapped from her train in front of hundreds of witnesses. When the railroad police tried to stop them, they held a gun to my niece's head and threatened her life."

"I see," he said quietly.

"No, you don't," the professor replied. "When Cornelia told them that the Army would be looking for her, Mr. Wall handed her a telegram. The governor personally arranged extra leave to keep my niece in Florida as a favor to Mr. Wall."

Mrs. Lawless gasped.

"Did you call the police?" Tommy asked.

"The ones who are ignoring the kidnapping? Think about it, Mr. Lawless. Even if we convinced the police to intervene, there's little they could do except be killed. She is safer with the gangsters. Wall has guards with her twenty-four hours a day. Any one of those so-called "hoodlums" will defend her to the death because that's what their boss wants."

"So, we just order dinner and act like nothing is wrong?"

"Tommy, we all know how brave you are," Teddy added. "But the bravest thing you can do is leave this to Cornelia. We would all like to come out of this alive, so please don't try heroics."

Tommy picked up his menu.

Thankfully, no avid readers were bypassing dinner for an extra hour of immersion in a good book. The dark-paneled reading room was empty when they entered. After being tugged through the hallway, Sal felt like an errant

139

schoolboy. The cool, dimly lit room reminded him so much of his headmistress's office that Sal could swear he smelled the crisp scent of Sister Lucia's starched habit mingled with that of old books and lemon oil.

Miss Pettijohn's expression did nothing to dispel the mood. It was hard to resist holding out his hand and waiting for the sting of a wooden ruler smacking his palm.

Cornelia's voice was low and menacing. "Why are all of you here?"

The woman was exasperating. Sal counted to ten before opening his mouth. "I have the photographs you requested. I wanted to look at them with you and hear your thoughts. More importantly, Miss Pettijohn, there have been three murders. The last one was inches from you. The killer knows you are looking for him."

"You think he is coming for me next."

"I think we have to be prepared."

Sal nodded to Eddie the Hat.

Eddie opened his jacket and pulled Cornelia's pistol from the waistband of his pants.

Sal took it from him and passed it to Cornelia. "I took the liberty of reloading it."

Cornelia gave him a wry smile.

Nobody said anything for a long time.

Sal pulled one of the chairs out and held it for Cornelia.

She sat down and laid the gun on the table in front of her.

Sal took a seat across from her while the two younger men remained near the door.

"I've spoken to the other dancers. Neither of them knew Liza was involved. They are pretty broken up about their friend, but they are willing to talk to you if you want."

"I don't think that's necessary," Cornelia said. "We know now that Chago was indeed framed. The killer knows we know."

"That's how I figure it." Sal rubbed the dark stubble on his chin. "I think we can rule out the women. None of them are strong enough to have moved the body alone.

Speaking of which, these are the photographs and witness statements you requested."

Cornelia opened the envelope and took the pictures out. She flipped through them quickly, pausing when she found the one showing the bullet wound. She put them back into the envelope and put them in her purse.

"I agree with your assessment of the women. None of them could have moved the body alone, at least not without becoming covered in blood. This killer doesn't have an accomplice. The way this killer is wiping out people who can finger him, any accomplices would have been murdered by now."

Cornelia pulled the list Mr. Baldwin had made from her purse and scratched off the women's names. "Blind Billy can be ruled out as well; there is no way he could have shot Liza and gotten away that fast. We also have to rule out Baldwin himself."

"He was there this morning. He could have shot Liza and disappeared into his office."

"No," Cornelia replied. "He had the opportunity to do the shooting, but lacked the ability to get away with the crime."

"How do you figure that?"

"Mr. Baldwin is a little older than you, heavier, and I think a lot less athletic. He could not have fired that shot, run back to his office, hid the gun, and returned to the dressing room without breathing hard or working up a sweat."

Sal grinned. "Yes. I see now. If it had been Baldwin, his appearance would have given him away."

"That leaves us with five possible suspects: the three Garcia brothers, Lefty, and the bartender, Tajo."

"I'll let the boss know," Sal replied.

Her face paled at the realization that Charlie Wall could see the whole list as expendable. "They can't just disappear, Sal, or show up floating in the river."

His eyes narrowed. "Are you sure you want to say that to the boss? It could be unhealthy to tell Mr. Wall how to manage a problem."

"Please do. I know life doesn't mean much in Ybor City. But I have spent my life saving the lives of others. I won't be part of innocent people vanishing because they *might* have done something wrong."

She could see the doubt in his eyes.

"Mr. Borrero, I know my peace of mind is not important to Mr. Wall. But killing the lot of them won't save Chago. Not without evidence that identifies the real murderer. He can watch them, and make sure nobody runs, but to save Chago, we need proof."

"How do you propose we find proof?"

Cornelia's brow furrowed. "The ring. The killer put his ring on her ring finger. It was his way of saying she belonged to him."

"You mean he thinks she was his wife?"

"I don't know if his delusion goes that far. But one of those six men has twisted reality into a vision of Chago as a villain. In his mind, Chago *made* him kill his beloved."

"*Beloved* is a strange word to apply to such a monster," Sal said.

"Monstrous acts are frequently committed in the name of love." She removed the envelope of evidence from her purse and laid it out on the table. "Look at those photographs. They tell a story of what happened in that alley. Despite the damage, there's no blood splattered on her dress or around her. She had been dead for a while before that bat was used. Whatever he did to cause her death was unintentional. She was his love. That's what he was telling the world when he put his ring on her finger."

"He did horrible things to her and dumped her in an alley." Sal sputtered.

"No, the rage came after. He didn't have the bat when he put her there. He put the ring on her and left."

"Why would anyone do such a thing?"

"He had probably seen Chago walk away. He knew he would not return for a while. At some point, he remembered the baseball bat he kept in the trunk of the car he drove. In his mind, Chago was the reason she was dead. Chago made her stop loving him. He was going to show them both what

142

happened when they betrayed him. So he stole Chago's bat and used it to beat her lifeless body until it broke. Then he left pieces there so everyone would see that Chago was evil."

Sal picked up the list and looked at the names. "I know all these guys. It's hard to believe that any of them could do such a thing."

Cornelia started putting things back into her purse. "I have seen much of the world, Mr. Borrero, and rarely have I seen life less valued than it is in Ybor City. Gambling, drugs, rum running, moonshine, prostitution, all the rackets are bathed in blood. I see the sides forming. There is a war tide rising, Mr. Borrero. People are dying all around you. A beautiful girl with the voice of an angel is dead, a bright future snuffed out because she dated a gangster."

"You see us all as evil," Sal said.

"No Sal, I don't." Cornelia picked up her purse and started to leave. The confused expression on Sal's face made her stop. "If I could see your mob as evil, I would have run. I would have felt justified in letting Chago rot in jail."

"It would not have been easy to escape."

Cornelia grinned. "I could have let my uncle shoot you."

Sal laughed at the memory. "I did not know how clever your uncle was at that time. I thought him harmless."

It was Cornelia's turn to laugh. "Uncle Percival, harmless?"

"It was a mistake I will not make again," Sal said. "The boss says I'll have to pay for the hole I put in the hotel ceiling. But, if it wasn't for us, what made you stay? Was it for Chago?"

Cornelia thought for a moment. "Teddy wanted to help. She thought we owed it to Chago for the help he gave her. But mostly, I can't stand to see authorities who accept bribes or choose the quick solution over the right one. If the police were capable of doing their job, I would have left them to it."

"You're a strange woman, Cornelia Pettijohn. You don't like gangsters or police on the payroll. You say the rackets are bathed in blood and that a war is coming, but you don't see me as evil?"

"I suppose I am," Cornelia replied. "The way I see it, that girl who sang the blues and her brother who sold *Bolita* tickets are early casualties of this war. Their mother is also a casualty. She will never recover from her grief. But I can't say Mr. Wall or any of you are worse than the politicians who made Ybor City have two Cuban Clubs. I don't know if Prohibition is better or worse than the evils of alcohol. I don't even know if it is more evil to kidnap me from a train or let your friend be beaten and tortured for a crime he didn't commit. In the end, does it matter?"

"Not if we can find the proof you seek. Do you know what we are looking for?"

"That ring is unique. If we could find who made it, that might lead to the owner. Conversely, if I could find the receipt for its purchase ... Do you think your boss could persuade our suspects to let us search their belongings?"

"It could be done. I still need to call him."

He motioned to Eddie the Hat. "Escort Miss Pettijohn back to her family and stay with her. Tell Clevon to get some sleep. Tomorrow is going to be busy."

Professor Pettijohn was trying to remain calm as they waited for Cornelia to return. When he realized that she was not coming back before the dining room closed, he caught the waiter's attention and waved him over.

"May I help you, sir?"

"My niece has been detained. Would you have the kitchen prepare a cold tray for her before they close? Then bring me the check."

The young man's shoulders relaxed. "Right away, sir."

"If you'll excuse me, I need to call a taxi," Tommy said.

Julia clutched his hand. "Tommy, couldn't you stay at least tonight?"

"Now Mother, we talked about this earlier."

"That was before I knew about the gangsters."

144

Tommy didn't know if she was frightened or trying to manipulate him. He decided to offer her an alternative. "If you are that worried, you can stay with me. I have plenty of room."

"You're not staying at this hotel?" the professor asked.

"I spent too many years at sea to be comfortable on land. *The White Tortuga* has all the comforts of home plus the motion of the sea to lull me to sleep."

"My brother practically lives on his yacht, dear," Teddy said. She stood up and slipped her arm around the professor's. "If you promise not to tinker with the engines, I'll ask him to introduce us to the love of his life. I'm sure the photographs he sent me don't do her justice."

"If you aren't too busy with wedding plans and whatever it is your niece is doing, I would be happy to take you yachting while I'm here. We could make a day of it."

Teddy squealed.

"I believe that was my lovely bride-to-be's way of saying that a day at sea sounds wonderful."

He smiled. "I look forward to welcoming you aboard."

Tommy offered his arm to his mother. "May I walk you to your door, Mother?"

"Have you decided where you're staying tonight?" he asked as they walked out of the dining room.

Teddy sighed.

"Is something wrong?" the professor asked.

"No, just a little disappointing." She squeezed his hand. "I couldn't hear Mother's answer. I would sleep much better if I knew she was sleeping under a different roof."

Quite a Conundrum

Over breakfast, Cornelia filled her uncle in on her discussion with Sal and her plans for the day.

He blanched at the thought of her confrontations with five potential murderers.

"Cornelia, this plan of yours is dangerous. One of these men is a killer. Who knows, all of them may be killers. That seems to be a popular local occupation."

She tried to put on a brave face. "Sal gave my pistol back last night. Besides, Lobster will be with me."

"I should go with you."

"Don't you dare try that, Uncle Percival. You just want to escape being the buffer between Teddy and her mother. You need to be here to keep the two of them from killing each other."

"They managed to stay civil through dinner. I think your pack of gangsters has put a healthy dose of fear into Mrs. Lawless. The last I heard, she was thinking of staying on Tommy's yacht."

"I wish she had stayed in Pennsylvania," Cornelia grumbled. "Why did she barge in, anyway?"

"She hasn't said. I expect she wants to get Teddy alone and grill her about me."

Cornelia could see the mischievous twinkle in his eyes. "You are going to make that difficult, aren't you?"

"Of course, I am. The woman ignored her daughter for decades. And the first time she sees Teddy, she belittles her."

"Uncle Percival, you're an old softy. I love you for that."

"Only where you're concerned, my dear. You are the closest thing to a daughter I will ever have. So be careful out there today. Rummaging through people's homes is a good way to get yourself killed."

"On this trip, Uncle, we have found any number of ways to get killed. I can't say any of them are good."

He laughed. "True enough, but be careful anyway."

"Are you and Teddy going to be able to check out the jewelry stores without alerting Mrs. Lawless? I left Teddy's drawing on the nightstand for her."

"We'll figure something out. Teddy has a talent for clandestine adventure. Besides, if Mrs. Lawless is anything like her daughter, she'll have a passion for shopping. Perhaps Teddy can distract her while I speak to the jewelers."

He hesitated for a moment before speaking again. "Yesterday in Mr. Baldwin's office, I noticed fresh bloodstains in the seam between the baseboard and the floor. I can't shake the feeling that we were lied to about where Mr. Zayas was shot."

"That's why you were crawling around on the floor yesterday. You think he was murdered in Baldwin's office?"

"We need to know who needed to hide where the murder took place and why. If Mr. Baldwin moved the body to cover up his own culpability, he certainly isn't going to tell me. Lobster isn't in Mr. Wall's inner circle. He wouldn't be aware of whether their boss gave the order to move Mr. Zayas' body."

"I suppose you could call Mr. Wall directly."

Cornelia mulled his suggestion over. "If he gave the order, it was because he didn't want us to know where Zayas was and what he was doing. The same could be said about Baldwin. Nobody was covering up the murder. Our knowing the location was a problem for someone. So, how do we figure out who didn't want us to find out without letting them know what you discovered?"

"That's quite a conundrum, Corny. Any idea of how to approach the problem?"

Her brow furrowed. "No," she admitted. "Let me mull it over. Maybe an idea will come to me later in the day."

Cornelia refused to let Lobster drive her Dodge. Lobster complained, argued, and then sulked, not that she gave a fig. She had learned to drive before he was born. Her uncle taught her to drive in his shiny red steam buggy. She had driven tractors and trucks around the farm, and ambulances in war zones. The traffic of this urban landscape was nothing to worry about.

"Either get in or stay here. I have work to do." She pressed the starter.

Lobster ran to the passenger side of the sedan and climbed in. "You can't go into those neighborhoods alone. They're dangerous."

"Young man, I promise I've been in more dangerous situations than you can find anywhere in Tampa."

She put the dark green touring sedan in gear and headed down the drive.

Lobster sulked.

He didn't stop sulking until they stopped at the curb in front of Fernando Garcia's apartment.

All three brothers met them at the door. None of them looked happy to have Lobster knocking on their door.

She hadn't expected to be welcomed. Cornelia also hadn't expected them to stand smiling at her as they made crude and sometimes cruel comments in Spanish. Their words hurt, but she played the fool. They were a lot more likely to say something incriminating if they did not know how well she understood them.

Lobster searched each man they visited and made them turn out their pockets. He turned a bright red at their insults but said nothing.

Their rooms yielded a wealth of information about the three young men. She went through each of them with as much attention to detail as she would have used inspecting the nurses' quarters before a visit from the commander.

The kitchen still held the aroma of *huevos rancheros* and *café con leche*. They must have just finished breakfast. The dishes were still draining on the rack.

Roberto must be the cook, she decided after seeing their bedrooms. His was as neat and orderly as the kitchen.

After every inch of the apartment was searched, she sighed and stepped outside where the three Garcia brothers were talking to Lobster. So far, her morning's work had uncovered nothing of use to Chago.

"Who's next?" Lobster asked.

"The bartender is closest. Let's get some lunch before we pay him a visit."

Tajo wasn't any happier to see her than the Garcia brothers had been, but he didn't seem worried about them, either. He growled about the fuss that was being made over a man who was leaving, but he let them do what they wanted. Once Lobster finished the body search, he stuffed his things back into his pockets and told him to lock up when they finished. He was late for work.

Lefty was next on the list. If the drummer was home, he didn't answer the door.

Lobster knocked louder and shouted his name.

He looked at Cornelia and shrugged. Then he took something from his pocket and, within seconds, the door opened.

Cornelia started to go in, but Lobster caught her by the arm.

"Stay here," he said. "Let me check the house out first. The boss told all of them to wait for you. If he's willing to cross Mr. Wall, who knows what else he's capable of?"

He took out his gun and made a careful search of the house.

Cornelia took a seat in one of the old rocking chairs on the front porch. She could hear Lobster inside, still calling for Lefty.

150

When he came back outside there was an odd expression on his face. "There's nobody home." He hesitated a second, then said. "I think you should check the upstairs bedroom first. It's creepy."

Calling the room creepy was an understatement. The entire room was a shrine to Jackie Dart. Posters of her events, photographs, and newspaper clippings filled the walls. A wedding dress hung on a dressmaker's dummy; the veil was laid out on the bed. Flowers and candles were decorating the mantel. On the bedside table were pieces of jewelry that he had probably stolen from her dressing room. Her make-up case from the club sat open on the dressing table. He must have taken that after they left yesterday. It had still been in the dressing room when Liza was shot. Beside it, a new silver-plated vanity set lay on a silver tray.

Cornelia picked up the brush and stood looking at it for a moment. *What did he plan? If the girl had lived, would he have kidnapped her and locked her in this … place? Was he going to force her to marry him?*

She laid the brush back on the tray. Unconsciously, she wiped her hands on her skirt as if the act of touching the purchase of a madman soiled her hand.

The smudged writing on the torn note had been a double clue. Left-handed people smudged cheap ink unless they were very, very careful.

The bedroom door closed with a thump. Cornelia didn't care about the noise. Despite the painful burns on her legs, she took the steps two at a time in her eagerness to get out of the house.

She turned the corner and started down the hall to the front door. Something was seriously wrong. For a split second, it didn't register what that something was.

The exit was blocked.

She fought down the urge to panic.

There had to be a back door somewhere.

Cornelia turned around and headed back the way she came. Before she could find any sign of an exit, a door opened beside her, and strong hands pulled her through.

She screamed as she fell into the darkness.

151

Cornelia woke with the mingled taste of blood and dirt in her mouth. Her head was pounding.

There was no light.

Nothing to tell her if it was night or day.

Nothing here but the musty smell of a long-closed room.

How long had she been here?

Panic clawed at her. She was alone, in the dark, without food or water. She forced the fear back. That kind of thinking led to compounding rather than solving problems.

Cornelia closed her eyes and lay there on the cold dirt floor trying to assess the situation. The split lip was of little consequence. Her left wrist was clearly broken. Intense pain shot up her arm and she could hear the grinding sound as she tried to move her hand. She wasn't sure about the left ankle. It hurt something fierce, but it could just be a sprain from falling down the stairs. Either way, the injury would complicate any effort to escape.

She reached up with her right hand and did a cursory examination of her face and head. Her lip was swollen and there were a couple of bumps, probably from hitting stairs on the way down. At least neither of them was bleeding. A concussion wouldn't surprise her, not with the massive headache she was experiencing.

Cornelia tried to push herself into a sitting position with her right hand. A wave of nausea hit her. She nearly lost consciousness and her head throbbed as though it was going to explode.

"Definitely concussed," she said aloud.

The situation was far from ideal, but she'd been in worse. The important task was to remain calm. She needed to think clearly to get herself out of this.

Lobster was with her when they arrived. The young redhead wouldn't have left his post.

Cornelia listened for his breathing, but all she heard was the sound of some small creature scurrying through the walls. Too bad Teddy and her slingshot weren't here.

The thought of Teddy was comforting although she was glad that she wasn't with her on this misadventure. A fall like that might have killed her.

Teddy and her uncle were safer wherever their day took them. And, she reminded herself, they knew where she went and what she was doing. When she didn't show up for dinner, they would be looking for her. Depending on how long she was out, they might already be searching for her.

Then, she remembered, Lobster was also missing. Perhaps he was locked up somewhere else in the house. She refused to think of the alternative.

There was no point in sitting alone in the darkness waiting for whatever came next. What she had seen of the house made her shiver. Lefty was a madman. He had killed three people and mutilated a corpse. He was capable of anything.

Worst of all, he could still be upstairs. Not hearing him moving around was not the same as knowing he was gone.

She needed to try to save herself.

Cornelia began reaching out with her right hand, feeling along the floor. She'd had her purse when she was pulled through the door. It might still be here. She hoped with all her might that Lefty had not thought to take it.

When she had searched the area that she could reach with her right hand, she started inching her legs along the floor. Between the burns and the injuries, she sustained in her fall, it was a slow painful process. It seemed like forever before she located the stairs, and then the banister.

Tears formed in her eyes at the thought of escape.

Her fingers wrapped around the first baluster. Clutching it, she tried to pull herself up. Cornelia's head throbbed. She could feel a warm rush as she lost consciousness again.

Shopping Around

Teddy dressed with care. Today no stocking seam could be even slightly askew, no curl could be out of place. Her mother was sure to find something to chide her about but there was no fun in making it easy for her.

Why was she here?

The question had nagged her all through dinner the previous evening and was still echoing through her head. Her mother wasn't the sort to galivant down the coast on a whim. *She* would do that, but not her mother.

Whatever the reason, she was here. Teddy refused to let her mother stop her from helping Chago. She picked up the sketch from her nightstand and took it with her to the living room.

It made her smile to see the professor reading his morning paper. The old dear was waiting for her and trying to look like he wasn't. At this time of day, he would have read every news story of even the slightest interest. With his memory, there was no point in rereading anything. The details were etched into his mind. She had seen him demonstrate his "eidetic memory" more than once.

"Your mother said she will meet us in the lobby in ten minutes." The professor gave her a reassuring smile. "I'm sure a short visit will be fine. We'll have a coffee together and explain our plans for the day. Dropping in unannounced isn't going to change those plans. Cornelia is depending on us."

"You don't know my mother," Teddy replied.

He stroked his short beard as he considered that. "No, I don't. That won't stop me from intervening if she tries to bully you."

Teddy smiled. She didn't have the heart to tell him that bullying was only one weapon in her arsenal. He would find out soon enough on his own.

"Now, where is this list of jewelers and your sketch?"

She handed them over.

Professor Pettijohn looked at the list and then handed it back to her. He put the sketch in his pocket. "Give the list to Sal. Tell him we'll start with Mr. Beckwith. We already have his goodwill. I'm sure he will be cooperative."

"What are we going to tell the jewelers?" Teddy asked. "We can't very well tell them we're investigating a murder and think they might have designed a custom ring for the culprit."

The question gave him pause. They needed a cover story that didn't frighten the shopkeepers.

He snapped his fingers. "We will tell them my best man saw the ring and liked the ring so much, he sketched it for me because he wanted me to see the design. Unfortunately, he was out clubbing when he saw it and can't remember which club he was in at the time. I am hoping to track down the owner and see if he will part with it."

"Do you think they'll believe that story?"

He smiled. "When the tale is accompanied by a twenty-dollar bill for their trouble, I'm sure they will be accommodating."

Teddy giggled. "This is going to be fun."

"Teddy, dear," Mrs. Lawless said when they entered the lobby. "Mr. Pettijohn said the two of you are going shopping this morning. So, tell me all about it over breakfast."

"We need to leave soon," Teddy said. "I have several shops to visit."

156

"Surely we have enough time to eat," her mother insisted. "I stayed with Tommy last night. Now I'm absolutely famished."

"I am sure Tommy would have given you breakfast."

Her mother stopped and stared at Teddy as if she had lost her mind. "You haven't spent time with your brother lately, have you?"

Teddy would like to have pointed out that her animosity was responsible for the distance she kept away from the family. Instead, she shook her head and kept her mouth shut.

"A few years back your brother was having stomach problems. Nothing more than indigestion, in my opinion. He decided to spend some leave time at the Battle Creek sanatorium. I thought he would get back to normal after a few weeks away from those fanatics, but he's a true convert. It's been nearly a decade, and he still follows that biological living diet Dr. Kellogg invented."

She heaved a heavy sigh and started walking again. "His idea of breakfast is a bowl of soggy cold cereal. I need real food, and coffee. Lots of coffee."

Teddy followed her to the dining room. "So, what are your plans today, Mother?"

"I thought we were shopping," the older woman replied. "Is there something else you had in mind?"

"Teddy and I were planning to visit a few jewelry stores this morning," the professor said. "I thought you might prefer the amenities of the hotel to traipsing through shops while I search for a gift for my best man."

"Nonsense," Mrs. Lawless replied. "I'm here to visit my daughter. Besides, I love shopping. Tell me about your best man, Mr. Pettijohn; is he also a retired teacher?"

The professor ignored the intended slight of his profession. He waited until the waiter had seated them to give her an appropriate reply. "No, Mac is a young pilot and engineer I met while we were staying in St. Petersburg. You know the family, of course. Teddy was once engaged to his father."

"Ansel's son? You've asked Ansel's son to be your best man? That hardly seems respectful to my daughter, Mr. Pettijohn."

Teddy pressed her lips, doing her best to mimic the professor's casual expression. It took a great deal of effort. Inside, she was laughing at the sheer delight of seeing her mother so shaken.

"It is Professor Pettijohn," he said calmly, "although I did ask you to call me Percival. As for your question, Mac is a friend and business partner of mine. Why would Teddy or I hold his parentage against him? We all know that Ansel Stevens was a liar, a brute, and a bully. Mac must take after his mother's side of the family. I am just thankful that Teddy had the good sense to escape Ansel's clutches. You should have seen the bruises that monster left on his wife."

He waved the waiter over and ordered a pot of coffee and a pastry. It had been hours since he had breakfast with Cornelia.

The breakfast delay meant it was nearly noon when Sal pulled the Oldsmobile into the parking lot at W.H. Beckwith's Jewelry Store.

During the long ride, Teddy's mother had hardly spoken. She didn't know if her silence was because she feared the gangster behind the wheel or if the professor's blunt opinion about Ansel had finally gotten through to her mother. She hoped it was the latter. On some level Julia Lawless had to know how horrid being married to Ansel Stevens would have been.

Teddy waited for Sal to open the door for her mother and then for her.

She looked over at Cornelia's uncle. These past months she had gotten to know the professor. He was so different from the men she had grown up around. Thinking of those differences reminded her of the faded photograph he prized. She wondered what sort of fool Mildred Hamm had been to give him up. Maybe Mildred never realized how much she was loved. If she had, she might have waited for him to graduate from West Point.

The professor squinted against the bright noonday sun. He wondered if the jewelry store had any of those dark glasses. The ones he purchased in St. Petersburg were still in his luggage, but that hardly helped today.

It took a moment for his eyes to adjust to the indoor lighting. By the time he could see again, Mr. Beckwith was approaching. His smile beamed at the prospect of another huge sale. "Back again so soon, professor? What can I do for you and your lovely fiancée?"

"Today I'm looking for a specific item. My best man sketched this." He handed him the drawing. "He was out on the town and spotted it on one of the musicians. He liked the ring so much he made a sketch. But you know how young men are; it was not his first stop, and his memory is a little fuzzy about which speakeasy he was in at the time."

"It is very distinctive. I dare say unique. At least I've never seen one like it." Beckwith said.

"I was so hoping you had sold the ring. If I can find out who purchased it, I could contact them and see if they would be willing to sell it. I wanted to surprise Mac with it as a gift."

Teddy pretended to be disinterested in the professor's quest. She wandered down the aisle looking at the shop's wares. She was pleased to see her mother was doing the same.

"If you want to leave the sketch, I could try to duplicate it," she heard Beckwith say.

They moved to the next jewelry case and a sapphire brooch caught her eye. Five sapphires formed the large petals, against them a circle of small sapphires set in white gold surrounded a solitary diamond at the center.

"What do you think of that?" she asked her mother.

Julia Lawless's gaze followed the direction Teddy pointed. "It is beautiful, dear, but you have always favored more modern designs. Wouldn't you rather have Art Deco, to match your engagement ring?"

"I was thinking of Cornelia. She's retiring in a few months."

"It is an exquisite piece. Would you like to get a closer look?" Mr. Beckwith asked as he walked around the counter and pulled out his key. "The marquise cut sapphires are one and a quarter carat. The ten small ones are an eighth of a carat each, and the center is a half-carat diamond."

Teddy picked up the brooch and examined the white gold filigree leaves adorning the stem. The design was elegant. She was sure Cornelia would cherish the piece.

She sighed and placed it back in the tray. "Thank you for showing it to me, Mr. Beckwith. It is truly lovely. But today we're on Percival's quest."

"Shall we go, dear?"

Sal opened the door and held it until his three charges were back in the bright sunlight.

"Give me just a moment, Sal." The professor said as he hurried back inside the shop. When he returned, he started handing out dark glasses to the group.

Sal balked.

"I promise you will see better with them than without," the professor insisted. "At least try them on."

The Cuban looked at the round lenses and wireframes of the spectacles with disdain, but he accepted the professor's gift and put them on.

The old man slipped something inside his jacket before getting in the car.

Their next stop was Mayor's Jewelry. The professor was mesmerized by the display of fine timepieces in the shop window. Teddy tried to nudge him toward the door, but it took Sal's strong arm to get him to move away from the watches.

Julia Lawless hadn't bothered waiting while the professor window-shopped. Her daughter found her chatting happily with a sandy-haired young clerk who was holding a strand of champagne-colored Southsea pearls.

"I see you've already found something you like," Teddy said, admiring the perfectly matched strand.

She took a quick glance back at the professor to assure herself that he was being helped.

160

"I don't think I've ever seen natural pearls this color," Mrs. Lawless replied.

"Yes, they're one of the lighter shades in the yellow range; you should see the deep golden ones."

Her mother's eyes narrowed. "When did you become such an expert on pearls?"

"I'm no expert," Teddy said. "When we were in the Philippines, the general's wife had a strand of golden ones, though they were not as large and well-matched as these. She told me about a store where pearl divers sold their wares. It was just a little shop with loose pearls sorted into jars by color. The yellow ones often come from the Philippine Sea, and they had every shade in that range."

They were still chatting about pearls when the professor joined them. "I'm afraid that this is another dead end."

"We still have a couple of places left on the list." Teddy said.

While Teddy and the professor made their way to the front of the store Julia purchased the necklace. With the current price of pearls, she couldn't resist.

It was getting close to closing time when they reached Friedman's Jewelers. Mr. St. John, the manager, welcomed them into his shop.

The young man sweeping at the back of the shop looked less pleased to see them. Teddy suspected he would have to sweep again after they left. It was impossible to walk in Florida without tracking sand.

She looked around the shop with keen interest. The sign near the front door had listed custom jewelry, but to Teddy's eye, most of his wares were the chain store variety. Not costume pieces, but the size and quality of the stones told her that these were mass-produced and sold through suppliers. Nothing she saw was one of a kind. This was the type of store middle-class housewives and young professionals would frequent.

Much to her surprise, the manager went to the back office and returned with a receipt for the ring. Her curiosity was piqued. It took all her self-control to remain out of earshot. The worst part was that her mother would be in the front seat all the way back to the hotel. The professor wouldn't be able to tell her what they had discovered.

Sal looked at the paper the professor held. His nostrils flared. He recognized the signature on the sales receipt. His fists clenched so tight that he could feel his fingernails biting his palm. When he got his hands on that weasel, there wouldn't be enough left of him to throw in the hoosegow.

He let out a slow deliberate breath, trying to maintain composure. He needed to call the boss. His hand reached inside his pocket searching for a nickel. There was a phone box on the corner, which he'd spotted while parking.

"Stay put, Professor. I need to have a word with the boss."

He walked out of the store without waiting for an answer. That little old man was the least of his worries.

The conversation with Charlie Wall was short. Mr. Wall wanted that receipt in his hands right away. Now that geezer-sitting was nearly over, he could get back to his regular work. All he needed to do now was let the professor know that the boss was sending backup to help Lobster and the fireplug, take the geezers back to the hotel, and get that receipt to the boss.

Not Adding Up

Julia Lawless found the silence in their automobile to be annoying. There was tension in the air so thick that an invisible wall hung between her and the others. They were up to something. She was sure of that. She wasn't sure what exactly was going on. The conversation at dinner the previous evening had created more questions than it answered. Cornelia Pettijohn was the last person on the planet that she would have expected to be involved with criminals.

What was it about the Pettijohn woman that made her so indispensable to everyone around her? She was a bumpkin, plain and frumpish, totally lacking in social graces or refinement. She couldn't imagine any circumstance that would be worth involving the Governor of Florida to keep Cornelia Pettijohn in the state.

Then there was this strange shopping trip. It had started out well. Teddy was even asking for her opinion. Shopping might be the only thing she and her daughter had in common. But her intended kept showing his drawing of a ring to everyone. It made no sense to chase after some unknown person to get a piece of jewelry. The first shopkeeper they met had offered to make the ring the Professor wanted. Instead, they kept looking until he found where the original was purchased.

After he found someone who could answer his questions, things got very strange. Their gangster bodyguard ran off to make a phone call. She was also certain that he had given the shopkeeper money when he returned to the store. Her usually very curious daughter kept talking about merchandise and wandering further away from the men. Then Mr. Pettijohn ushered them out of the store with great haste.

The sense of urgency bothered her. She could see the tension in their driver's shoulders. His brows were drawn and the muscles in his jaw twitched. Even though traffic was moving at a snail's pace, Sal clutched the wheel so tight that his knuckles turned white, and he used every trick he could to get them moving faster.

Once or twice, she tried to start a conversation with Cornelia's uncle, but the man was so lost in his own thoughts that he didn't hear a word. Or maybe his hearing was just that bad. He had a hearing device in his breast pocket, but he rarely wore the earpiece. What was the point of having the blasted thing if he never wore it?

Teddy's behavior bothered her the most. She usually enjoyed talking. Today, her hands gripped the upholstery. Who knew where her mind was? She sat on the edge of her seat and stared at the back of Sal's head. Perhaps she was willing the traffic in front of them to clear a path. She remained in that position all the way back to the hotel.

Sal dropped the geezers off at their hotel and stayed long enough to find out that Cornelia had not returned. He told himself that Lobster was a big guy, more than a match for Lefty, but with three dead bodies in his wake, the drummer was a threat to be reckoned with.

He headed to the El Dorado to pick up guns and reinforcements. It took time that he wasn't sure Cornelia Pettijohn could spare, but he wasn't stupid enough to go after Lefty without backup. He pulled the Oldsmobile into its usual parking spot and headed to the casino.

Eddie the Hat and the boss were waiting for him in the office. Two shotguns and a box of shells were set out on Wall's desk. He handed the receipt to Charlie and picked up one of the shotguns and filled his pocket with shells. Eddie grabbed the rest of the ammunition and the other gun. Sal nodded to the boss and left.

He didn't like shotguns. They were messy. They were also efficient. A man could sometimes dodge a bullet. But when both barrels of a shotgun emptied into a man's midsection, it was over. A shotgun at close range would cut a man in half. He couldn't help feeling sorry for Lefty.

The man had to be crazy. There was no other explanation for his shooting people in one of Mr. Wall's clubs. Any man in his right mind would have known better than to cross Charlie Wall. Crazy had no boundaries, no stopping point. Somewhere in that messed up mind he had to know that there was no good way for this to end. He was a walking dead man.

If he had done anything to Miss Pettijohn, he and Eddie would be doing him a favor to take him out now. A gut shot wasn't pretty, but it was fast. In Charlie Wall's hands, Lefty's would be a slow painful death. For some reason, the boss had a soft spot for the old dame. For that matter, so did he. There was something about her that was honorable. Her kind of integrity didn't usually show up in his world.

He turned the corner and spotted Miss Pettijohn's green Dodge. There was no question that Lobster and Miss Pettijohn were here. Cornelia's automobile was parked across the street from Lefty's place. He pulled in behind her and shut off the engine. The two men climbed out of the Oldsmobile and headed for the ramshackle house on the other side of the street. Sal motioned for Eddie the Hat to head to the back door in case Lefty tried to do a runner.

Sal gave him a moment to get in place before he knocked.

There was no answer.

He opened the door and found himself staring at the backside of a piece of furniture. Who knew what was on the other side? Blowing a hole in the thing would attract more attention than he wanted. He lowered the shotgun to waist height and held it at his side. Sal used his shoulder to push hard on the cabinet, and felt it inching forward. There was no attempt to stop him. One more shove and he would be inside. Sal put his back into this final push and stepped forward. Sharp pain ran through his shoulder and down his arm. He wasn't sure, but he thought he might have broken something in that last push.

It was sunset when they reached the hotel. Teddy had hoped that Cornelia would be back before them. When they discovered she wasn't, her heart sank.

Sal ordered them to go to their rooms and lock the doors while he went in search of their companion.

Teddy Lawless was at the front desk requesting a taxi before Sal's backside disappeared through the hotel door. There was no way she was going to stay cooped up in the hotel while Cornelia was in danger.

Had she not been so worried about Cornelia, the shocked expression on her mother's face would have given her enormous satisfaction.

"You cannot be traipsing off through a strange city in the middle of the night."

"Really, Mother? Watch me."

"Theodora."

"Mrs. Lawless," the professor said, "you should do as Sal said. You will be perfectly safe locked in your hotel room. But Teddy and I are going to find my niece."

She shifted from one foot to the other as she watched the two of them walking across the lobby. Curiosity outweighed her fear, and Julia Lawless followed them outside.

Cornelia's hand still clutched the balustrade when she regained consciousness. Her head rested against the bottom step. She shuddered at the feeling of something crawling in the tangled cobwebs plastered to the left side of her face. She sat up and tried to bat whatever it was away. Her reward for trying to brush the sticky mess off was an instant reminder of the broken wrist. Hot, sharp waves of pain shot up her arm.

It was too dark to see how bad the injury was, but she could feel the swelling and tenderness. Her fingers were numb. Tears burned in her eyes. She didn't try to stop them from spilling down her face. The darkness and pain were just too much for her to endure.

After a good cry, she wiped her face with her sleeve and tried moving her leg over the floor in the hopes of finding her bag. Her foot hit something solid. She hoped it was her purse.

She leaned forward and reached out her good hand toward the object, feeling for the familiar square shape.

Relief rushed through her.

She found her flashlight and turned it on. The small beam of light didn't illuminate more than a small patch of the room, but the ability to see the stairs and the exit gave her hope of escape.

Slowly she moved the beam to the right, looking for something that she could use as a crutch. A few feet from the bottom of the stairs, the body of the burly young man they called Lobster lay sprawled in the dirt. His flaming red hair was dulled with dirt and his sunburned face seemed painted on, too red against the bloodless white skin.

Cornelia had never felt so alone.

She held the flashlight with her chin and rummaged through the purse with her good hand. The distal radius fracture was her first concern. With a couple of emery boards and her handkerchief, she fashioned a splint. She had a devil of a time figuring out how to tie the handkerchief and hold the splints in place at the same time. A lot of trial and error went into the job.

The next challenge was getting up the stairs. Her ankle could not bear weight. She didn't have the balance to hop up the steps without breaking her neck. Although she hated to give up the comfort of her small light, she turned it off and put it back into her bag. She used the uninjured hand and arm to lift her rear end high enough to scoot up the steps one at a time. Until she reached the door at the top.

To her surprise, it wasn't locked.

Lefty must have figured the fall would be fatal.

A Revolting Development

It wasn't difficult to figure out which house was Lefty's. Three police cars, an ambulance, Cornelia's Dodge, and the Oldsmobile Sal drove were parked at the curb. The Hillsborough County Coroner had pulled his vehicle into the driveway. Officers and officials were scattered around a two-story clapboard house that had seen better days.

"Are you folks sure you want to stop here?" the taxi driver asked.

"Anywhere along here will do," Teddy replied. "There's no need to wait. That's our car over there." She pointed at the Dodge.

The professor handed him a five and told him to keep the change.

Teddy was already out of the taxi and headed toward the police barricades.

Professor Pettijohn looked at Mrs. Lawless' pale face and stopped beside her. "You don't have to stay. I can have the driver take you back to the hotel."

She nodded and sat back down.

The professor handed the driver a second five-dollar bill and had him return his future mother-in-law to the hotel. He watched the taxi pull away before crossing the street where a small crowd of gawkers had gathered.

Teddy was at the front of the crowd scanning the faces of those on the other side of the barricades. He could see from her expression that she had not spotted Cornelia.

He slipped the earpiece of his hearing device into his right ear and turned it to the highest setting. He knew that the background noise would make it hard to pick up much conversation, but he had to try. There wasn't enough light for lip reading.

It took a few minutes to worm his way to where Teddy was standing.

"Eddie the Hat is over there talking to the sergeant. I haven't seen Sal or Cornelia. Have you?"

"Not yet," he said. "She was with Lobster. Have you seen him?"

She gulped. "I think that's him." She pointed to a body bag lying in the side yard. He could see the teardrops glistening in the corners of her eyes.

"Cornelia will be all right. I promise." He held out his handkerchief to her.

A disheveled Sal was sitting on the back bumper of the ambulance. His coat and hat were in his lap. Teddy wasn't sure where he had hidden his pistol, although she doubted his ability to use it. He had blood on his shirt, and his right arm was immobilized in a sling. She couldn't see any splints.

She waved at him.

When Sal spotted the two of them at the edge of the crowd he came over. "You shouldn't be here, Miss Lawless. It isn't safe."

Teddy ignored that.

"Where is my niece?" Professor Pettijohn demanded.

Sal flinched. "Miss Cornelia is alive, but she had a bad fall. They should be bringing her out on a gurney soon. They're taking us to Gordon Keller Hospital on North Boulevard. I can have Eddie drive you there if you want."

"Were you shot rescuing Cornelia?" Teddy asked.

Sal glanced down at the sling. "Nothing so dramatic. Somebody, the killer I think, had barricaded the door. The medic thinks my clavicle broke when I busted in. He's probably exaggerating, but I have to wear this thing until they X-ray me."

The professor's eyes narrowed. "The killer, not Lefty?"

Sal was quiet for a few seconds, then let out a long slow breath. "No. They found Lefty in a far corner of the basement behind some boxes. The medical examiner says he's been dead a while. A bullet to the head, just like the dancer."

All the color drained from Teddy's face.

Gordon Keller Hospital was not large; the campus had only the main hospital building and a training facility for nurses. The emergency waiting room was cramped and dimly lit. In Teddy's opinion, whoever chose the depressing shade of gray paint for the walls deserved to have one of those floggers sent to his door.

Teddy and the professor sat in hard wooden chairs and waited for more than two hours to see Cornelia. When a nurse finally called the professor's name, they were both so stiff it was difficult to stand.

Eddie the Hat stepped away from his position by the door to give the professor a hand.

The nurse explained that Cornelia was being admitted for observation due to a severe concussion. Her broken wrist would need to be kept immobile for the next five weeks, and she would probably find it weak and difficult to use for several more weeks. The ankle wasn't broken, but the sprain might take longer to heal than her wrist.

"Can we see her now?" Teddy asked.

The nurse frowned. "Visiting hours ended at eight. As I said, she is just being admitted now. She hasn't even been assigned a room."

The professor was so angry his ears burned red. He started to speak, but Eddie put a hand on his shoulder.

"Excuse me, Nurse," Eddie said. "May I speak to you privately for a moment?"

The two of them disappeared around the corner and less than a minute later the nurse's attitude had shifted dramatically.

171

"Miss Pettijohn will be in room 214; it is our very best private room. If you'll follow the gentleman, he knows the way."

"Out with it, Mr. Hat, what did you tell her?" Teddy asked.

Eddie grinned. "Just that my boss would be insulted if all accommodation wasn't made for his personal guest. I don't think you'll have to worry about visiting hours anymore."

Room 214 had the same white metal hospital bed with crisp white sheets and cotton blankets that Teddy had seen in every hospital she had been admitted to in the last decade. The similarities ended there. A pair of upholstered rocking chairs flanked a small white table by the window. A large silver -framed mirror hung on one wall above a white dressing table. On the other side of the room was a door that led to a private bathroom, and another that proved to be a closet. There was also a phone on the bedside table.

Teddy settled into one of the rocking chairs to wait for Cornelia.

She thought she was prepared for the worst, but when they wheeled the gurney into the room Cornelia looked more dead than alive. It didn't help that the hospital gown was a slightly lighter shade of gray than the emergency waiting room's walls. Bruising and abrasions covered her face and arms. At least, the part of the arms she could see. Her right hand, the dominant one, was in a cast up to the elbow. Only her fingers were exposed.

The professor tapped her shoulder. "We should step outside while they get her settled."

Eddie the Hat was still standing near the door. He too looked shaken at the sight of Cornelia's injuries.

"I'm sorry, Professor. We didn't do a very good job of taking care of her."

The professor rubbed his forehead. He didn't know what to say to Eddie. *Eddie wasn't the only one to fail Cornelia. My niece wouldn't have been here to be kidnapped by gangsters if I hadn't tricked her into coming on this trip. This is all my fault.*

"She's all tucked in now," the nurse said from the doorway. She joined them in the hall, allowing the orderlies to take their gurney back to the emergency room. "I'm afraid that she is not making much sense tonight. I'm sure it is just the aftermath of trauma. Head injuries are tricky."

The nurse smiled at them and waited for questions. When nobody said anything, she continued. "I will be sitting with her tonight. Her admitting form has the Tampa Bay Hotel as her current address. Is that correct?"

Teddy forced a smile. "Yes. Thank you. May I have a moment to say good night?"

Once Teddy and the professor had each had a short visit, they headed out the door.

"Are you ready to go, Eddie?" the professor asked.

"My orders are to stay; the boss will send someone else in the morning."

The professor nodded and turned away. He was halfway down the hall before he realized how accustomed he had become to having armed men standing outside their rooms.

Teddy fastened the clasp on the small suitcase she had packed for Cornelia. She had hoped to ask Cornelia about what happened, but last night wasn't the time. The fall hadn't made her as delusional as the nurse thought when Cornelia's fevered brain rambled on about gangsters and shootings, but she wasn't entirely aware either.

She sipped a medicinal dose of Mr. Scroggins's moonshine. It was important to have her wits about her today. Cornelia needed her.

When she opened the door to the suite, she saw Sal and Chago standing guard. She squealed with delight, dropped the suitcase and her cane, and hugged Chago. "When did you get out? How? You didn't crush out, did you?"

The young gangster laughed. "No," he said. "I didn't escape. The charges against me were dropped, thanks to my friends. When the judge was presented with pictures of that room, the receipt for the ring, and the journal Lefty kept, he ordered my release."

His smile disappeared and his gun came out at the sound of a door opening down the hall from them.

"Put that away," Sal ordered. "That's Miss Teddy's mother."

Chago's eyebrows shot up. "I'm so sorry. I was not told your mother was here."

"It's all right, Chago. Mother's arrival was a surprise to all of us. Besides, I know you wouldn't have shot her."

Teddy didn't dare look at her mother for fear that she would burst out laughing. The expression on her face when she saw Chago's pistol was a memory she would cherish forever. She couldn't have gotten better revenge on her for inviting herself to Florida if she had planned this moment.

Cornelia didn't know what to think when she woke up in the hospital. At least she *thought* it was a hospital. Wherever she was, it was better than that awful basement. She had clean sheets and a blanket. It occurred to her that she could be dreaming. Fear prickled at the edges of her consciousness. If she opened her eyes, would everything clean and comfortable vanish?

No, if she were dreaming her head wouldn't ache like this. She had vague memories of an ambulance, and someone shining a light in her eyes. At one point she thought she had heard Teddy talking to her. She wasn't sure if that was memory or wishful thinking.

The sound of a ship's whistle startled her into opening her eyes. The light was pouring through a large window. It was so bright that she needed to shield her eyes. Unfortunately, her attempt to do so ended with a plaster cast banging into her head. Now that her headache was exponentially worse, she remembered that her wrist was broken in the fall.

"Good morning, Miss Pettijohn. How are you feeling today?" A too-friendly voice was chattering on, making her want to scream. "I don't know if you remember much about last night. You took a tumble down a flight of stairs. They brought you here by ambulance. You're in the hospital."

Cornelia opened one eye and squinted up at her nurse. "I don't know if it is possible to strangle you with one hand, but if you don't stop talking so loudly, I am going to find out."

The nurse jumped back.

After a short pause, she spoke softly, "I'm sorry, Miss Pettijohn. Your head must be throbbing. I'll see what your doctor has ordered."

She returned with headache powder and a glass of water. "Dr. Wilson would like you to try the standard remedy first. He has written an order for morphine if you need it to sleep."

"I'll manage fine with this," Cornelia replied. She had seen too many casualties of drug dependence to trust using them for pain management of a headache. Cancer maybe, or some other horrible disease might be different.

The nurse helped her sit up and adjusted her pillows.

Rising was a challenge. Cornelia closed her eyes as the room started to spin. It was all she could do to keep herself from passing out from the effort of moving her head. She knew she was fortunate to be alive after falling down a flight of stairs. But she didn't feel very lucky this morning.

"Would you like an icepack for your head?" her nurse asked softly.

"Yes. Thank you."

"We will be changing shifts soon. Is there anything else you need before I leave?"

"Could you please close the window shade? I know I have a lovely view of the bay, but the light is painful."

The nurse pulled the shade and turned out the overhead light before leaving.

Sal closed his eyes and leaned back against the wall. Having the two Lawless women bickering in the hallway made it hard to resist the urge to groan. Perhaps he should have let Chago shoot Mrs. Lawless.

175

There was a lull in the conversation that made Sal's eyes open. To his surprise, everyone was looking at him.

"What?" he growled.

"Do you want to sit down?" the professor asked. "You really shouldn't be working so soon after surgery."

The old inventor was worried about him. This was the last thing Sal needed.

Last night was rough. He doubted he had been able to get a solid twenty minutes of sleep. The shoulder injury was painful, what with the bones being held together by brass plates and screws. But being treated like an invalid by the professor was wrong in so many ways. The man was old enough to have been the engineer who designed the first wheel. He should be the one who needed a soft chair. Instead, the professor spent his time devising ways to cause trouble.

"What I want is to let Miss Cornelia know that her job is finished. Are we ready to go?"

"Are you that anxious to be rid of us?" Teddy asked.

"Nonsense, Miss Teddy," Chago insisted. "He is just happy to have me back to boss around. Right, Sal?"

Sal glared at him.

This only made Chago laugh.

"You're leaving again," Mrs. Lawless protested.

"Only for a little while. Cornelia won't be up to a long visit." Teddy told her. "The poor dear was unable to sit up last night when we left the hospital. I doubt that she is much better today. Head trauma is hard to recover from."

"Head trauma? Where was her bodyguard?"

Teddy turned to face her. Tears welled in her eyes. "Dead, Mother. Lobster was murdered yesterday. Cornelia nearly met the same fate."

Professor Pettijohn handed her his handkerchief. "There, there, now. Dry your eyes. You know you need a brave face for Cornelia's sake. She has enough to worry about without our worrying her."

"I'm sorry, Percival."

"Think nothing of it, my dear. You go powder your nose or whatever you ladies do to always look so lovely." He

176

patted her arm. "Meanwhile, I'll walk your mother back to her suite."

When her nurse woke her for the next round of medicine, Cornelia's headache was less fierce. Thankfully, the dizziness and double vision were gone. Now that she was feeling better, it dawned on her that she was not in a regular hospital ward. This was one of those fancy private rooms reserved for dignitaries, famous, important, or high-ranking patients.

She had been mistakenly included in that group.

The hospital room was beginning to resemble a florist shop. When the nurse handed her the cards, she discovered that Mr. Wall had sent two dozen red roses and a box of chocolates. The pink roses and white carnations were from the governor. *The St Petersburg Times* sent a rainbow of calla lilies. She was sure Mitch was behind that delivery. The reporter was one of a handful of people she considered friends. To her surprise, there was even a potted peace lily from Sal.

Teddy and her uncle arrived with a basket of fruit and a box of pastries from the hotel. "Hospital food is always terrible," Teddy said, as she set the treats on her nightstand.

"I wouldn't know, they haven't offered me any," Cornelia replied. "So far I've only been allowed liquids."

"You're looking better," her uncle said.

"You're losing your eyesight, Uncle Percival. There is a huge mirror behind you. I know that most of my face is purple or black."

"Yes," he said, grinning, "but I much prefer that to the ashen look it wore last night." He reached down and held the exposed fingers peeping out of her cast. "You are the luckiest person I know. I am amazed that you went down a dozen steps, face first, and only broke your wrist."

"Lobster wasn't so lucky."

"Do you have any idea who attacked you?" Teddy asked.

Cornelia's brows furrowed. "I didn't get a clear look at his face, but it was Lefty's house."

"It couldn't have been him. They found his body in the basement. He was dead before you arrived."

Cornelia stared at her, unable to believe what she heard. She had spent hours in that dank cold basement with two dead men. "Lefty had a shrine with things he either pilfered from her or bought for her. He had to be the killer."

"Oh, he killed Jackie," her uncle said. "We found the receipt for the ring he put on her left hand. When they were searching his house they also found a journal that was quite damning. The charges against Chago have been dropped. He is outside waiting for us to finish visiting so he can thank you. Your nurse wouldn't let us all in the room at once."

Cornelia shook her head and instantly regretted the action. She closed her eyes for a moment to allow her vision to clear. "Are you telling me that the murders weren't connected after all?"

Teddy sat down on the edge of the bed, being careful not to touch Cornelia's injuries. "I believe they *are* connected, just not the way we thought. Percival and I were talking about how Mr. Zayas's body had been moved. The only reason we can deduce for the move is that there was something in that office his killer didn't want us or the police to see. It had to be something he couldn't just pick up and take with him. Which means it is probably still there."

A familiar twinkle was back in Teddy's eyes. "Please don't go off investigating on your own," Cornelia said. She knew Teddy well enough to know that was exactly what she had in mind. She also knew that there was nothing she could do to stop her.

"We promised your nurse we would keep the visit short," her uncle said. He bent down and kissed her forehead. "Teddy packed a bag with some things she thought you might want to have while you're here. I'll set it in the closet for now."

He left the room to give Teddy a moment alone to say goodbye.

For a moment she just sat there holding Cornelia's hand. "Our room is very empty without you. I miss your snoring."

Cornelia smiled. "I missed you, too."

"You need to get better quickly. I was so worried about you yesterday that I forgot to have even a medicinal dose of alcohol."

"The world may end," Cornelia teased.

Her voice lowered. "Cornelia, I haven't said anything to your uncle about this, but there's something you need to keep in mind. The killer doesn't know you can't identify him. There is a good chance he could come after you again."

"That thought had crossed my mind. I am at a serious disadvantage right now. I can neither fight nor run away. You are going to have to hope Mr. Wall's guards don't meet Lobster's fate."

Teddy hugged her gently. "I'll be back this evening. Call if you need anything."

"I will," Cornelia promised. "Look after Uncle Percival."

Chago Aldama showed no ill effects from his time in jail. Now that he was a free man, his dark hair was again combed and waxed into place. His white suit was freshly pressed. He held his white boater hat in his hands and smiled down at Cornelia.

"I won't stay long," he said softly. "Miss Teddy told me you have a headache. I am just grateful that you still have your head. That was bad business last night."

"I am glad the charges against you have been dropped and Miss Duarte's killer has been found."

The smile vanished from his face. "I'm sorry to have caused you so much trouble. Mr. Wall should not have dragged you into this search for a murderer. If I had been consulted, I would have told them not to involve you or Miss Teddy."

Cornelia closed her eyes and leaned back against the pillows. "I don't approve of his methods, but he was right in believing the police would not look further. A quick arrest mattered more to them than the truth. Is everyone in Florida corrupt?"

179

"Not everyone, but too many are." Chago started to say more, but this wasn't the time. "Thank you, Miss Pettijohn. I'll leave you to rest. I'm just outside if you need me."

It was late afternoon when Tommy Lawless docked his yacht and walked to the hospital. He made a short stop in the gift shop to purchase flowers, then asked for Cornelia's room number. He was surprised when the front desk asked for his name and had him wait until they spoke with her nurse.

Surprise turned to shock when he saw a young man with a suspicious bulge under his left shoulder standing outside her door. He didn't know what was going on, but he was going to get to the bottom of it.

"Mr. Lawless?" a middle-aged nurse in a starched white uniform asked.

Her iron-gray bun and square set of her jaw reminded him of Cornelia. He wondered if there were Pettijohn cousins in Florida.

"Yes."

"The first forty-eight hours after a head trauma are the most dangerous. Miss Pettijohn is not to be exposed to loud noises, bright lights, stress, or long visits. Do you understand?"

"Yes. How serious are her injuries?"

Her jaw tightened as she scrutinized him. "I am not at liberty to say, sir, except that she is stable and allowed brief visits."

He could feel the young gangster at the door watching him as he crept into Cornelia's room and closed the door behind him.

She was propped up with several pillows into a half-sitting position. Her head rested on the uppermost pillow and her eyes were closed. The parts of her face that were not bruised or bandaged were very pale. The lower part of her right arm was in a cast and propped on its own pillow. The steady rise and fall of her chest was the only indication she was alive.

180

He cleared his throat.

Cornelia's eyes opened. "More flowers," she said.

Tommy looked around the room and smiled. "You do have a lot of admirers. I'm beginning to think you're secretly one of the rich and famous. Private room, a guard at the door, a personal nurse and more flowers and gifts than you have space to display."

"It is all above my pay grade," she said. "Do you think I've been given a couple of stars, and nobody told me?"

"At least you haven't lost your sense of humor. Though you would make a good general if the military allowed women to rise to that level."

"Alas, I shall retire as a lowly captain. I don't think I will live to see any woman rise that high."

He pulled one of the rocking chairs close to the bed. "Cornelia, can you tell me more about Mother has pulled me into the middle of? Your uncle said that you had been taken from your train at gunpoint."

Cornelia sighed. "That's true. But I agreed to stay. I can't really explain all the twists and turns but the young man guarding the door is Chago Aldama. He is a friend of Teddy's, and he was arrested for a murder he didn't commit. Now that we have proved him innocent, the charges have been dropped."

"So, it's settled."

"I wish, but no. I am in the soup up to my eyeballs. There is a killer out there that thinks I know who he is, and he is probably plotting to kill me." Cornelia waved her left hand over her body. "As you can see, I'm in no position to deal with him."

"Why aren't the police involved?" Tommy asked. "Have you talked to them?"

"I have had three police interviews since arriving in Tampa. I don't expect any assistance from that quarter." She gave him a wry smile. "Can we change the subject, please?"

He leaned back in the chair. "All right, tell me about your uncle and my sister."

Cornelia winced. "I asked for that, didn't I?"

181

"I could ask them, I suppose, but my impression is they are both quite practiced at bending the truth to suit their needs."

"You're right about that," Cornelia said, "But before I answer your question, I need to know that what we say goes no further."

"You have my word," Tommy promised.

"Bending the truth to suit their needs is how this whole marriage plan got started. A little lie to the St. Petersburg police to explain why Teddy was staying in the same suite as my uncle, since she was not related to either of us."

"This whole thing, the wedding plans, that expensive ring your uncle gave her, is all an elaborate lie?"

"Not anymore. My insane uncle has persuaded your crazy sister that their getting married was a good idea. When your mother called and said she was coming to the wedding, well, that was the final straw. I have given up trying to change their minds."

Tommy rested his chin on his knuckles. "Cornelia, we have a long history of being honest and direct with each other."

"Of course."

He took a deep breath and let it out. "You have never said anything, but I have always thought you and Teddy were more than friends. Have I been wrong about that all these years?"

"No."

"But she is marrying your uncle."

There was a note of bitterness in Cornelia's voice. "She could hardly marry me."

"No, I don't suppose she could." He put a hand on hers. "I am sorry."

There were tears in the corners of her eyes. "I think their decision is wrong, I've told them both that, but it is their decision. My uncle is right about one thing, though. It will make our being together look more respectable. Not that I give a fig. But Teddy—her mother's rejection hurt her more than you know. She has always wanted the life she thought she would have growing up."

"What does your uncle want?"

"To live his life on his terms."

"I don't understand."

"My uncle is wealthy, well respected, even admired in his field. He is kind and generous. You wouldn't believe how many young people he has helped, including me." She grinned. "He also has been turning seventy-five every year for a long time. The old dear knows that he is getting too old to live as he wants without help. He is looking at this marriage as the kind of window dressing he needs to protect his dignity in his final years."

"Are you sure of his intentions?" Tommy asked.

"Where women are concerned, I have always been sure of my uncle's heart. To him, there is only *the* woman."

"Oh!"

Cornelia smiled. "When I was a girl, there was a police sergeant in Lexington who loathed my uncle. He must have found a dozen different reasons to arrest him. I never understood why until I found out the sergeant's wife was the love of Uncle Percival's life. When he went away to West Point, she was unwilling to wait for him. She married the policeman while he was away. They had a couple of boys and, as far as I know, had a happy life together. Uncle Percival never tried to approach her, but I think her husband knew he never stopped loving her. She's been dead for more than twenty years, but Uncle still keeps a photograph of her on his nightstand."

Tommy was still holding her hand when he stood up. "Your nurse will be in here to throw me out if I stay any longer. But Cornelia, I would be proud if you considered me your brother." He squeezed her hand and left before she could reply.

Missing a Pair of Aces

Tommy Lawless brought his yacht to the dock outside the Tampa Bay Hotel and walked across the lush lawn to the hotel lobby. He had promised to meet his mother for dinner even though he hated the kind of lavish meals his mother always ordered. The building was magnificent, even in the slow decline of Victorian buildings in this modern age. He still remembered the picture postcard his sister sent him when she stopped here on her way to Cuba.

Her postcards were a gateway for him to follow her adventures in faraway places: New York, Tampa, then Santiago, and Havana, Cuba. He replied with postcards from Key West, Nipe Bay, Pensacola, the Canal Zone, Ireland, Amsterdam, and later Algiers. Joining the Navy was a decision he had never regretted, not even in the worst of the Great War.

He used the house phone to call his mother's room, and then the professor. Soon the four of them were settled around one of the hotel tables looking over the menu. The waiter brought their drinks: sweet iced tea for the professor, unsweetened for Mrs. Lawless, and lemonade for Teddy and her brother, his without the added rum. Tommy wasn't impressed with the menu, but settled for the cream of celery soup, followed by a lettuce salad and cheese and crackers. The professor chose the lobster, as did Teddy. Mrs. Lawless started with the *bouillon en tasse* followed by chicken croquettes.

"I stopped by the hospital to see Cornelia earlier," Tommy said. "She still has a guard at her door, but I noticed there are none here this evening. Now that Teddy's gangster friend has been released, I suppose you are feeling safer."

"How was Cornelia when you visited?" the professor asked. "She was still a bit groggy when we saw her this morning."

Tommy noticed that the professor had ignored his question. "We talked a little about your upcoming nuptials. Have the two of you set a date?"

"Not yet," Teddy replied. "I was thinking late June after Cornelia retires."

Her mother stared at her as if she had lost her mind. "What? Isn't Cornelia leaving soon? You can't possibly stay without a chaperone. Think of your reputation."

"Mother you made it quite clear that my reputation was ruined years ago." Teddy countered.

"There is no need for that to be dredged up in the papers," Mrs. Lawless replied. "I'm not going to allow you to drag the family name through the mud again. If you wish to wait until June, I shall have to call your brother and let him know that I am staying with you until after the wedding."

Tommy lowered his head. He really hadn't intended to instigate the kind of drama he'd left home to avoid. He took a sip of his lemonade and felt it hit the acid churning in his stomach.

The professor waited until their waiter left to speak. "I am sure Theodora won't object too much to moving our wedding forward a few months. Once Cornelia is out of the hospital, we will speak to her and Mac and figure out a date that will work. Is that acceptable to you, Mrs. Lawless, or would you prefer I call you Mother?"

Julia Lawless was in the middle of drinking her tea. She gasped at the thought of a man of Mr. Pettijohn's advanced age calling her *mother*. Iced tea went down her windpipe and caused her to cough so hard that it dripped from her nose and mouth.

Sal didn't often let Eddie the Hat drive, but between the pain in his shoulders and back and the fever he was developing, driving was too much for him tonight. Still, the boss wanted him to swing by Club Tropical and have a look around. Too many things that had happened in the last two days didn't add up. He thought about the list of names Miss Pettijohn had, and how interviewing those men became a fight for her life.

It was clear that Lefty killed Jaquinda. It was clear that he was crazy and twisted. Who knew what he would have done if he had brought the girl to that awful room? Her death was an accident, made to look like murder to frame Chago.

Everything that happened after that was planned. What didn't make sense was someone else learning what Lefty had done, and using that knowledge to keep everyone's attention on Jaquinda instead of Zayas.

There was an outside chance that Zayas was murdered by Lefty, but that was looking more and more unlikely. There was no way the drummer could have killed Liza or Lobster. He was already dead when those crimes were committed. He wasn't the one who threw Miss Pettijohn down those stairs. The only thing that made sense was someone thinking they could use Lefty's insanity to cover up killing Geraldo Zayas. Then Miss Pettijohn got too close to finding out what happened.

He leaned back in the seat and closed his eyes as Eddie pulled the big Oldsmobile into the parking lot of Club Tropical. "We're here, Mr. Borrero."

Sal wiped the sheen of sweat off his face. "Park by the rear door. If we're lucky, I have a little time to look around before anybody knows I'm here."

The back hall was unlit. Sal made his way to the ladies' dressing room. He stood where he thought the dancer had been standing when she was shot and looked out into the hallway. There was only one place the shooter could have hidden to make that shot. He had to have been hiding in the men's dressing room.

187

He thought about the statements that had been given to the bulls when Liza was shot. Lobster and the professor were outside, the ladies were interviewing Liza, but Baldwin had been in his office when the shot was fired. If the man had run toward the exit, he would have run into Lobster. If the killer had headed deeper into the club, he would have gone right past Baldwin's office. Baldwin had to know more than he'd said in his statement, more than he told Mr. Wall.

He needed to rest a moment, then he would go confront Baldwin.

Sal stopped to wipe the sweat off his face. Despite the heat radiating off his skin, he was feeling chilled, shivering, and more tired than he had felt in ages. He leaned against the wall and mopped his forehead with a handkerchief.

Eddie the Hat knew the rules. He was supposed to keep his mouth shut and follow Sal's lead. Sal wasn't leading, though. His face was flushed and covered in sweat. He had been wiping it with his handkerchief most of the day, but the sodden cloth was having little effect now.

Sweat had soaked through his shirt and left rings under the arms of his jacket.

He had stayed close, watched the older man, and tried to make himself useful. But, when he saw Sal leaning against the wall mumbling to himself, he decided to act.

He caught him by the waist, led him back to the Olds, and then drove him back to the hospital. Sal hadn't put up much of a fight. Today he didn't have much fight in him.

Eddie wasn't under any illusions about what could happen to him for disobeying orders. It was the kind of thing that could leave a man floating face down in the Hillsborough River. He didn't think this would go that far. The boss might fire him later, but he would rather be out of work than have another dead friend.

An hour later, Eddie called the boss from the hospital to let him know that Sal was being admitted. The sawbones had said something about sepsis. They were going to treat the wound with carbolic and give him plenty of fluids.

The boss hadn't replied with anything that could be repeated in mixed company. He wasn't sure but it sounded like he kicked the trashcan across the room. Eddie hung up the phone. Profanity was still ringing in his ears when a couple of orderlies wheeled Sal's gurney toward the elevator. He grabbed his hat and followed. It looked like this was going to be his second night in a row spent at the hospital with someone out of their head.

Teddy took a deep breath and swallowed down the lump in her throat before entering the hospital room. She had convinced Percival that she should speak to Cornelia alone. Now that the time was here, she wasn't sure how she was going to tell Cornelia that her wedding plans had changed. For a woman who had no mechanical skills, her mother was an expert at throwing a wrench into her plans. There was nothing to do but brazen it out.

"You are looking much better," Teddy lied. Most of the unbandaged part of Cornelia's face was a deep eggplant purple and her split lower lip was double the usual size. "How are you feeling?"

Cornelia's eyes narrowed to slits as she watched Teddy cross the room. She waited until Teddy had pulled one of the padded rocking chairs close to the bed and settled into it before she said anything. "What's going on?"

"I don't know what you mean. I told you this morning that I would come back during the evening visiting hours." She took a small silver flask out of her purse and had a sip.

"Theodora Lawless, don't play word games with me. I've known you far too long. You're upset about something. Now out with it."

Teddy sighed. "When do you think they will let you out of the hospital?"

"Tomorrow, unless some unseen complication arises. I'll soon be past the forty-eight-hour mark, so the window for concussion risks is closing. I'm not sure how I will get around yet, but there is no point in lying abed all the time."

Cornelia finished the short speech and looked at her. "Now can you answer my question?"

Teddy studied her hands. "Your uncle thinks we should move the wedding forward a few months."

"Why?"

Teddy didn't dare look at Cornelia's face. Her heart was racing and the lump in her throat had grown three times the size it had been when she entered the room. "When I told Mother that we were thinking about late June, she announced that she was staying with me until the wedding because it was unseemly for me to be alone with Percival after you return to Colorado."

"I see."

"Do you?" Teddy asked. "I don't know what to do. I can't spend three months living with Mother. One of us would have to die."

"If I had to spend three days with your mother, I would murder her."

"You're not angry?"

"I'm not happy. I still think marrying my uncle to protect our reputations is a crazy plan. But, no, I am not angry."

Teddy hugged her. "You are wonderful. I'm going to find you a beautiful dress for the wedding, or perhaps a gown for an evening wedding. What do you think? Your uncle would look very distinguished in a tuxedo."

The smile that spread across Cornelia's face caused the wound on her lip to reopen. "I think Uncle Percival isn't going to know what hit him. It serves him right too ... Since getting married was his bright idea."

Cornelia Gets the Chair

When Teddy left to visit the hospital, Professor Pettijohn was in full engineering mode. Crumpled sheets of paper were tossed toward the trash bin, most failing to land inside. Every now and then one of the sketches met his approval, and was added to a growing pile in the center of the table. He was still hard at work when she returned to the suite.

She came over to see what sort of invention he was working on this time. "May I?" she asked, picking up the stack of paper.

"It is a work in progress. I haven't quite figured out the framework."

Teddy flipped through the pages illustrating detailed dimensions of parts to some machine. She recognized the wheels. There was a motor mounted to long metal pipes. Behind it was a battery. "What is it?"

He took the pages from her and one by one laid them out on the table. Piece by piece, a motorized vehicle of some sort started becoming apparent.

"When I telephoned young Mac to ask him to be my best man, we got sidetracked talking about Cornelia's injuries. Her ankle isn't going to heal for some time. That broken wrist will make it impossible to use crutches. There are wheelchairs, of course, but she would need someone to assist her. That is a problem all on its own. She isn't going to stand for bringing an unsuspecting stranger into this mess, and neither you nor I are up to the job."

"So this is going to be a motor-powered wheelchair?"

"More than that. The design needs to be portable. See how the engine and batteries are positioned under the folding seat? The whole design will feature the ability to fold so it fits into the back seat of her sedan. Once her driver unloads and unfolds the device, she will be able to get around unassisted."

"What a wonderful idea. I do hope you can build it successfully. But Cornelia thinks she will be discharged tomorrow."

"Your brother has offered to take me to Mac's workshop this evening. It's Saturday; no one else is likely to be there. Going across the bay will be faster than driving, and we can stay on his yacht. Three sets of hands should make short work of the task. Mac is assembling the parts now."

The trip to St. Petersburg took less than an hour; Mac Stevens met them at the pier.

Tommy didn't know what he had been expecting but the tall, broad-shouldered young man in dungarees and a leather pilot's jacket wasn't it. He bore little resemblance to Ansel and had none of his father's polished style. Maybe he wouldn't hate him after all.

His shop was much like Mac himself: practical, efficient, and organized. He had set up a workbench in one corner of the room with an assortment of parts laid out for their use.

"This is the seat I was telling you about, professor." Mac held up what looked like a metal box about four inches deep. The lid was taller than the bottom and had a handle that ran the length of the top. "I thought I could start with this. I got it sanded and cut the upholstery boards before you got here. What do you think?"

"It is just what we needed. Have you thought about the frame problem?"

Mac picked up the sketch of two long pipes with a sprocket attached to each side and studied it for a moment. Too complicated and inelegant. He took a pencil out of his

192

pocket and began to sketch. "It should be more like a motorbike design, a single sprocket chain with one set of chainrings on the rear hub and one at the motor. I see you've gone for a grip brake. That will be good for a smoother stop. What is the purpose of the switch here?"

The professor pointed to the wiring. "See here, how it connects? Centered, the chair will go forward, back for reverse. It will also turn right, or left and if you press forward, it applies the brake."

"That's ingenious," Mac said.

The professor's chest swelled at the praise. "I can't take full credit for the switch. It is just a natural progression from William J. Newton's toggle switch. Instead of flipping a switch to make one thing happen, I've set directional toggles. The same switch can be moved into distinct positions, each with a single function."

Mac laughed. "It may be a logical progression to you but, believe me, the potential of that idea is enormous. I could think of half a dozen uses on the machines I build."

"How would we support the motor and batteries in a single drive configuration?"

"Take that second pipe and cut it in half. Mount the shorter pipes three inches from either side of the center pipe. That gives you room for the motor and battery mounts."

Tommy left the engineers to do their design and found the parts laid out to finish the seat and cushions. First, he painted the folding seat and set it near the fans to dry. Stevens had already done thin plywood cutouts to the shape of the back and bottom of the folding chair. The shop had several shades of leather for use on his speed boat seats. He chose a rich red leather covering and cut layers of cotton padding. Then he went to work on the two leather-bound pillows. It beat spending more time under fire with his mother and sister.

By the time he finished hand-stitching the seat, the engineers had welded their frame together and mounted the engine. The professor was working on a battery charger that could convert ordinary electric current into twelve-volt power for recharging the chair batteries while his friend completed the folding joints for the wheel array. Once the frame was painted, they called it a night.

The professor was up in time to watch the sunrise slowly change the calm waters of the bay from black to wine red, then violet. The sun crept above the horizon and the sky was alight with shades of pink and lavender, blue, and orange, all of it reflected to him by the water. It was as if all the color in the universe was spread out on the Florida coast and illuminated by the sun. It made him want to hold out his arms so the breeze could splatter him with the colors of the morning sun. It was good to be alive.

"Beautiful, isn't it?"

"Good morning, Tommy. I didn't hear you come up."

Tommy noticed the black wires of the professor's hearing device hanging uselessly and grinned. "I was getting breakfast. Would you like to join me?"

After hearing his mother's complaints regarding Tommy's dietary habits, the professor was keenly interested in discovering the nature of the Kellogg Cure. "I would be delighted."

"Good," Tommy said. "Have a seat on deck and I'll fetch a tray from the galley."

When he returned to the deck, Tommy carried a tray laden with bowls of strawberries, sliced bananas, and blueberries along with a pitcher of milk and a large white box labeled "Kellogg's Toasted Corn Flakes" in red letters.

The professor watched his host fill a bowl with thin flakes of cereal, then smother it with milk. Then he spread an assortment of fresh fruit over the flakes and started eating. The concoction was crunchy and slightly sweet. In the professor's diet, it would never replace bacon and eggs, but it certainly wasn't the horror Tommy's mother believed. The only thing he really missed was his morning coffee. Once they had finished, Tommy took the tray back to the galley.

Mac was hard at work on the wheel assembly when they returned to his shop.

"What do you think, Professor?" Mac asked, gesturing.

The professor came over to examine the wiring while Mac was mounting the last tire. "Are the batteries charged?" He asked. "It looks like we're ready to test it."

Mac grinned. "Do you want to do the honors?"

"I would like to see it folded. If you have a scale, I would also like to know how heavy it is."

Mac nodded. He released the lock on the back axle, and let the seat slide down the back legs until they rested just above the tires. When the crab-like front legs were unlocked they pivoted backward over the engine.

"As you can see, Professor, the wheels are the widest part of the folded chair. Thirteen-inch rims were the smallest I could find on short notice. Then we have to add another two inches for the tire. We're looking at fifteen inches thick, thirty-eight inches tall, and thirty inches wide.

He fastened a small hook on the side of the chair and then lifted it off the floor. "I don't have a scale, but I would say it is between thirty-five and forty pounds."

"Lighter than a sack of potatoes." The professor came over and caught hold of the bar, then tilted the chair toward himself. A slight tug on the handle and the chair rolled closer. "Easy to move once it's unloaded. Let's open it up and see how it runs."

Once the wheels were locked into place, Mac opened the seat and all three men stood back to admire their work. Professor Pettijohn settled into the red leather seat and moved the switch forward to apply the brakes. He pushed a small red button on the arm of the chair and the engine whirred.

"Here goes," he said as he released the brake and let the wheelchair move forward. The chair moved easily across the concrete floor of Mac's shop. Professor Pettijohn grinned as he switched the direction right, and spun in a circle. He moved the switch left and did two more circles before testing reverse, laughing like a schoolboy when the two younger men had to move out of his way.

"You are going to be a horrible influence on my little sister," Tommy said when the professor finally applied the brake. "Do you do this kind of stunt all the time?"

The professor stood up. "Would you like to give it a try?"

Tommy walked around the machine looking at it from all angles. The red seats made an excellent contrast to the sleek black frame. "Elegant is a good word for this design. It is smaller than the old wooden wheelchairs and less cumbersome."

He sat down and released the brake allowing the chair to move forward. "Easy to operate with one hand," he called over his shoulder. "How long do you think the batteries will last before needing to be recharged?"

"An average person could get through the day before needing to recharge," Mac said. "Someone who is heavy or very active might need two sets of batteries so they could switch them out when the charge is low."

Once Tommy was through putting the wheelchair through his testing, he parked it in front of the workbench.

Mac immediately started folding the chair.

"You aren't going to try it out?"

Mac shook his head. "I've got work to catch up on this morning. Especially if I'm going to take time off to be your best man."

The professor slapped him on the back. "I'm grateful that you were willing to drop everything to help me. Thank you. And thank you for agreeing to be my best man."

"I'm looking forward to watching Miss Teddy walk down the aisle. I hope the two of you have many happy years together."

Leaving the hospital was a more arduous process than Cornelia expected. That surprised her. In all her years of nursing, she had never considered how much waiting was involved in being discharged. She had to wait for the doctor to visit, and for the nursing staff to go through a long checkout list. When that was finished there were all the outpatient instructions. It was no wonder that so many patients were grouchy and impatient to leave.

When Eddie the Hat arrived to replace Chago, she felt relieved and guilty at the same time. She had been afraid all night that she had helped the young Cuban dodge a flogging only to get him shot protecting her. Chago didn't deserve that. Not that *Eddie* did, but she knew Chago better. He was a sweet boy who stayed to drive her back to the hotel instead of going home to sleep after his shift. He also agreed to take the flower arrangements in her room to the nurses' station and ask them to distribute them to patients who had no family and friends near enough to visit. She had seen how much difference a bouquet of flowers could make in a patient's recovery. Besides, she didn't need half a dozen flower arrangements in her hotel room. There would be plenty of blossoms there for the wedding.

While he was gone, she tried to shake the feeling that she was being watched. It was a foolish notion. The killer had an impossible task getting past the nurses and the guard at the door. Still, the fear lingered in the back of her mind. Someone had known she was going to be at Lefty's home. They had arrived before her, waited, and tried to kill her.

Being discharged only added to her anxiety. Teddy had driven herself to the hospital for her last visit. She had not had a bodyguard. In fact, she had said none of Charlie Wall's men were at the hotel. It was as if they all thought that Chago's release ended the risk to her family. The hotel had over five hundred rooms. It would be much harder to secure than one hospital room.

More worrisome was the fact that Sal was in the hospital. He was dependable and smart. He kept the young men who worked with him on their toes. Without him, she had less faith that Mr. Wall's protection was enough. She wasn't particularly surprised that the open clavicle repair became infected; they often did. The infection turning to sepsis, however, was an ugly surprise. It was not easy to recover once the infection spread to the bloodstream.

She stopped brooding when the nurse arrived to help her get dressed. While struggling with her smallclothes, Cornelia realized that she would not have been able to dress herself. This was an unexpected problem. At least Teddy had brought a dress with sleeves that fit over her cast, but the nurse had to do up the back and comb her hair.

How was she going to get back to Colorado when she could neither stand nor use her arm? She was not going to be able to return to active duty. While the shock was still setting in, the nurse compounded it by bringing a wheelchair to take her to the exit. She sulked all the way to the Oldsmobile.

The nurse pushed her as close as possible to the open car door and assisted her in standing. She was relieved that she could hold herself upright by putting all her weight on her uninjured foot and clinging to the door with her right hand. Movement was far from graceful; she managed to turn and sit down on her own. However, her nurse stayed close in case she needed help.

Chago put her things in the back seat before closing the door and walking to the driver's side of the vehicle. Eddie the Hat followed him and climbed into the back seat.

Neither of them said much on the way to the hotel. Cornelia could tell that her companions were tired. There was far too much happening for any of Mr. Wall's men to rest.

With the warm noonday sun pouring through the windows Cornelia closed her eyes and dozed. She didn't wake up until they stopped outside the hotel.

The families, hers and Teddy's, were standing unnaturally close together in the hotel parking lot. If they were posing for a picture, she was going to give them a piece of her mind. She didn't like having her picture taken when she was at her best. A photo of her burned, bruised, battered, and bandaged was not going to show up in anyone's photo album. And, if her uncle was hiding his motion picture camera behind him, he had better be prepared to have it broken over his head.

Before she could work up a full head of steam, Teddy and the professor took a couple of steps to the left. Meanwhile, Tommy and his mother stepped to the right. Between them was a chair that resembled nothing she had ever seen before. It was small and black with a red leather seat and an electric motor. The professor sat down in the seat and pushed a button or two. The contraption started rolling toward her. He moved the switch and it turned and stopped beside her.

"What is that?" Cornelia asked.

The professor's eyes danced with merriment. "It's a wheelchair, of course. The doctor said you shouldn't put any weight on your ankle, and I just couldn't picture you being confined to your bed. I made a few sketches and gave Mac a call. He was more than happy to help, and Tommy took me over to St. Petersburg on his yacht last night. Mac, Tommy, and I built you a motorized wheelchair that can be folded and carried in your sedan. Do you like it?"

"You went to all that trouble for me? I don't know what to say."

"You don't need to say anything. Just hop on and try it out." Her uncle stood aside so Chago could help her get settled in the chair. "That red button starts the motor, but before you do that you need to make sure the switch here is pushed all the way forward. That locks the brake." He showed her how the directional switch worked. "You can control it with one finger, and it is small enough to go down any hallway or sidewalk. I'm afraid steps are an obstacle we haven't overcome though, so you will have to drive around to the other side of the hotel to get in."

Cornelia noticed a small crowd had gathered to gawk at the motorized chair. She wasn't comfortable with the attention, but she understood the interest. She waved to the audience, started the engine, and released the brake. There were cheers as she drove across the parking lot and headed to the other side of the building.

The crowd outside had become a larger crowd inside the hotel. There were so many people crowding around her to get a closer look that Cornelia had to stop and wait for them to disperse. She didn't have to wait long. A few men asked about the machine and the professor was soon lecturing on the mechanics of the chair. Within a couple of minutes, his passion for the subject took the conversation beyond the average person's understanding of non-engineers.

Cornelia took advantage of the thinning audience to head to the elevator. Eddie, Chago, Teddy, and her family followed, leaving just her uncle holding an impromptu lecture in the hotel lobby.

The elevator operator's eyes bulged when she rolled her new chair into the car and stopped just inches from the wall. He quickly schooled his face when he saw that none of his other passengers seemed to notice anything unusual.

Chago carried her things to the door. When he insisted on having a look around the hotel suite before leaving, Cornelia protested. He had been up all night watching over her while she slept.

He ignored her objections. "Someone tried to murder you. I am not going anywhere until I know he is not lurking in a closet waiting for you like he did before."

There was nothing to do but move aside and let him look for killers behind every door.

He was still searching the suite when her uncle arrived.

"Cornelia, you'll never guess what happened after you left. One of the gentlemen I was discussing your wheelchair with has a son at the hospital where you work. He was a cavalry officer who was injured while on patrol on the Mexican border. He has asked to purchase the chair, after you are through with it, of course. I explained that the chair was a gift I designed for you and not mine to sell. He has offered an exorbitant amount of money if you are interested in selling."

"How exorbitant?" Teddy asked.

He took a folded sheet of paper out of his pocket and handed it to Cornelia. "This is his offer."

Teddy put on her reading glasses and leaned over Cornelia's shoulder as she unfolded the paper.

"That's more than I make a year," Cornelia said. "Shucks, I paid less for my sedan than this."

"It is certainly much more than it cost me to build. You need to think of it in terms of what it is worth to a father to give his son the gift of mobility. His spine was broken in the accident. He is never going to walk, even on crutches." The professor replied. "I built the chair because I didn't want you to have to depend on others to do ordinary daily activities for the next couple of weeks. I can't imagine what it would mean to a young man who was used to commanding others, to be totally dependent on someone else to cross the room. Anyway, I told him we would let him know in the morning."

The excitement of getting back to her family was a bit more than Cornelia was ready to endure. She didn't like having everyone hovering around fussing over her. It took a little effort, but she convinced Teddy that she should go shopping with her mother. There was a lot to be done if the wedding was indeed going to take place.

Cornelia was getting used to the idea, although she could not bring herself to like seeing them play the happy couple. She really didn't know if she could ever adjust to this new arrangement.

Before she left, Teddy brought a stack of books from the hotel's reading room. Cornelia looked through them and chose the new one by Agatha Christie, *The Secret of Chimneys*. She was perfectly happy to have a quiet afternoon in her room reading. She had foolishly thought that her leave would be an excellent time to catch up on her reading. That had not turned out to be the case.

Maybe she shouldn't have chosen a mystery. She still couldn't shake the uneasiness that had plagued her all day. Every shadow made her jump. Every sound the old hotel made reminded her that someone wanted her dead.

She set the book aside and tried to organize her thoughts. Every line of reasoning she followed in Geraldo Zayas' murder came back to the traces of fresh blood her uncle found in Mr. Baldwin's office. *Why move the body before calling the police?*

In Mr. Wall's profession, it was not uncommon to hide a body or dump one in the river, but gangsters didn't go to the trouble of moving a body and cleaning up a murder scene or calling the police. That just brought unwanted attention to their activities.

She closed her eyes and tried to picture where her uncle had found the blood. Mentally she placed Geraldo Zayas into the picture. The shot was likely fired from the doorway. Zayas didn't have time to turn around before he was shot. That meant that he had been standing behind the desk. She needed to have a more thorough look at the evidence from Zayas' murder. Unfortunately, her purse and the evidence envelope were several feet away on her dressing table.

Was it worth the trouble of getting up and getting into the wheelchair just to get those pictures?

Of course it was. Something in that envelope could tell her the identity of the killer.

Mother Hat

Percival Pettijohn was always a shrewd businessman. He hadn't realized that his multi-function toggle switch would have the number of uses Mac saw. Nor had he thought much about a need for motorized wheelchairs. Now he realized the process for obtaining patents needed to begin immediately for the switch, the chair, and the recharging device. He contacted his attorney in Lexington and asked him to file the needed caveats with the federal patent office while he attended to the specifics, uses, and professional blueprints. The switch and battery charger should be in his name exclusively, but the chair was in conjunction with Nimrod McKinley Stevens.

When he finished giving the particulars of the caveats to his attorney, he hung the earpiece back in its cradle, then picked it up again and asked the hotel operator to connect him to the St. Petersburg exchange. Mac needed to be aware that their design was sparking interest and that he had begun the patent process. "I have asked my attorney to file documents for me for the switch and the recharging device. However, your input on the chair and its design was invaluable. I asked him to file a joint caveat for the two of us. Do you consider equal shares fair?"

"That's more than fair, Professor. The whole project was your idea."

"Don't sell yourself short, Mac. Your modifications made it much lighter and easier to transport. I had never considered wheelchairs as an industry before, but someone must manufacture them. Once we have secured our patent, we can either create a factory or sell the design to another manufacturer and collect a royalty on the product for the next seventeen years. I have many such agreements, and my attorney is particularly good at looking out for my interests."

"Professor, are you trying to get me to build wheelchairs?"

"Not if you have no interest in adding another form of transportation to your business. As I said, we can work out a deal with another manufacturer. I was giving you options." The professor paused for a few seconds to give Mac a chance to consider what he was saying. "This chair is much simpler to build than your speedboats or your private aeroplanes. It also has a market that already needs this kind of product."

"I have more orders now than I can fill," Mac said.

"Yes, but what happens to those orders if the land boom becomes a bust? Your business is great for boom-time Florida. Poor men have no money to spend on luxury items. But a man who is feeling useless because he can no longer support his family could, with the help of that chair, live a productive life."

"I'll think it over," Mac replied.

"While you think it over, can you ask your draftsman to draw up exact detailed blueprints of our invention to submit with the patent application?"

Mac laughed. "I'll do that, but you are paying him."

"You have a deal."

Cornelia read through the witness statements and then sorted the photographs on the foot of her bed. She set aside the ones at the nightclub. Since the body had been moved, it didn't matter how he was positioned. They might be of use later; she would just have to see what happened.

The wide-eyed look on Lefty's face was interesting. He had clearly been surprised by the killer. But death must have come quickly. He hadn't had enough time to turn. The bullet entered his back just below the right shoulder blade and created a sucking chest wound that would have bled out in moments. She had seen a few men survive this kind of wound when care had been immediate, but it was rare.

There was a knock at the door that made Cornelia jump. This trip had shattered her nerves as well as her body. She was beginning to think she was too old to keep up with her perpetually seventy-five-year-old uncle.

"I hope I'm not waking you," the uncle in question said. "I'm ordering room service. Are you hungry?"

"Starving," Cornelia replied. "I'll be right out."

She gathered the evidence and put it back into her purse. It might be hard to convince Eddie the Hat, but she really needed to get a look at Mr. Baldwin's office. There was something in that office that made someone decide to move Mr. Zayas's body back to his own office. Maybe it was still there. If not, she might be able to deduce what had been removed.

An unhappy Eddie drove the old guy and his niece to Club Tropical. Even the nice lunch they provided before the trip didn't make up for having to go back to that place. The last time he was in the club, Sal had keeled over. Miss Pettijohn looked worse off than Sal. She couldn't even walk, but she was determined to keep going. Eddie gave up fighting and drove her to the El Dorado to get the key.

Club Tropical was closed. The sign on the door said, "Closed due to unexpected death." The ugly truth was, there were too many police around. The boss couldn't risk opening it until the eyes of the police were elsewhere. Mr. Zayas' and Liza's shootings made it hard to bring liquor in without some overzealous cop raiding the place.

The Pettijohn woman was relentless. It didn't matter that someone killed her bodyguard and threw her down a flight of stairs. She didn't seem to care that she couldn't run away or hold that pistol she carried. She'd solved Jaquinda Duarte's murder and got Chago released. Anyone in their right mind would have left town. Not her; she was full of vinegar over being attacked. He was beginning to feel sorry for the guy who tried to kill her. He didn't know how much trouble he was in.

The uncle was double trouble. He was too smart for his own good. First, there was that pipe gun that Sal shot a hole in the ceiling with. He would've liked to have seen Sal's face when that happened. When he heard that Miss Pettijohn was going to be confined to a wheelchair for a couple of weeks, it set the old man off again. If his niece couldn't get around on her own, then he had to fix the problem.

He got a wild idea and ran off to St. Petersburg to make her this weird chair that folded up when she wasn't driving the thing around. Eddie couldn't help wondering what the old guy would come up with next. Having him for an uncle must make Christmas morning interesting. You would never know what would come out of the gift box.

Eddie took the chair out of the back seat and unfolded it the way the professor had shown him. Then he helped Miss Pettijohn get situated before he unlocked the back door of the club. He found the light switch. It was still pretty dark, but the old people insisted on looking around Mr. Baldwin's office.

Miss Pettijohn took a flashlight out of her purse and handed it to her uncle. "You're about the same height as Mr. Zayas. When you find the bloodstain, try moving back far enough so your chest would hit the floor on top of the spot."

"Mr. Zayas was found in his own office," Eddie said. "It's back there."

"He was found there, but he wasn't shot there." The professor shone the light on the floor behind Baldwin's desk. "If you look close, you can outline the blood stain from the blood still visible in the seams between the baseboard and the floor."

"Huh," Eddie said. "You've got good eyes for an old guy."

The professor laughed. "Thank you, I think."

"Back to work, Uncle. Picture your chest right in the middle of that stain. Then stand where you think he was with your back toward the door."

"I can't," the professor replied. Not without moving the desk."

206

"Mr. Hat, could you move the desk for my uncle?"

"Just Eddie, Miss Pettijohn. The boys gave me that moniker when I got this hat. It's a nickname."

The corner of her mouth quirked. "So, I should stop picturing Mother Hat?"

He sighed. "Where do you want me to move it to, Professor?"

"About three feet in that direction." He pointed to the wall.

Eddie gave the desk a shove.

"That's good." The professor took his position and turned his back to the door.

Cornelia spotted something reflective in the beam of the flashlight. "What's that?"

Both men looked where she was pointing.

The professor got down on his knees. "Eddie, do you have a knife?"

"I do," Cornelia said as she reached into her purse.

He opened the borrowed pocketknife and pressed the blade down on a small brass strip hidden between the floorboards. The tip of the blade sank about half an inch as a small brass lever rose from the floor. Three boards popped up when the professor tugged at the lever. When the section of the floor was lifted, a large compartment and stash of items was revealed. The professor began taking out envelopes that he presumed were cash, then a ledger and a small black journal, a couple of larger envelopes followed, and finally two bundles of hundred-dollar bills that were still in the bank wrappers. "I think that's it," he said. He fitted the boards back into place and closed the latch.

Eddie helped the professor to his feet.

"Can you find something to put this in, Eddie, and then move the desk back?"

"How much money do you think that is?" Eddie asked as he stared at the bundles of cash.

"In your line of work, I would have thought that you saw large amounts of money regularly," Cornelia said.

"Not that large," Eddie the Hat exclaimed. He pointed to the two square bundles.

"Are we just talking about the bundles?" the professor asked. "Those are standard treasury issue: one hundred bills to each band, ten bands to the bundle, exactly two hundred thousand. The rest I would have to count."

Eddie let out a long low whistle. "If Baldwin is hiding that kind of dough, he must be stealing the boss blind."

Cornelia looked up from the ledger she was examining. "You're supposed to be getting me a box for this stuff. Now, please. Baldwin could show up at any time. I do not want to have to explain what we are doing in his office."

"What do you think, Cornelia? Is Baldwin our killer? He comes in, spots Zayas raiding his secret safe, and shoots him?"

"I don't think Mr. Baldwin knows anything about the stash," she said. "The handwriting in the journal doesn't match the sample Baldwin gave me. I would say Mr. Zayas was the one keeping these records. It looks like he was running a blackmail racket. The ledger is full of dates and amounts. Some of them go back years."

"Why would he put his stash in Baldwin's office instead of his own?"

"I don't know," she admitted. "Maybe that's a question Mr. Wall can answer. The ledger doesn't give names, not even an initial. We need to take this file to Mr. Wall and see if he can shed some light on the operation. Barring that, if we can sit down and study his records, we can probably figure out who some of his blackmail victims were."

The professor pushed the desk back to its original position. "Whoever killed Zayas knew that he recognized the ring. He probably recognized it too and knew that Zayas had found himself a new victim. All he had to do was wait and watch until Zayas collected his payoff. Then he could follow him to his stash to rob him."

"Maybe, but if that's the case, something must have gone wrong. Otherwise, he would have cleaned out the box and left Zayas where he fell. If the killer wanted the cash, why did he shoot Zayas before he found his stash?"

"Why do you think he didn't find the money, Corny? Zayas had already moved the desk. Wouldn't he have been able to see the latch just like we did?"

"I didn't realize it was a latch when I spotted it. That tiny flash of brass looks like the head of a nail. I spotted it because you were holding the flashlight directly over it in a way that reflected the light. I don't think I would have found it otherwise."

Eddie the Hat returned with a liquor crate he found behind the bar. "I see you've moved the desk. Should I load the mazuma up?"

"Yes," Cornelia said. "Then I think we should pay your boss a visit."

Decoding a Crime

Eddie the Hat handed the crate to the professor and closed the back door of the Olds. He wasn't sure how the boss would feel about that pile of cash landing on his desk, but he was having trouble thinking about anything but what *he* could do with that much money.

The closer they got to the El Dorado, the more he wanted to turn around and head the other way. Two things kept him from acting on that urge. One was his fear of the boss. Charlie Wall was not a man to cross. The other was the old bat sitting beside him. She might look like someone used her as a punching bag, but in the brief time he had known Cornelia Pettijohn, he had realized nothing stopped her. He wondered if she was some sort of secret military weapon the government developed and not a real person.

He pulled the Oldsmobile into its usual spot in front of the El Dorado. Then he set up the chair for Miss Pettijohn. Once they were inside the café, he had them wait there until he spoke to the boss.

"Leave the crate with me," Cornelia said. "I want to look over the books again."

He hesitated a moment, then handed it over.

Cornelia started with the little black journal caught on a loose nail in the bottom of the crate. She pulled the book free without damage and noticed it wasn't the first item caught on the nail. A long string was stretched across the bottom of the crate. She pulled it free and tucked it into her pocket before opening the journal.

"This is all some sort of code or cipher. I can't make any sense of it." She flipped through the pages twice before deciding that the author hadn't provided any clues to how to read the journal.

"Let me see," her uncle said. He looked through the book a couple of times and then closed his eyes. "A cipher. Not a complex one, just a patristocrat monoalphabetic substitution cipher, I can decipher the notes when we get back to the hotel, or if you want to do it yourself, I can write you a key."

"Showoff," Cornelia teased. She handed him the ledger. "What do you make of this?"

"Mr. Zayas was a lucky man to have lived as long as he did. These entries started seven years ago, and he has fifty-four different symbols that I presume are different blackmail victims. I would say his saving grace is that no individual amount is huge. Instead, his scheme is monthly payments that rarely end."

"They likely only end when the person dies or finds a way to disappear. Quite a piece of work, our Mr. Zayas," Cornelia replied, as she flipped through the contents of one of the large envelopes. "Compromising photographs and stolen correspondence. Some of these items confound me: this napkin, for instance. What possible purpose does this serve a blackmailer?"

Her uncle looked up just in time to see a lacy ladies' garter fall to the floor. Enough heat radiated from their faces to toast marshmallows.

"Yes, well," the professor said. "I imagine his marks knew what the items meant. I should pick that up before Mr. Hat comes back."

He picked up the garter between two fingers and held it at arm's length until he could drop it back into the envelope. "Maybe you should put all those away for now. Someone could walk in at any moment."

Their meeting with Mr. Wall was brief. Judging from the busted knuckles on his hands and the freshly mopped floor, talking to them had been squeezed into his schedule

212

after a much less friendly encounter. Eddie the Hat presented him with the liquor crate and left the room. Mr. Wall took the two bundles of cash and handed the crate back to Cornelia.

"Those small envelopes are cash as well," the professor said.

"Consider it a finder's fee." Wall said dryly as he stood up and came around the desk to get a better look at Cornelia's chair. "An impressive piece of work, Professor. I highly recommend that you stick to this type of invention rather than firearms."

A sheepish grin peeped through Professor Pettijohn's short snowy beard.

"Miss Cornelia," Wall said, "you know how valuable the information you are holding is to a man like me. However, I gave my word that I would not involve you in my business. I won't ask anything about the contents except that if you find it, you give me the name of the killer. Once I have that, our business is concluded, and you can do what you want with that box. Is that agreed?"

"I thought our business was concluded when Chago was released."

Wall looked directly into her eyes. "I think we both know that it's for your benefit as well as mine that Mr. Zayas' killer is unmasked. He has reason to believe you know who he is and has tried to kill you once. If you don't find him, he will find you."

Cornelia nodded in affirmation.

"Then we're done here. My men will keep trying to protect you until this is over. For both our sakes, I hope that's soon. There have been too many dead bodies." He opened his office door and watched them leave.

When they left the casino, Clevon was waiting beside the Oldsmobile. His eyes widened when he saw Cornelia, but he didn't say anything.

"Change of shifts?"

"Yes Ma'am, the boss has something else he wants Eddie the Hat to do."

"Could you help me stand up?" Cornelia asked.

"Yes, Ma'am. I'm sorry, Ma'am." Clevon hurried over, but had no idea of how to help.

"Come beside me here," Cornelia pointed to the spot she wanted him to stand. She put her good arm around his waist and held on to him until she got off the chair.

Once Cornelia was situated the professor took over, demonstrating to Clevon how the wheelchair folded and locked so it could be placed inside the Olds.

"Ain't that a wonder?" Clevon said. "Where did you find a thing like that?"

Professor Pettijohn's chest expanded, and he stood a little taller. "My partner and I designed it for Cornelia. There isn't another like it in the world."

"Is that a fact?" Clevon said.

"Uncle Percival, I know you are proud of your work, but I would like to get back to our hotel. Teddy and her mother should have finished shopping by now. Maybe we could all have a quiet dinner in our suite."

"I am sorry, Corny. You must be exhausted."

"I was exhausted before I left the hospital. I should have rested today and picked up the investigation tomorrow. But I was worried that a delay would get us killed."

The professor turned his hearing device off, leaned back in the seat, and closed his eyes. Driving back to their hotel never took less than an hour. That was plenty of time to decipher the small black journal. In his mind, the pages spread out in front of him, row after row of letters with no indication of where one word ended and the next began. What he did have was a working knowledge of the frequency of a letter being used. If the writer was using English, as he believed, then the three most frequently used letters in the language should break the cipher. At West Point, they had learned this as the "EAR" method of breaking ciphers.

Once he could see the cipher in his head, he opened his eyes. They still hadn't reached the bridge. Cornelia, the poor dear, had fallen asleep with the side of her face pressed against the window. There was no point in waking her. He took out his notebook and wrote down the key for his niece.

There was time left before they reached the hotel. Professor Pettijohn turned the page in his notebook and started writing out the text of the journal using the correct letters. Without spaces between words, it was still just a jumble of letters. Later, when they were not creeping along in bridge traffic, he would try to parse the text. He was still writing when the Oldsmobile turned into the hotel's parking lot.

Theodora Lawless had looked through about half the dresses in the bridal shop before she found one that she liked. The ankle-length Art Deco gown was made of champagne-colored silk satin and beaded. Cornelia was going to scream at the sleeveless, open-backed dress, but it was so beautiful, and she adored the heart-appliqued train and the pearl crown. This one, she had to try this one. First, she would need gloves, opera-length ones that matched the gown.

The shopkeeper was happy to oblige her. He returned in an instant with the requested gloves and showed her to the dressing room.

Her dress was not the easiest to try on, with snaps on the side and back. It took assistance from her mother to get the back ones fastened. Teddy didn't dare look until she had the crown and gloves in place. She preened in front of the three-way mirror, admiring the dress from all angles.

"What do you think, Mother?"

"Shoes," her mother said. "We have to get shoes to match. Everyone is going to see your feet."

"So you like the dress."

"It is beautiful, my dear, and so stylish."

"Cornelia is going to hate it. She thinks sleeveless is inappropriate for someone my age."

Mrs. Lawless smiled broadly at the thought of annoying Cornelia Pettijohn. "I wouldn't let sour grapes spoil your day, dear. With her build, she will never be able to carry off the latest styles."

"She has never cared for styles," Teddy replied. "Her dress uniform is usually her first choice for formal events."

A sharp retort balanced on the end of Julia Lawless' tongue, but she resisted the urge. This had turned into a splendid day with her daughter, and the venom she had for that woman wasn't going to spoil their fun.

"Let me help you out of that. We have shoes to find, and new night clothes and foundation wear." She paused for a moment and looked at Teddy. "Have you even thought about your bridal trousseau? Do you have clothes set aside for your rehearsal dinner, or honeymoon? What about items for your home? What is the Pettijohn house like? Bachelors never think of things like linens or silver."

Teddy laughed. "Slow down, Mother. We are almost a thousand miles from his home. Any updates to the household goods will have to wait until we go back to Kentucky."

She paid the shopkeeper and headed down the street with her mother.

Julia Lawless was not thwarted. While Teddy looked at shoes, she continued to press.

"But you can't just go into a marriage without a proper trousseau. It isn't done. Now tell me about this farmhouse."

"It is a big white house." Teddy stretched out her foot. "What do you think of these?"

"They're more ecru than champagne."

Mrs. Lawless looked up at the young man assisting them. Then she pointed to the shelf behind him. "Let's try the third pair from the left. Size seven, please."

She turned to Teddy. "You can do better than that, Theodora: what kind of house?"

Teddy sighed. "His house is a lovely white brick colonial with black shutters and wings at either end. There's a whistle walk from the house to his workshop, which was the original kitchen. There are two-story white columns along the front porch of the main house. The bedrooms and the ballroom on the second floor open to a long balcony that

I have been told was used as a place to sleep when it was too hot to sleep indoors."

"Hmm. How old is this house? It takes work to maintain an older property."

"Honestly Mother, you forget how inventive Percival is. His home has been cared for by generations of his family. Percival has provided all the modern conveniences, and he has a staff for the farm and the house. If there are any changes needed, they will be to décor. I doubt any new furniture has come through the door since his mother was alive. His kitchen belongs to the twentieth century, as does the wiring and plumbing, but the rest dates to the eighteenth century. The main house was built before Kentucky was a state."

Her mother grabbed her arm. "Theodora, are you telling me that your intended has a large house furnished with nothing but antique furniture? If that's true you should not change a single piece until you have had a proper appraisal of the entire home!"

"I'd be more likely to add a few items. Like a piano."

Teddy tried the next pair of shoes on, then compared them to the color of the dress. "Perfect. I'll take these and two pairs of matching stockings."

"Where to next?" her mother asked.

"The hotel. I need to rest before dinner. Tommy says he is planning something special."

"You can't trust your brother with food, Theodora. He probably plans to take us grazing in a field somewhere."

"Really, Mother."

"I am serious. Your brother has turned a little dyspepsia into an obsession with food."

Teddy laughed. "Percival had breakfast with him in St. Petersburg. He said the food was fine, but not very filling. A couple of hours later, he was ready to eat again. I'm sure we can order sandwiches if that happens. Tommy was nice about dining with us. The hotel has very few choices that are on his diet. We owe him a dinner of his choosing."

Her mother frowned but said nothing.

Cornelia was napping when Teddy returned to their room. She stacked her parcels in the closet, slipped her shoes off, and stretched out on top of the covers. It had been an odd day, the first she could remember with her mother in years that didn't end in screaming. Of course, it wasn't over yet. If Tommy did show up with twigs and leaves for dinner, the evening could still end with the famous Lawless verbal fireworks.

"I see you survived," Cornelia said as she turned over. "How did it go?"

"Mother is on her best behavior today. She didn't even lose her temper when I told her that Tommy was bringing dinner tonight."

Cornelia chuckled. "I'll bet she had something to say about that."

"Nothing major. How was your day of leisure? Have you spent the entire day in bed?"

"No, Uncle Percival and I went out for a while. He is deciphering a journal we found. I expect he will want to talk to us about it after our guests leave this evening."

Teddy gave a huff of exasperation. "Cornelia, what were you thinking? You just got out of the hospital this morning."

"Don't yell. My head still hurts."

"Would you like a headache powder?"

"That would be lovely," Cornelia said.

Teddy fetched her a packet. "Well, this is a reversal of roles."

Cornelia poured the powder on her tongue and took the glass of water Teddy was holding. She frowned at the taste.

Teddy sat down beside her and placed her hand on Cornelia's uninjured one. "What happened to resting and reading today?"

"I shouldn't have started reading a mystery. I kept getting distracted by thoughts of the murders at Club Tropical. After lunch, Eddie the Hat drove us to the club to have another look at Baldwin's office. Under Baldwin's desk, we found a secret hiding place. There was no lock or anything. It seems that Mr. Zayas lied to us because he wanted to add Lefty to his list of blackmail victims. He has been running quite a racket at the club. Some of his shakedown victims have been paying him for years. Uncle Percival has the ledger and journal. Hopefully, he can make sense of it, because I couldn't."

"Why would Zayas hide stuff in Mr. Baldwin's office? That doesn't make sense."

"I don't know, Teddy. That's one of the details that bother me."

"What are the others?"

"Why Zayas would double-cross Mr. Wall. Also, why did he blackmail dozens of people if he wasn't desperate for money? It's risky. His ledger kept track of how much he took in, but the man wasn't spending the cash. He had thousands of dollars stashed away in brand-new bundles of hundred-dollar bills."

"That's a real boodle." Teddy tried to come up with an explanation but could think of nothing useful. "You're sure all the money was there?"

"He kept a ledger with every payment in the last seven years. There was no lavish or self-indulgent spending. He was just hoarding the money."

"That is strange," Teddy agreed.

"So was his blackmail scheme: nobody paid out a huge sum of money at one time. Zayas wanted monthly payments from everyone. There are different starting dates for each symbol but after that, they paid him every month. The amount of money in a single payment ranged from two dollars to three hundred dollars. Who would risk jail for two dollars a month?"

Teddy thought about her question for a moment before answering. "You're thinking about it wrong. If I was asked to choose between paying someone two dollars a month or having my deepest secret revealed, I would be inclined to pay. Most people would."

Tommy Lawless spent the day exploring the small coastal towns around the bay. The weather was perfect, sunny with a slight breeze. His yacht cruised over turquoise waters along the coast. He had promised to bring dinner and was looking forward to introducing his family to some new treats. He knew his sister would love trying new dishes, though he doubted that his mother was going to be happy with the picnic he'd planned. The Pettijohns were the wild cards. He would just have to wait and see. The professor had found the convenience of his breakfast choices acceptable. Maybe the old guy would enjoy having something different again.

The elevator boy was looking hungrily at the heavy baskets. He couldn't blame him. The scent of fresh baked bread and the fragrance of fresh herbs filled the car. The door opened and he took a deep breath before stepping out into the hallway. A day on the water had given him quite an appetite.

Clevon knocked on the professor's door before Tommy got there, and the old gent was waiting for him.

"What have we here?" he asked as Teddy's brother brought the baskets into the room.

"I thought I would introduce you to another of the local cuisines. There's a Greek community on the other side of the bay and I arranged for their local café to prepare some of my favorite dishes." Tommy opened the lid to the first basket and began setting the table for the five of them.

"May I help?" the professor asked.

"You might want to knock on Cornelia's door. I'll give Mother a call."

It didn't take long for everyone to gather around the small table.

Tommy set out two thermoses followed by baskets of bread. The first was a crusty white bread cut into slices, the other was a round flat bread sliced in wedges. This was followed by two glass jars. "*Skordalia*, and *tzatziki*," he said, pointing to each. "This one is a garlic and potato blend, and the white one is yogurt, cucumber, lemon, and spices. I also brought olive oil and fresh herbs if you prefer that on your bread."

Two tins came out of the baskets next. "This is a *horiatiki*, which you can see is a type of salad, and this one is *dolmades* with *avgolemono*. The outside is a grape leaf, the inside is rice and herbs, and the sauce is a lemon and egg mix. And this," he said as he lifted a large baking pan, "is *spanakopita,* which is a blend of spinach and cheese baked in a flaky crust. Dig in, but leave room for dessert. I have *baklava.*"

"Is that leaves or twigs?" his mother asked.

"Nuts and tree bark," Tommy deadpanned.

Teddy laughed.

"Don't encourage him, Theodora."

Her mother's admonishment made her laugh hard enough to kick off a fit of coughing.

Mrs. Lawson glared at her son. "Now see what you've done."

"Would you prefer coffee or iced tea?" Tommy asked.

Cornelia tried one of the grape leaf bundles. The warm rice was mixed with dill, mint, and parsley, wrapped in tender grape leaves, and smothered in creamy lemon sauce. "These are delicious."

The professor didn't need any encouragement. He was busy filling his plate with a little of everything.

"Go easy on the *skordalia.*" Tommy cautioned. "The garlic and onion are quite strong."

"I will grant that it's a bold flavor, but don't see it replacing butter," the professor said. "May I try the olive oil and herbs? They look interesting."

Tommy sliced into the spinach pie and served a corner piece to his mother. "Give this a try, Mother. If you don't like it, I will order room service for you."

She poked at it with her fork, breaking off a small portion of the crust and an even smaller amount of the filling. "The crust is light and buttery." She tried a more substantial bite. Then took a small portion of salad. By the time Tommy brought out dessert they were all feeling well fed.

The Seven-Year Plan

Cornelia tried not to think of Teddy driving her Dodge Brothers sedan. She had been on her best behavior about taking only the medicinal doses of alcohol, but that only made her worry more. Theodora Lawless was one of those rare individuals who became less dangerous behind the wheel of an automobile when she was drinking.

There was no polite way to refuse to let her take the sedan. Cornelia couldn't claim that she needed it. She was in no condition to drive. Even if she were, Mr. Wall had placed his Oldsmobile at her disposal and provided her with a driver. Besides, her job was to figure out exactly what got Mr. Zayas killed.

She and her uncle spent most of Tuesday morning poring over the pages of letters he had deciphered. The utter lack of punctuation coupled with the absence of blank spaces turned the chore into a worse headache than the Gertrude Stein novel. At least in the novel, she could tell where one word ended and another began.

It wasn't particularly surprising that her uncle made better progress. She had never known anyone with a greater grasp of visual clues. She didn't know if that was part of his eidetic memory or if it stemmed from his mechanical aptitude. Maybe his quirky mind just saw things differently.

She had spent a good portion of her childhood comparing her abilities to those of her uncle and feeling stupid. It had been quite shocking to start school and discover that her classmates struggled to grasp concepts she found simple. School bored her. When her uncle realized how little she was learning, he convinced her father to let her attend Campbell's Academy, in Lexington. She didn't fit in any better with the students there, but the teachers found ways to challenge her.

Her uncle's voice startled her out of her ruminating.

"Mr. Zayas was very well organized. His record keeping is better than many businesses. I believe these symbols in the ledger indicate either a profession or an identifying characteristic."

He held out one of the pages of the cipher for her to examine. "The information in his journal has nothing to do with the blackmail racket. It's titled, 'Plan de Siete Años.' Seven-year plan?"

She nodded. "The two pages I finished are related to labor and wages in different occupations. The more information I recognize, the less I understand what he was doing." Cornelia set the pages down and closed her eyes for a moment.

"What if the blackmail was just a means to accomplish this—seven-year plan?" She asked. "This scheme of his was so important he was willing to risk crossing Charlie Wall by running a blackmail racket in one of his clubs. He could be arrested for what he's doing. One of his victims could turn on him. There are any number of reasons he could be killed. He still goes on year after year, finding new blackmail victims and stockpiling the money."

Her uncle took the two sheets from Cornelia, and studied them. "He may have been crazy, but he was considerate. I believe he was basing his demands on what he thought his victims could afford. So far, the only thing I can say for certain is that he was preparing to leave the country. He had no family here besides his late wife. What does that tell us about his murder?"

Cornelia was quiet for several minutes as she looked over the information they had in front of them. Then she sighed. "I think we need more information."

"What?"

She reached out with her good arm and pulled him close, kissing him on the forehead. "You are the best uncle in the world. Thank you for decoding this." She backed her chair up and turned toward her room. "Would you tell whoever is guarding the door today that I need to go out?"

"I will, but you aren't going anywhere without me."

The Oldsmobile pulled over in front of Mr. Zayas' house. He had lived in one of the small wood frame houses that were built in the late 1800s for the cigar factory workers. The houses lining both sides of the block had the same white wood fences broken by wooden steps leading to nearly identical front porches. There were no front lawns, no shrubs, or flower beds, and only a couple of feet separated one house from the next. Over time there had been slight changes in the shingles used or the color a porch was painted. Now and then, someone added touches of color to their porch in the form of potted plants or welcome mats. Otherwise, the cookie-cutter neighborhood looked much the way it had in the last century.

Cornelia took one look at the row of steps leading to the front door and sighed. There was no way she was going to be able to search inside. She doubted that she would find anything there that was of any more use to her than the view from the curb.

"What am I looking for?" her uncle asked.

"I don't know, exactly."

"Then why did you insist we come here?" Her uncle said. "I thought you had figured out what was going on here."

"I'm interested in why he needed so much money. He might have a will or other papers that might explain it." She turned to Chago. "How well did you know Mr. Zayas? Mr. Baldwin told me his wife died several years ago. Does he have any other family?"

"I don't believe he did, at least none in America. He was from Spain. His wife was Cuban."

"What will happen to his house?"

225

Chago was quiet for a few seconds. "This I have not heard. Is this important for you to discover?"

"Perhaps Mr. Wall will know," the professor suggested.

"The blackmail is out of character for him," Cornelia replied. "Mr. Zayas was a frugal and careful man. He lived with his wife in a working-class neighborhood. I would be willing to bet that when he started working for Mr. Wall, he was one of the cigar factory employees. Only interested in making a little extra money selling *bolita* tickets."

"Yes," Chago said. "The boss offered him several opportunities, but he liked being the lecturer at the factory. He was not interested in more responsibility."

"Then his wife died, suddenly," Cornelia said. "From the timing, I suspect she died of Spanish flu."

"I did not know him then," Chago said. He opened the car door. "Wait here. I will go look for his will."

"And any other papers that look important, like a deed or title," she called after him. "See if you can find his passport or anything related to travel."

The professor waited until Chago disappeared into the house. "He may not have thought to write a will. How will you proceed if he neglected that?"

Cornelia turned in her seat so she could see her uncle. "He was an intelligent man, but it doesn't matter. The only reason he took the job at the club was to set this scheme in motion. He had lived here all these years with little to show. The only family he has would be back in Spain. That was when he decided he had to prove himself. For the first time in his life, he wanted money. Enough to return home as a rich man. At the club, he kept his eyes and ears open and in a quiet, deliberate way built his blackmail racket. The notes he kept were all about how much he needed to finance his new life."

Her uncle rubbed his beard as he pondered her remarks. "If it wasn't the blackmail, what did get him murdered?"

"Greed," Cornelia replied. "The worst part is that Liza was killed because we were nosing around in Baldwin's office. The killer wanted to keep us focused on Jackie's murder. He planned to make Lefty's death look like a suicide, but something went wrong. I don't know if Lefty put up a fight or if there was another reason he was delayed. Maybe Lobster and I just arrived sooner than he expected. Whatever the reason, he was still in the house when we got there."

"You said Lobster searched the house."

"Lobster didn't do the best search of the house." She sighed, feeling guilty. "Oh, that isn't fair; I'm sure he did his best. If he looked at the basement at all, he couldn't have seen much. That place was dark as a tomb." Cornelia shivered. "It almost was *my* tomb."

Chago returned with a stack of papers from Mr. Zayas's house. "This is everything I could find."

Cornelia flipped through the stack and pulled out the passport. "He recently renewed his passport. That lines up with my theory that he was planning to return to Spain. These receipts also tell their own story. We should contact Mr. Wall now. I believe we have all the pieces. Although, our killer may be smart enough to have left town."

They were all surprised to see Sal sitting in the boss's office when they arrived. He looked pale and thinner, but Cornelia was glad he had beaten the infection. Over glasses of Planter's Punch, Cornelia ran through all the events that followed the tragic accident that killed Jackie Dart. She could see how difficult it was for Chago to hear about the lack of respect given her body in the attempt to frame him. With Lefty dead, there was no outlet for his anger. She wished that Teddy were with them. She knew what to say to Chago. Cornelia had never been able to soften the blow of grim news.

Then she laid out what she and her uncle discovered about Mr. Zayas's blackmail scheme. "He didn't keep any written record of the secrets he was being paid to keep. His cryptic notes only addressed what he estimated he needed to reach his goal. He'd made a down payment on a beachside property in Valdés and was looking for a boat. He planned to leave for Spain soon."

Wall frowned. "You haven't told me anything about who killed him or why."

"Can you answer one question for me first? I have not been able to figure out why Zayas used Baldwin's office to stash the money."

Wall smiled. "The hiding place predates either Mr. Baldwin's or Mr. Zayas' involvement with Club Tropical. The building was a pool hall until Prohibition ran it out of business. The storage space was behind the bar, where we kept the *bolita* balls until it was time to draw. I had forgotten it was there until you found it again."

Cornelia knew it was time to live up to her part of the agreement. "The bartender, Tajo, killed Zayas. He had his own key, so he could come in early on Mondays to take liquor deliveries. From his place behind the bar, he could hear Zayas moving things around in Baldwin's office when the club manager was busy in the club. Tajo started watching Mr. Zayas. He had to have seen certain customers hand envelopes to him. The bar area is a direct line of sight with the stool where Zayas watched the crowd. He either heard or figured out that Zayas was blackmailing customers."

"What makes you think it wasn't one of the other waiters? They're all out there walking around where they could also see what was happening."

She shook her head. "No, they couldn't. They might have seen a few envelopes change hands, but they couldn't hear what went on in Baldwin's office. They also didn't have keys to the club. They couldn't come and go as they pleased. Tajo knew that Mr. Zayas was planning to return to Spain. He probably used his access to the club to listen in on Zayas' telephone calls. I believe he wanted to take over the blackmail racket, and Zayas refused to let him."

"How do you figure that?" Wall asked. "Any fool would have known that the cops would be all over a killing in the club."

"He likely didn't intend to kill him at the club, but he saw Zayas go into Baldwin's office with a canvas bag. Tajo knew that he was going to take the money and leave; he had to act. Besides, Lefty had set himself up to be the perfect cover. He saw the opportunity to kill Zayas and let Lefty take the fall. He took the gun that was under the bar, shot Zayas, and used the canvas bag to staunch the bleeding until he could get the body moved to Zayas's office. The bullet didn't go through; there was no splatter. All he had to do was clean up the blood that pooled on the floor. Then he could wait and search for the money and ledger when everyone cleared out."

"Then we started snooping around Baldwin's office," Sal said. "He needed to direct us back toward Lefty."

"Exactly," Cornelia said. "He shot Liza just as she was about to tell us that Lefty had paid her to deliver those gifts. He thought that we would conclude that it was Lefty who shot her. Which is what we did."

She frowned before continuing. "His first big mistake was when Lobster and I came to search his place. He threw us the keys and told us to lock up when we finished, that he was late for work. He couldn't have been late for work; it was just past noon. Instead, while we searched his place, he was at Lefty's. That was where his plan derailed. He'd killed Lefty, but was still at the house when we got there and hadn't had time to make it look like Lefty killed himself.

"The rest, we all know. Lobster was killed. Sal and I ended up in the hospital." Cornelia said. "It's a tragic mess. If Tajo has any sense, he's getting as far from Tampa Bay as possible."

The Nuptials

The rest of the week was a flurry of activity. Uncle Percival and Teddy went to get a marriage license. Afterwards, the professor and Tommy went to procure proper attire for the ceremony while Teddy and her mother argued over its location. The bride would have been happy to rent a room at the Cuban Club or one of the other secular establishments, but Julia had her way in the end. The ceremony would be held in a church. They found a Saturday venue with the assistance of a large donation to the building fund. It wasn't the big church wedding with the Venetian lace gown Julia had planned for her daughter in the previous century, but it would have to do.

Other errands needed running. Teddy went back to the bridal shop to check the alterations to the gown. A multi-tiered wedding cake was out of the question with such short notice, so Cornelia and Julia contacted local bakeries to see what they could provide. The widow Lawless was further appalled by the need to render invitations by telephone.

The morning of the wedding, Teddy and the professor breakfasted in their separate rooms before dressing for the event. Shirley and Anna Wheeler arrived a short time later. Shirley was the maid of honor. Her mother, Anna, closed their beauty shop for the day and they crossed the Gandy. Shirley helped the bride with her gown, while Anna styled Teddy's hair and arranged her veil. It was her gift to the couple.

After they finished with Teddy, Shirley coaxed Cornelia into her new lavender gown and matching jacket. The old nurse would have preferred her dress uniform, but it had been sent to Colorado with her luggage. She hoped Ruth's aide had already picked it up.

There was a knock at the door.

"Who is it?" Anna called. "It had better not be Percy out there."

"No, it's Tommy. Everyone decent?"

Shirley let him in. He was in dress uniform, Cornelia noted enviously. He wore the dark blue double-breasted coat of a naval officer, with gilt buttons and four gold stripes on his sleeves.

"The groom sent me. He has a gift for the matron of honor."

Cornelia stared. "Me?"

"Yes. He and Teddy chose it together. He hopes you will wear it today."

Teddy's eyes widened. Had Percival...? Of course he had. He was good at hearing things when they were important.

The sapphire brooch was inside the small dark box. "This is ... so expensive," Cornelia gasped. "Too expensive for an Army nurse."

"I think it will perfectly match your outfit," Julia Lawless said. "It should pick up the blue tones in your dress."

"And your eyes," Teddy added. "I'd love to see you wear it."

"Since you asked so nicely, I will."

When Mac showed up, they bundled Uncle Percival into his room. It had been decided that once the men were ready, they would go to the church. If they waited until Teddy and her mother were ready, they'd be there all day. Better for the groom to be at the church as an incentive.

Mac was taking the men in his car; Sal would be driving Cornelia's car when the ladies were ready.

Cornelia was tempted to suggest he put his feet up. It would be a while.

Lulu, Opal, CJ, and the Gemstones sat behind the white guests as segregation required. They wore their Sunday best, although Diamond Fingers only seemed to have the one dress. It made Cornelia smile. Despite the strictures of society around them, these women had created the world they wanted. They sat on the bride's side; Clevon sat on the groom's.

She was surprised to see Peter Rowley in the pews. Since Uncle Percival had invested in his business, it was appropriate, but they were a long way from Homosassa. The man next to him, older, wrinkled face turned brown from decades exposed to the sun, seemed familiar, but Cornelia couldn't place him at first. When she mentally removed the jacket and tie, though, she recognized him at last. It was the jailer from her uncle's time in the Crystal River hoosegow. The sheriff hadn't come with them, but somebody needed to maintain order in Citrus County with the jailer gone.

And bless her stars, there was Mitchell Grant. He must've slipped the nurses in the hospital. Mitch had intervened in a shootout between Cornelia and a murderous hairdresser and received a bullet for his trouble.

While the guests got situated, the cellist and pianist Julia had hired for the ceremony began to play. It was an arioso, probably Bach. Teddy had played a lot of Bach for the brass when they visited the Army hospital. When she played for the doughboys, though, she preferred popular songs that would lift their spirits.

The first person to walk down the aisle was a little girl. Her hair had been done in ringlets, and she wore a bright yellow dress. The child flung flower petals enthusiastically at the guests. Cornelia couldn't help but smile; Shirley's cousin bore a strong resemblance to her, and the girl had good aim. She accepted being socked with flowers graciously.

Her brother, dressed in a tiny black suit, was the ring bearer. He held the pillow up in front of his face in embarrassment, nearly tripping over what had to be his first pair of long pants. When he paused at the altar, confused, Mac made a "psst" and the boy took the pillow to him.

The girl plopped in the pew next to Cornelia, basket empty. The boy headed for the groom's side of the company and sat between Anna Wheeler and Sal.

Shirley was next, in a tea-length dress. The pale blue went well with the brilliant, but probably not natural, red hair. Unlike the children, she had a measured, graceful step. She glided to her proper place near the altar.

The musicians paused, then began playing the familiar notes of Wagner's "Bridal Chorus." Everyone stood and turned to watch Teddy proceed down the aisle with one gloved hand tucked into the crook of her brother's arm.

Cornelia had to confess that she was beautiful. The gown accented her slender figure and coloring, and the sunlight streaming through the stained-glass windows of the church gently illuminated the pearl headpiece and the beaded veil.

Uncle Percival met her at the altar, splendid and distinguished in his tuxedo. Mac stood nearby, ready with the rings.

Her sight blurred and she snatched her handkerchief from her jacket pocket. She didn't know whether it was grief or anger that brought the water to her eyes. To justify her closeness to Cornelia, society required that Teddy marry a man in her family. Sharing a tent as Army nurses in Cuba was excusable; living together on her mother's farm had already started gossip. How many times had she been forced to lie? She wondered, sometimes, whether the world was intentionally cruel.

Julia, less conflicted, was prettily weeping into a lace hanky beside her.

The ceremony itself was brief; Uncle Percival had emphatically informed the priest that long services were for people who didn't need a cane. The vows covered the basics, although Cornelia noted that Teddy put one hand behind her back and crossed her fingers when she promised to obey her lawful husband.

She managed to smile. Teddy would always be Teddy.

When the church doors opened, their photographer carried his camera down the stairs and prepared to take more pictures. Mitch followed Chago, who was carrying the professor's motion camera. Julia Lawless took charge of the wedding party and began arranging people into poses.

The photographer raised his camera to take the first picture and caught Teddy scowling, hand pointing at someone behind them.

Bobby Hornbuckle! What are you doing here?

The reporter, dressed in a smart navy suit, smiled cheerfully at them. "Just getting a photograph for the society pages."

The bride started down the stairs, bouquet gripped like a club, but her mother held her back. "Teddy, let the lady do her job. It's for the society pages."

"She wants to find a new way to humiliate me."

"She's not going to do that. Humiliating a bride would be bad for business."

Teddy continued to protest, but Julia bullied her into posing.

Once the stills were taken, the photographer got to play with the motion camera. He had the wedding party wave to an invisible audience, then had Teddy and Shirley skip on the stairs. Cornelia worried that one of them would trip in their heels, but they were up for the task.

The man backed up with the camera so he could record the traditional bouquet toss. Teddy stood at the top of the steps, while the women clustered below. There hadn't been many invitees, due to the rush job, but some of the church staff joined the pack.

At least no one will think Teddy had to get married, Cornelia thought.

Shirley grinned at Cornelia. "If I catch it, I hope my marriage doesn't take as long to happen as it did for Teddy."

"I never expected it to happen at all," Cornelia said, truthfully.

The girl started forward, then turned. "Are you coming? I'll make them give you room."

"No, dear. I'm about to retire; I don't want a new job."

The girl laughed and ran to the crowd.

Teddy leaned over, talking to CJ. Cornelia admired the pleased blush on the bride's face. She giggled like a girl Shirley's age. Even after all they'd been through in body, Teddy's spirit had never grown old.

She turned now, silver hair gleaming under the lights, and flung the bouquet over her shoulder. It shot high into the air, spinning stems over blossoms ...

... and knocked Eddie's hat off. It bounced on his forehead and landed in his hands.

Eddie grabbed his hat and crammed it back on, but his secret was out: he had little hair left on top. It was a secret many men had.

"Aww, they're your color!" Sal said. "Who's the lucky lady?"

"I'll let you know when I figure it out," Eddie growled. "Hey, any of you gals want a flower?"

The reception was held at The Black Opal in Ybor City. The kitchen staff came out to cheer when the wedding party made its grand entrance. The El Dorado wasn't suitable, since it was a casino, and Club Tropical was still closed. The Tampa Bay Hotel would have excluded half of the guests because of the segregation laws, so it was unsuitable for their company. Teddy's mother had wanted to use the church hall, but Teddy flatly refused.

"No wedding reception of mine is going to be dry."

Julia Lawless arranged for platters of sliced fruit, cheese, crackers, and divinity to be delivered to the reception. When the caterers complained about the Ybor City location, she was properly haughty with them. The centerpiece was a large Strawberry Charlotte. Tea, lemonade, and punch were the beverages. The punch didn't start as alcoholic, but Eddie and Shirley made contributions to "improve the flavor."

Instruments had been set up on the stage. Once the guests had settled down, four men filed in. They wore three-piece ivory suits with wide lapels and flap pockets. Their

236

designated leader, a slender man with slicked-back hair, introduced the group as the Minott Brothers. He spoke with a faint lilt to the voice that suggested a Caribbean background.

"It's our pleasure to be here to celebrate the marriage of this fine couple. We're honored to share in this occasion. May your years together be as sweet as the songs we're about to sing."

The music began, and the bride and groom danced for the first time as husband and wife. Cornelia hoped that Teddy and Uncle Percival hadn't just made a huge mistake. Still, having another official family member around would be helpful if something happened to her uncle. By her estimation, the old dear had to be nearly ninety.

She felt a nudge on her shoulder. It was Chago. He'd brought her a cup of punch and a plate of cheese and crackers. "Here. Take this so you don't starve."

She thanked him. "I'm so glad they released you quickly."

"Well, the boss greased the wheels a little. Miss Pettijohn, I wanted to say thanks. For helping me."

"Thank Mr. Wall and Sal. They kidnapped me instead of bribing the cops."

"You're the one who hoofed it everywhere on my behalf. And almost got killed."

They ate. Teddy was dancing with her brother now.

Cornelia took a sip of the punch and tried not to choke. How many people had spiked the bowl? "I think I was safer getting shot at in France during the War."

"And yet you live. And *senora* Teddy is a *mujer afortunada*. I hope she doesn't dance your uncle to an early grave. She's a handful."

"No, that's what you're here for. You should claim her for the next song."

"If you could stand, *senora,* you would be the one I would ask."

"Be glad I can't, for the sake of your feet."

He clasped her hand and squeezed it. Then he headed towards Teddy.

"Felicidades! I want a turn."

The dancing stopped when the appetizers were served. Shrimp cocktail, mullet spread with crackers, and deviled eggs were placed on the tables.

Mac stood once everyone had settled in and addressed the assembled company. "I've only known the bride and groom for a short time, but they are both extraordinary people," he said. "Professor Pettijohn is best known for his clever inventions and handiness with a hammer, but he is also devoted to his family and friends. I've seen how far he will go for someone he loves."

There was polite clapping.

"And Miss Teddy—she spent years as an Army nurse, and one of her patients was me. She read letters from home to soldiers who were flat on their backs, and played piano so we'd have something to enjoy. Her wit was our good fortune. Professor Pettijohn's niece was her closest friend—and no doughboy wanted to cross the Iron Petticoat. Here's to the happy couple!"

Cornelia drank with the others. It was kind of Mac to remember her in his speech, short as it was. Teddy and her uncle were not the traditional bride and groom, but the marriage was going to change things for all of them. There would be roles Teddy would be expected to step into, and ones Cornelia would need to give up. However, two of them would be caring for Uncle Percival, sharing the burden.

The meal was primarily fried chicken and fish, although beef tenderloin was provided for northerners who didn't follow Dr. Kellogg's regimen.

Cornelia was enjoying having yet more food she couldn't get in the barracks, and noted that Tommy was trying the greens, despite their being cooked with fatback. Cornbread sat beside it on his plate, and someone had found him a tall glass of milk. Cornelia immediately requested one also.

As the plates were emptied, they were quietly cleared. More toasts were made to the new couple while the Charlotte was sliced and served. Shirley declared that Teddy was her sister "once or twice removed," Tommy got choked up confessing that he was glad the family had been brought back together for such a good reason, and Sal announced that now they were each other's problem instead of his.

After the next round of dancing, Teddy and the professor stood at a separate table with the wedding cake while everyone took pictures. Then, the bride cut a slice from the cake so she and Percival could feed one another. The men shouted for them to smash the cake into each other's faces, but Sal opined that they shouldn't start their marriage with a fight. "I'd hate to see you two at war. Him with his inventions and you with your slingshot."

The old nurse sat back in her motorized chair and watched the guests dance. Clevon was doing double time as a partner for the Gemstones. Her uncle was dancing with Anna Wheeler, and Eddie was squiring Shirley. Julia Lawless was speaking with Mac. In a different world, he might have been her grandson. But this world was better.

She noticed someone else in the room, a slender stranger leaving through an open door.

She wasn't positive, but she thought the woman wore red shoes.

'til Death Did They Start
By Roberta Hornbuckle
The Evening Independent
March 14, 1926

After a tumultuous time in Saint Petersburg, during which she was charged with murder, Miss Theodora Lawless, originally of Harborcreek, Pennsylvania, became Mrs. Percival Pettijohn on Saturday afternoon. Professor Pettijohn is retired and resides in Midway, Kentucky.

The bride wore an Art Deco gown of champagne-colored silk satin with a train and opera gloves. Shirley Wheeler of Saint Petersburg, Nimrod Stevens (son of the late Ansel Stevens), Captain Thomas Lawless (retired), Julia Duvoth Lawless (widow of the late Henry Lawless of Harborcreek) and Nurse Cornelia Pettijohn of Fitzsimons Army Hospital in Colorado were members of the wedding party. The wedding was solemnized at Laurel Street Methodist. The church was decorated in cut flowers provided by Downs Nursery and Florist. Attendees of the ceremony were a motley crew: they included Mitchell Grant of the *St. Petersburg Times*, Morgan Cosgrove, Esquire (who ably defended the bride in court), Elmer Farrell of Farrell Brothers' Yachts, Peter Rowley (Homosassa), Rena Orlov (Sarasota), and musicians from Opal and the Gemstones (Ybor City).

The new couple will be returning to Kentucky. We at the *Evening Independent* will miss Mrs. Pettijohn. She graced our pages with her fashionable clothing and provided more interesting stories than the average socialite.

Body Found on Rocks at Ballast Point
By Mitchell Grant
St. Petersburg Times
March 22, 1926

Two fishermen discovered a human corpse snagged in the rocks at Ballast Point on Sunday. The body was identified as Tijo Ibarra, an employee of Club Tropical in Ybor City. This is the latest unfortunate incident in a series for Club Tropical. Ibarra is the third employee to die under questionable circumstances. Geraldo Zayas, a club manager, and Liza Boling, a dancer, died of gunshot wounds in separate incidents. Authorities have not released Ibarra's cause of death yet.

Club Tropical's manager, Lester Baldwin, is seeking new employees. He states that this time of high turnover has ended and business should be back to normal in a week or so.

THE END

EL PRESIDENTE

 This cocktail was named for either Mario García Menocal or Gerardo Machado; both served as president of Cuba during the 1920s. Slightly bitter with a citrus orange flavor, it's not as well-known as the Mojito or Daiquiri, but it's still popular with locals and visitors to Cuba. The original recipe called for blanc vermouth (sweeter), but dry vermouth is often used instead. The recipe also calls for grenadine, but some modern mixologists substitute pomegranate syrup.

1 1/2 ounces white rum
3/4 ounce dry vermouth
1/4 ounce orange curaçao
2 dashes grenadine

Add the white rum, dry vermouth, orange curaçao and grenadine to a mixing glass with ice and stir until it's well-chilled, then strain into a chilled cocktail glass.

AUTHORS' NOTES

Charlie Wall was born into one of the wealthiest and most prominent families in Florida. However, his mother's death and his father's subsequent marriage to a younger woman whom Charlie loathed led to a troubled home life. His father died when Charlie was ten years old, leaving him in the care of his stepmother. At thirteen he had his first run-in with the police when he shot and wounded the family cook. He was sent to military school, where he did well with classwork but was expelled for visiting a brothel. Instead of returning home to his stepmother, Charlie chose a life of crime.

By his fifteenth birthday in 1905, Charlie's rap sheet included fighting, using abusive and profane language, running a gambling house, and associating with prostitutes. Before he was twenty, he had built a mob and taken over the Tampa underworld. He had also taken over control of the popular *bolita* games, a precursor to the lottery.

Prohibition allowed Wall to cement his position as the crime lord of Central Florida. He purchased the El Dorado Hotel in Ybor City and turned it into a combination speakeasy, casino, and brothel.

Tampa Police The 1920s were a challenging time for the Tampa police. Between 1920 and 1925, the population of the city more than doubled. With the new residents came a surge in crime, including highway robbery, theft, property damage, burglary, and, of course, murder. Bootleggers were pervasive due to Prohibition, narcotic sales surged, and gambling houses were everywhere.

Unfortunately, the police department's funding and staff did not expand to deal with these crimes accordingly. In 1924, there were only nine or ten patrolmen active on each shift. Worse, some officers were on the payroll of the criminals. Between the low staff and the amount of graft, many crimes went unsolved. The public did not trust the police and sometimes called upon outside help.

For example, car theft was one of the most pervasive and brazen crimes. One of the bolder thefts was a car stolen from the police department itself in 1924. The insurance underwriters used their network to locate the vehicle. With their help, it was found about six months later in a suburb and returned to the police department. Not only did the car still display its City of Tampa plate, four gallons of liquor were found inside.

Also in 1924, the president of the Bank of West Tampa was robbed while making a transfer to the Exchange National Bank. When the Tampa police suspended their investigation, the Exchange National Bank hired private detectives to investigate. They located one of the robbers and, upon his arrest, he implicated employees with both the city police and the sheriff's department.

The lack of confidence Tampa citizens had in the local forces of law and order led to extralegal solutions, but justice was still only available for those who could afford it.

The El Dorado Hotel started as a hotel for cigar factory workers. It ended as the base of operations for Tampa's homegrown mob. Crime boss Charlie Wall purchased the El Dorado Hotel during the cigar factory's labor strike. He gave free room and board to the striking workers while labor negotiations were stalled. His actions during the strike endeared him to Ybor City's working class. The strike marked the beginning of his political power in Florida. No politician could win the Ybor City vote without his support.
Along with an impressive array of gambling tables the El Dorado hosted the richest *bolita* drawing in the country. Wall

held a near monopoly on *bolita* in Central Florida. By the 1920s, the El Dorado was a booming speakeasy, casino, and brothel. The upper floors of the old hotel became a thriving bordello. Prostitutes were smuggled into the country through the port of Tampa along with rum from the Caribbean and European spirits. Prohibition was in full swing, but at the El Dorado there was never a shortage of the best alcohol.

Ballast Point is the entrance into a small 7–9-foot channel that connects Hillsborough Bay to the mouth of the Hillsborough River. It is unclear when the term "Ballast Point" came into common usage, although it appeared in Bay area newspapers in the early 1800's. The name was coined because schooners had to drop their ballast to keep from running aground in the shallow channel. The steady accumulation of rock near the channel created an unplanned sea wall at the edge of the bay that frequently snagged bodies floating between the river and the Bay.

La Union Marti-Maceo Initially, when the club began, it comprised both black and white Cubans that fought side by side in the war. The *La Union Marti-Maceo* was comprised of both black and white Cubans that lived happily together. However, the introduction of the Jim Crow laws prompted the separation of the black and white Cubans. In 1900, the club got divided along racial lines leading to two separate organizations: *El Circulo Cubano* and *La Union Marti-Maceo*.

El Circulo Cubano became an exclusive white Cuban club, while the *La Union Marti-Maceo* became a black-dominated Cuban society. The social halls developed by *La Union Marti-Maceo* were used to provide cultural, social, and medical support to cigar workers and their families. Though the club has ceased providing medical benefits, it continues to facilitate social activities such as excursions, parties, and dances regularly. The site is significant, especially to black/Afro-Cubans, since it contains the history of their undeniable role in historic Ybor City. For many years, they have been isolated from Italians, Spaniards, and white Cubans living in the region. Afro-Cubans form only a small proportion of the larger Ybor City, and it was very easy for their influence to be forgotten. For a long time, journalists and local historians neglected the history of Cubans of color and the *La Union Marti-Maceo*. Besides, they were not included in the official records of Ybor City. However, the site of the *Marti-Maceo* was incorporated as a "significant structure" in the official documents and maps of Tampa. Though the *La Union Marti-Maceo* is a sign of remembrance for Cubans of color, it also serves as a mutual aid society.

El Circulo Cubano (Cuban Club) When segregation forced the Cuban community to break away from being a single organization, the decision was made for white Cubans to build a new clubhouse and leave the old one to the Afro-Cubans. 1902 white Cuban workers founded "El Circulo Cubano" which means "Circle of Cubans." It was a mutual aid society to "bind all white Cuban residents to Tampa into a fraternal group, to offer assistance and help to the sick." The club provided a gathering place for community members and served as a unifying force in the Cuban community. The irony of the name, considering the reason for the club, seems to have escaped the founders.

Fire destroyed the first clubhouse in 1916, and soon afterward its members started plans for its replacement. The present four-story yellow brick building with Neoclassical design elements sits on the original site. Constructed in 1917, the building contained a two-story theater, pharmacy, library, ballroom, and cantina. Imported tile, stained glass windows and elaborately carved sgraffito spandrels decorated the structure and the Grand Ballroom ceiling displayed elaborate murals. It once housed a gymnasium complete with lockers, a swimming pool, and two bowling lanes.

The Tampa Bay Hotel is not only a stunning example of Moorish and Turkish architecture, but also served as the headquarters for the United State Army's invasion of Cuba during the Spanish-American War. Constructed between 1888 and 1891 by Henry B. Plant to draw tourists to Florida, the massive hotel and its expansive grounds proved extremely useful during the Spanish-American War. Henry B. Plant, railroad magnate, successful businessman, and founder of the Plant System of railroads and steamboats, brought the railroad to Tampa in 1884. Plant's railroad connected downtown Tampa to the rest of the east coast and to Port Tampa, where people could board a Plant steamship to Havana, Jamaica, New Orleans, New York, Bermuda, or other destinations.

With the arrival of Plant's railroad and steamships in Tampa, new businesses and markets burgeoned. The fishing industry prospered, new products filtered into Tampa's market, and Tampa's tourist industry began. Newly founded Ybor City (also featured in this itinerary), an area of Tampa that quickly developed into one of the cigar manufacturing centers of the world, benefited from using Plant's trains to ship fine Cuban cigars to the rest of the U.S. market. Plant's trains and steamships forever changed the sleepy village of Tampa, Florida and brought it fast into the 20th century.

The Tampa Bay Hotel continued operating as a hotel until 1932, even after Plant died in 1899, and his heirs sold the hotel and 50 acres of land to the City of Tampa in 1905. In 1933, the City signed a lease with the University of Tampa giving the university the right to use the building for 100 years at the cost of one dollar a year. Today, a portion of the building and its grounds serve the University of Tampa, while the Henry B. Plant Museum in the south wing of the old hotel and Plant Park provide visitors with the opportunity to experience this historic place.

ABOUT THE AUTHORS

Hair and Photo by Jay Martello

Gwen Mayo is passionate about blending her loves of history and mystery fiction. She currently lives and writes in Safety Harbor, Florida, but grew up in a large Irish family in the hills of Eastern Kentucky. She is the author of the *Nessa Donnelly Mysteries* and co-author of the *Three Snowbirds* stories with Sarah Glenn. Her stories have appeared in *A Whodunit Halloween, Decades of Dirt, Halloween Frights (Volume I)*, and several flash fiction collections. She belongs to Sisters in Crime, the Short Mystery Fiction Society, and the Independent Book Publishers Association.

Gwen has a bachelor's degree in political science from the University of Kentucky. Her most interesting job, though, was as a brakeman and railroad engineer from 1983-1987. She was one of the last engineers to be certified on steam locomotives.

Sarah E. Glenn is a Jane-of-all-trades. She has a B.S. in Journalism, mostly because she'd rather write about stuff than do it. She also spent time as a grad student in classical languages, boning up on her crossword skills. Past occupations include: interning at a billboard company, helping doctors navigate a continuing education website, and updating listings in telephone books. Her most interesting job was working Reports Desk for the police, where she learned that criminals really are dumb.

Sarah loves mystery and horror stories, usually with a sidecar of humor. Her baby is the *Strangely Funny* series, an annual anthology of comedy horror tales by talented authors. Sarah's great-great aunt served as a nurse in WWI, and she was injured by poison gas during the fighting. After being mustered out, she traveled widely. A hundred years later, 'Aunt Dess' would inspire Sarah to write stories she would likely not have approved of.

Books by Gwen Mayo and Sarah E Glenn

Murder at the Million Dollar Pier

Murder on the Mullet Express

Ybor City Blues

Books by Gwen Mayo

Concealed in Ash

Circle of Dishonor

Books by Sarah E. Glenn

All this and Family Too

The Strangely Funny Anthologies

www.ingramcontent.com/pod-product-compliance
Lightning Source LLC
Chambersburg PA
CBHW030107260626
47156CB00008B/2564